A DYING TRUTH EXPOSED, BOOK FOUR

THE MISSING PUZZLE PIECE

HE HAS HIS MOMMA'S SMILE...

MARCUS ABSTON

CHAPTER 1
The Evil Wolf

THE WRINKLED HANDS OF ALBERT Brooks opened the old photo album, exposing more letters next to pictures. "Annabelle had survived many things in her life," he said. "First, she ran from the plantation, leaving behind her family and the few friends she had. She escaped to Missouri with the help of Ruthanne and Elizabeth, but that hope of family and freedom was taken from her. Her first husband, Benjamin, along with her firstborn, Benita, were murdered. To further escape slavery that had found her once again, she was taken to Indian Territory to live with the Cherokee."

Albert's daughter looked at her father with lowered eyebrows and a frown. "She experienced so much at such a young age," Liz said. "I wouldn't have blamed her for ending it all."

"I'm sure it crossed her mind, but she kept pushing forward. She struggled and fought. It takes strength to heal."

"I think that's what allowed her to fall in love again. John was a good man. Did he get revenge for Joseph being taken from them?"

Albert looked down at one of the letters encased in plastic. "John actually wrote this. They weren't sure if Joseph was even alive after the kidnapping. Annabelle was grief-stricken. She'd fought against being enslaved, and now her baby boy was forced into the system. The family had to hold onto faith. I've already told you about the two wolves, and at this time, the wrong wolf was getting fed. Our family was now at war. The uncertainty of Joseph's condition echoed in Annabelle's and John's minds. The only one with answers was Hunter Sawyer, a racist Indian agent with a self-righteous complex."

"They killed him…didn't they?"

Albert nodded. "Let's continue with the legacy of our family. On that horrific day of June 1, 1860, Hunter was now strapped down to the crooked tree by both hands. His wounds had been treated, but he was unable to stand because of his wounded knee. John and the rest of the men in the family stood before that hateful White man, hoping to get the answers they needed to bring Joseph home."

⎯⎯⎯◆⎯⎯⎯

"Tell me now! Who helped you kidnap my son?" John asked in a roaring deep tone.

"I have no reason to give you any answers," Hunter growled. "What do you think is going to happen to your sister for putting two arrows in me?"

John kicked over the water bucket sitting in front of Hunter and stepped on his injured kneecap. Hunter screamed in anguish while John continued putting pressure on the wound. "Now tell me who took my son. Is the person worth dying for, Mr. Sawyer? I'm not leaving you alone until you give us answers."

"Go to hell, prairie nigger," Hunter said.

John took his foot off Hunter's kneecap and turned to George. "Please prepare the orange arrow, Uncle George."

George nodded and set a fire, then placed an arrow so its copper head rested in the center. Eli, George, Jacob, John, Luke, and Samuel waited for the arrowhead to burn bright orange. The burning fire was a manifestation of their anger, and its glow reflected off their furrowed brows. George and Luke stood by the fire with their gazes fixed on the arrowhead. Jacob and Samuel quietly spoke with each other in an attempt to calculate how far Joseph could've been taken by then. The howling of coyotes could suddenly be heard while John's and Eli's gazes remained on Hunter. The sound of the coyotes became louder, and the man began to look to either side as his shoulders began to tremble.

"Do you not hear them?" Hunter yelled.

"I trust those coyotes more than I trust you, Mr. Sawyer," Eli said. "Maybe we'll let them take a chunk of you."

Hunter spit on the ground. "Damn you redskins to hell!" he said.

John's right hand curled into a fist and he rushed toward Hunter, but Eli and Jacob held him back. "Not yet, brother," Jacob said.

Eli and Jacob released John, who then shook his head, kicked the dirt, and turned his back to Hunter.

"I'll make sure your sister sees chains for the rest of her life," Hunter said. "She attempted to take my life with those arrows."

"If it were anyone else, you'd be dead," Samuel bellowed. "Be grateful Grace thought to spare your life."

Hunter scoffed and pursed his lips, and the coyotes howled again. He gasped and quickly turned to his left. He turned back and exhaled, his brown eyes now fixed on the scowling faces of the Cherokee men. His gaze then went to his injured knee and remained there.

A few minutes later, Luke gave the smoking arrow to John, who then resumed standing before Hunter. "Tell me where my son was taken and who helped you."

"Do you think that's really enough to break me? I'll never tell," Hunter said.

John frowned, then poked Hunter on his wounded kneecap with the smoking arrow. Hunter screamed in pain as John poked him two more times. John was about to poke him again when Hunter started pleading.

"Wait! Wait! I'll tell you what I know."

John's face twisted. "Then you need to start talking, Mr. Sawyer."

Wide-eyed, Hunter replied in a higher-pitched tone, "I promise I'll talk. Please let me go, and I'll tell you everything."

John's eyes narrowed. "We no longer have patience, and I

don't trust you. Now where's my son? If I have to go inside to tell my wife and children there is no hope of getting him back, you won't live to see the sunrise."

Sweat dripping down his forehead, Hunter looked wildly from one man to the next and back to John again. "There are slave traders very willing to sell Indian children and half-breeds. There are certain plantations in Tennessee, Mississippi, and Georgia with Indian slaves. Many of the owners feel that an Indian's intelligence and strength are valuable. Some of them have already mixed bloods and gotten children that don't know how to be Indian. The mixed bloods are a good stock because they don't get sick like full-blooded Indians. They have the smarts of the Indians and the strength of both peoples."

"So you don't even know which plantation my nephew was being sold to?" Uncle George asked.

Hunter answered, "No, because the boy has to go to an auction. Good luck finding which one he's being taken to."

John punched Hunter.

"We should hang him," Samuel said.

John replied, "No. There is more he needs to tell us. Who was the other man? Who was the man driving away in the wagon? And don't lie and say you don't know."

Hunter looked at each man again, this time as if he were analyzing their serious expressions. Looking back to John, he replied, "Simon is his name, but I don't know his last name."

"How do you not know his last name?" Luke snarled.

"Brock set this trap," John said. "Ain't that right, Mr. Sawyer?"

Hunter nervously replied, "I have no idea of what you're talking about."

John's eyes narrowed, and he punched Hunter. He took out his knife, but Eli and Jacob restrained him. "Let me go," John yelled.

"Calm down, John. This is what he wants," Eli said. "Please calm down. We will find Joseph."

John slowly relaxed as the men released him. "We'll dump

him off at the courthouse tomorrow," Jacob said. "I hate to say it, but killing this fool will only bring us more trouble."

Hunter began to laugh.

George punched him hard across his cheek. "Be grateful it was my niece that took the shots with her bow. If it were me, I would've killed you."

Hunter snobbishly replied, "That woman is the smartest one out of all of you. I suggest you listen to her, Mr. Strongman."

George sarcastically replied, "I know, Mr. Sawyer. She is a great planner. I do have a gift for you from my other niece though. I doubt she would've been merciful to you either." He reached down into a bowl and came out with a handful of salt that he then smacked onto Hunter's wounded shoulder. As Hunter screamed, George said, "Sleep well."

Eli, George, Jacob, John, Luke, and Samuel walked inside and told the others what they had gotten out of Hunter.

◆

During the night, the sound of insects echoed through the land. Simon had set up camp by a tree and was busily eating beans in front of a crackling fire. The moonlight and stars gave even more light to the wilderness and cast a surreal glow on Joseph's body leaned against a tree with his head slouched forward and his hands tied in front of him. Suddenly he gasped and took a deep breath. His eyes slowly widened, his head slowly lifted, and he saw his wrists were bound with rope. He saw Simon eating, but the White man's eyes remained on his beans. Joseph's breathing became heavier. He struggled to balance his head, causing him to slightly jerk it back. He clenched his teeth, reached to the back with his tied hands, and touched the back of his head. He brought his hands back in front of him and saw blood on his hands. He yelled for his mother, and Simon's steely glare immediately locked on him.

Quickly annoyed with the boy's shouts, Simon took his revolver out and pointed it at his head. "Keep on screaming, boy, and I'll end you here," he said.

Tears flowed down Joseph's face while he watched Simon take another bite. "Please take me home, sir," he begged.

"It's too late for that, boy. It should make you feel proud to know that they fought for you. I'm sure they killed Hunter Sawyer. Those fools felt that for some reason we couldn't take you at night. Well, it certainly cost them."

"Please take me home. I'll tell my family I got away and you couldn't find me. Please let me go home. I'm Cherokee. I'm not a slave."

"I know what you are, boy, but who's going to tell the difference? In the South, you're a nigger, a half-breed nigger. You're not a rarity, boy."

The moonlight reflected off Joseph's tears. "I did nothing wrong to you. My family has done nothing to you."

"You speak good English, boy. I suggest you speak more like a Negro unless you want to get beat. You're nothing but a profit, and someone wanted you gone. So there's your answer. Someone wanted you gone, and I want my money. The only way I'm getting my money is at the auctions."

"My family has money. They can pay you."

Simon laughed. "I doubt they have enough to cover you, boy."

Joseph scowled as he sat up against the tree, slowly trying to pull his hands free. "God is watching you."

Simon quickly smacked Joseph, knocking him onto his side. "What do you know about God? God made your people to work the land and for mine to govern. What they been teaching you in Indian Territory?"

"I'm Cherokee, and my momma said God loves all people the same. White people lie because they think they are better than us and want to control us."

Simon stood up and kicked Joseph in his stomach, causing the boy to moan. "Your momma lied to you, boy. So you're proud to be Cherokee, eh? You know...the men I'm taking you to don't care. They want a strong young boy that will grow into a strong slave man. It don't matter if he's a nigger or a grass nigger. It will be interesting to see how much you sell for."

Still holding his stomach and trying not to cry, Joseph glared up at the man and said, "My family will come for me."

Simon leered. "Is that right? I would love to see them try, especially after killing a White man. I would love to see them try."

✦

Throughout the night, Annabelle spent most of her time comforting the distraught twins. When the twins finally fell asleep, she entered her own room and found John sitting on the bed. She sat down next to him and laid her head on his shoulder.

"The twins are finally asleep," she said in the Cherokee language. "I feel so powerless. The girls are scared to go anywhere alone. They shouldn't be scared to go anywhere alone on our own land."

"I promise we're bringing Joseph home," John said in his native tongue.

Annabelle's lips quivered. "My baby is out there alone with some crazy White man. I know Brock knows where they're selling him. That evil man has to suffer for what he's done." She began to cry on John's shoulder, and he embraced her. "They stole my baby. I can't lose another child." Now rapidly breathing, she gasped between her words, "I can't. My soul can't handle it. I can't lose him like I lost Benita."

John deeply exhaled while he held his sorrowful wife. "We will find him. I promise you this." John kissed her on the cheek as his eyes began to well up.

✦

Suddenly, Lizzie came out of the shadows and walked toward Hunter, still tied to the tree. The moonlight reflected off her drying tears, emphasizing her rage. Her grip tightened around the tomahawk she carried, and her hands began to shake.

"What are you doing here?" Hunter asked, staring at the weapon in Lizzie's hand. "Your brother said no one is to kill me."

Each word deepening in timbre, Lizzie replied, "My brother does not control me."

Hunter pulled at his restraints and tried to stand up.

"Someone help me!" he yelled. "Please don't kill me. I told your brother everything I know."

Lizzie replied in Cherokee, "Stupid White man. I should spill your blood right now for lying."

Hunter's eyes widened, and he stopped struggling to free himself. "What did you say?"

"They won't come to your screams, and I think you're lying." Lizzie placed her tomahawk against Hunter's belly. "Did you know that if I spill your guts, you would still be alive?"

Hunter struggled to break his restraints as he looked into Lizzie's merciless eyes. "God, please help. Please help me!"

"How dare you ask for help! What went through your mind when my nephew screamed for his mother? Why would the Father save you now? He only has so much patience! Didn't you know that?"

"No, ma'am, I didn't know that."

Lizzie lifted her tomahawk and placed its blade on Hunter's injured shoulder. "I'm going to ask you questions, and if I think you're lying, I'll cut pieces of you off. Screaming won't save you."

Hunter gulped. "Please don't do this. I never did you wrong. It was always Brock. It was always him. I was just doing my job."

Lizzie leered, reached into her pocket, and brought out a pinch of salt. She looked into Hunter's frightened eyes and pressed her finger onto his injured shoulder. Hunter howled in pain, and Lizzie lifted his chin with her tomahawk.

"I will take pieces of you if I think you are lying, and you should consider that the only warning you'll have. Did you know that in every person there are two wolves always fighting each other? The wolf we feed is the one that wins. I'll tell you a secret. My weakness is that I don't feed just one wolf."

"What are you talking about?" Hunter asked with a higher-pitched tone as his eyebrows drew together and he leaned away from Lizzie.

"In all people there is good and evil. One wolf is good, and the other wolf is evil. I have on occasion fed the wrong wolf. Now, who else helped you take my nephew?" She placed the blade of her tomahawk in between his legs.

Hunter's body began to tremble. "His name is Simon. That's his name. It's Simon!"

"What is his last name, Mr. Sawyer?"

"I don't know his last name. I was only told he was one of the kidnappers taking Indian children to the auctions."

"Who told you about Simon?"

"I already knew about the man. We never came across him until today."

Lizzie placed her tomahawk on Hunter's black vest and cut the top part open, exposing his chest. With another swipe, she cut his chest.

Hunter screamed in pain, "You crazy woman…you took more than a piece of me!"

"Don't insult me. A piece of clothes isn't part of you, and I don't believe you. John said there were two separate tracks. Who was the other man? I know Brock had to be involved, even if he wasn't here."

"I don't know who he was. I'm sorry. Please have mercy. Please have mercy. See that I meant to do you no wrong."

Lizzie's voice deepened as she replied, "You wronged me by taking my nephew…an innocent, loving little boy. I want to make you suffer for everything you have done to my family." Tears of rage rekindled in her eyes. She grabbed a handful of salt and pressed it onto Hunter's shoulder, making him scream again. "My only reason for not killing you is that Jesus has helped me change, though it has been hard."

Hunter shook his head. "I understand changing is hard."

Lizzie sliced Hunter's bicep, a cold glare in her eyes.

He screamed.

"Don't patronize me," she scoffed as she flicked her long braid back over her shoulder. "You probably didn't believe I knew that word. Lisa told Brock if he ever returned to my family's farm, she would kill him. I will make the same promise to you. Now, where is he taking my nephew?"

"I don't…I don't know," Hunter said, sobbing.

"Why are you so loyal to men that left you to die?" Lizzie

swiped her tomahawk above Hunter's injured knee, cutting his thigh.

Hunter cried in pain and tugged at his restraints again.

Lizzie grabbed a handful of salt and smacked the salt on his knee.

He squealed in agony and urinated on himself. "Please stop. I beg you." He looked into Lizzie's brown, coldblooded eyes.

She lifted her tomahawk to swing again.

"Tennessee. He's taking him to Tennessee, and the slave owners go to the auctions."

"Is that where all the other Indian children have been taken?"

"I don't know because it depends on the men who take them. Some of them are in Tennessee, some are in Missouri or Mississippi. I swear that's the truth."

"After this, I hope you won't look for revenge." Lizzie turned around and headed back toward the kitchen door. She looked back at Hunter. "When I was a child and forced to come here with guns pointed at my head, I lost all of my grandparents. I lost Kay, my cousin William, and then my momma walked on soon after we got here. You're more than hypocrites. You're fake Christians. You use the truth in the Bible as a weapon, in an attempt to control us. That's nothing like what Jesus did. The only thing you White men know how to do is *destroy*. That's your culture…your curse. I know some of my own people have a misunderstanding of us who are believers, thinking we gave up our culture for a White man's religion, but it was never yours in the first place. You're nothing but death. Jesus is life, and I've heard the voice of the Holy Spirit before."

"All I ask is for mercy, Miss Lightning. Please show mercy."

"If we don't find my nephew, you should be fearful for your life." Lizzie leered and let out a little cackle. "You never know. I might go a little crazy if we don't find my little Joseph."

CHAPTER 2
Separation

A s their new reality dawned with the sun of the next day, the family struggled. John stood on the spot where Joseph's bow had been found on the trail, his brown eyes anchored on the trail and his hands tightened into fists. Lisa and Maria spent their time trying to juggle Jonathan and Sunni while getting the girls to eat. The girls sobbed at the table, wanting only to question the likelihood of Joseph's return. Luke helped Tsula nurse Michael as he lay in the bed, while Jacob and Samuel quietly ate and David picked at his food. Annabelle stood staring at her son's bed with her hand on her heart until Lizzie finally coaxed her away and into the kitchen.

George watched his nieces enter the kitchen as he sat at the table and put Jannie on his lap. He turned to Lisa, "Where is John?"

Lisa replied, "He's been staring at the practice field's trail. He hasn't come in to eat."

George's brow lowered. "I see." He looked at Jannie and gently pinched her cheek. "Uncle George will be right back, sweetie."

"Okay," Jannie said with watery eyes.

George looked at Jacob. "Jacob, come with me."

Jacob nodded and the two men left the house. With the morning sun outlining the land, George and Jacob walked up to John, who turned around with a furrowed brow.

John sighed and shook his head. "I have to get him back," he said.

"I believe you will," George said.

"I failed my son, the family. I failed on the most important thing, protecting them."

George pointed at John and bellowed, "You have always done the best you can do! Don't allow this evil we've experienced to stop you now, boy."

"What if—"

"No what-ifs, John," Jacob said. "Joseph has a strong spirit and has learned how to survive from a strong man. We must have faith. No matter how long it takes."

George stepped up to John and put his hand on his shoulder. "The Father will guide us on bringing Joseph home," he said.

John nodded.

"Now, go comfort your wife before you go to war. You have a difficult journey ahead of you, but I believe in all of you."

"Thank you, Uncle," John said.

The two men patted each other on the back, and then Jacob and John patted each other on the back. The men entered the family house. John sat down with Annabelle and put his arm around her. After the family had prayed together, John, Luke, and Samuel rode off to Tennessee to retrace the trail Jacob and Luke had tried to follow yesterday.

George, Jacob, and David went to work in the fields while Lizzie and Maria worked the supply store and Annabelle, Tsula, and Lisa remained home to take care of Michael and the children.

◆

Grace and Eli walked through Tahlequah, leading a battered Hunter. The townspeople took notice but kept on with their business.

"Your crazy sister will pay for what she did to me," Hunter said.

"I doubt it, Mr. Sawyer," Grace said. "You have no proof that she did anything, and your wounds could be from your fighting Michael.”

Hunter growled, “It is my word against your word.”

Grace arrogantly replied, “Yes, it will be, and the fact that Michael is in danger of losing his life is in my favor. Mr. Gross has already been informed by Maria of Joseph’s kidnapping.”

“Why didn’t you let me go? What are you people planning?”

Eli replied, “We never told Mr. Gross that Joseph’s kidnapper was caught, and giving you to the council probably wouldn’t have given us the answers we needed. You’re alive, Mr. Sawyer, and your wounds were cleaned, so don’t complain.”

They arrived at the courthouse and were about to enter when Mr. Gross shouted, “Grace!”

Grace and Eli looked to their right and watched as Mr. Gross and Mr. Smith quickly approached them with their canes in their right hands.

“Grace…Eli, what is the meaning of this? Release Mr. Sawyer,” Mr. Gross commanded.

Grace replied, “Mr. Gross, this is the man who took Joseph, and the other one is being hunted.”

Clutching his cane, Mr. Gross drew closer to Mr. Sawyer and threw off his black top hat. “Our people have been terrified because of the kidnappings over the years, and all this time it was you?!”

Hunter replied with a tired tone, “To be honest, Mr. Gross, I have never aided in the kidnapping of a Cherokee child.”

Mr. Gross angrily replied, “Until yesterday. Do you understand the stress that has been going on in my head? To have a Mexican woman run up to me and tell me about the attack on her husband’s family was beyond disturbing. Grace, how is Michael doing?”

“Michael is doing better. The wound was deep, but Lizzie was able to get the bullet out. To be honest, he could have died. We’re watching him closely.”

“Did you see these wounds, Mr. Gross?” Hunter asked. “I want both of the Lightning sisters hanged.”

Mr. Gross replied, “We will make sure your wounds are further taken care of, Mr. Sawyer, and the US Secretary of Interior will be informed of your actions. I'll make sure you're removed from Cherokee territory permanently. There are a lot of answers we need, especially if you know the locations of any Indian children."

Hunter spit on the ground and said, "I know no such thing."

Mr. Gross narrowed his eyes. "How can we be certain of this?"

"I give you my word. I have no idea where the other children are."

Mr. Gross replied, "I think the rest of these discussions need to be held before the council."

"Mr. Gross, we need to know how the council will help us find Joseph," Eli said.

Mr. Gross sighed. "We need to take Mr. Sawyer inside first, and then we will be able to give you answers. Please wait inside."

Eli and Grace waited anxiously by the front doors of the courthouse as Mr. Gross and Mr. Smith escorted Hunter away. After some time had passed, Grace paced around the hallway.

Eli walked up to Grace and placed his hands on her shoulders. "We have to be patient," he said. "I know time is against us, but we must have faith that we'll get Joseph back."

Grace's lips quivered as she looked at Eli and said, "You weren't there. I've never heard him scream like that. It was pure fear...nothing but fear in his voice. Joseph is a sweet boy. It'll ruin him if we don't find him."

"I know we will find him. I promise you that."

After several minutes went by, Mr. Smith approached Grace and Eli. "We wanted to thank you for catching Mr. Sawyer. It will certainly help us give answers to the other families."

"Mr. Smith, what about Joseph? We need help finding my nephew," Grace said.

"Grace, as far as the court is concerned, finding the Cherokee children is a priority over finding Joseph. We've only found two children out of forty-four now missing."

"What do you mean, Cherokee children?" Grace asked with an enraged tone. "Joseph *is* a Cherokee child."

"You know the agreement of your brother's marriage to Annabelle. As far as we are concerned, he is a Negro child who lives in our territory. He isn't a Cherokee citizen, and he'll never be considered a citizen."

Grace lunged for Mr. Smith, but Eli caught her before she could grab him. "How could you? How could any of you deny us help when he was taken from us?! You shame our ancestors. You're not Cherokee," she yelled in Cherokee.

"Grace, I need you to calm down," Eli said.

Grace continued trying to break Eli's hold on her, tears now streaming down her face.

Eli said, "Listen, we will get Joseph back. I promise we will find a way."

Grace glared at the blue-eyed Cherokee councilman. "Mr. Smith, the council owes my family. The least you could do is give us the locations of auctions held in Tennessee."

"Like I told you, our priority is the other children, not Joseph."

"Did it ever occur to you that finding Joseph could lead us to other children of the tribe?" Grace challenged.

Eli's brow furrowed as he said, "It must feel good to travel to the South and have the White men not recognize who you are." He placed his arm around Grace's shoulder and coaxed her to leave the courthouse.

As they walked away, Grace glanced back at Mr. Smith with a furious gaze. It was the first time she'd actually felt betrayed by her own tribe.

<hr>

For three days while John, Luke, and Samuel charged toward Tennessee in hopes of finding Joseph and Simon, a beaten and exhausted Joseph walked alongside Simon's black horse with his hands tied. The two arrived in a city with buildings made of brick and wood. Joseph had never seen buildings so tall, and as wagons and carriages passed him, he noticed some of the townspeople watching him. While he was forced to move along the dirt road of the city, he could feel his heart race.

"Where are we?" Joseph asked.

"If you must know, we are in Memphis, Tennessee, and that's all you need to know," Simon said. "Now walk faster." Simon jerked the rope, forcing Joseph to speed up.

"Why are we here? I want to go home."

Simon stopped the horse and pulled Joseph closer to him. "You will learn when to shut your mouth, boy. When I said that's all you need to know, that meant to keep your mouth shut!"

"I asked a simple question."

"Keep it up, half-breed. I'll beat the life out of you before you question me again."

Joseph scrunched up his face but remained silent.

Simon resumed pulling Joseph through Memphis, soon stopping at a red-brick building where he dismounted and tied his horse to a post. Simon pushed Joseph forward, coaxing the boy to enter the red-brick building. Joseph reluctantly walked to the entrance and saw a sign on the top of the building that read, Waters' Auction & Negro Sales. Joseph's eyes bulged, and he felt his throat tighten as he entered, then passed a few White men who stared at him. Joseph's face scrunched up, and he put his tied hands over his nose to escape the scent of musty bodies filling the air. The low-lit building had wooden flooring and two large, square dirty windows on each side of the entrance. He walked slowly and felt his chest tighten when he saw a large wooden podium surrounded by wooden chairs. *What is that for?* he thought. Joseph turned his head to his right upon noticing someone was there.

"Ah, Simon Bane, you always bring something interesting to these auctions," a chubby man said.

"Mr. Waters, I'm hoping for some strong bidders," Simon said. "It was an unbelievable amount of trouble to retrieve this half-breed brat. Cost a man his life."

"How did such a thing happen?"

Simon scoffed. "Those Indians, such savages, are nothing but trouble."

Mr. Waters examined Joseph's face. "So this isn't a mulatto after all, but one of the mixed-blood Indians. He looks like he's in good condition, and how old is he?"

"I'd say he's about eight years old."

"I'm nine years old," Joseph asserted.

Simon smacked Joseph.

"Careful, Simon," Mr. Waters said. "Be careful not to strike him so strongly. He is a specimen. I'm sure you don't want his value dropped by a petty wound."

Simon arrogantly replied, "The boy knows too much. Those Indians don't even follow their own laws. He doesn't know his place."

Mr. Waters sighed. "Well, I'm sure whoever bids for him will teach him how to behave."

Joseph replied, "I'm Cherokee. I'm not a Negro."

Mr. Waters slapped Joseph. "Now you listen here, nigger. You're not home, and you're never going home. Here, you ain't no Indian, half-breed or not. All I see is a nigger…a smart-mouth little nigger that's going to learn fast or be punished. It doesn't matter if you want to be called a nigger or a grass nigger."

"My name is Joseph Lightning, and my family is going to come for me."

Mr. Waters kneeled down in front of Joseph and gave a sadistic grin. "They can come for you if they want, but I promise each of them will catch a bullet unless they buy you. You can take him to be greased down like the others, Simon."

Simon pushed Joseph to walk toward a stall that was on the left side of the building. The stall door was already open, leading to an outdoor rectangular pen with a wooden floor and tall wooden walls that allowed air through, but because there was no roof, the sunlight filled the space. "Move, boy," he commanded. "Keep fighting back. The next time, it will be a punch you get instead of a slap."

Joseph complied, moving to stand in the stall.

"Take off your clothes, boy."

"Why would I do that?" Joseph asked.

Simon grabbed Joseph and began ripping off his beige cotton shirt.

"Stop it! I'm not taking my clothes off!" As Joseph struggled against Simon, he fell.

"You little brat, I'll teach you." Simon kicked Joseph in his stomach.

Joseph lay on the floor holding his stomach and moaning in pain.

"Now, take off your shoes and your trousers unless you want another kick."

As a pouting Joseph stood up and took off his shoes and trousers, two men came in the stall carrying a bucket full of grease.

"What do we have here, Simon?" one man asked.

Simon replied, "Another half-breed Indian child. He has certainly cost us."

"He looks healthy. I don't think we need to do much with him," the other man said.

Simon huffed. "Grease the boy up anyway. He won't need as much as the rest of these Negroes, but I'm not taking any chances. I want full price for the trouble this boy has given me."

One man replied, "What kind of trouble could this boy have given you?"

Simon replied, "His family put up one hell of a fight for him, and it cost one of my partners his life."

"Well, I guess that's what you would expect when going against redskins," the other man said. "After all these years, they are still out there being wild."

The men approached Joseph with the bucket of grease, causing him to take a step back. He glanced at the stall door and thought, *Am I fast enough to get to it?*

"I suggest you stop thinking, boy," Simon said. "I promise, if you give us any more problems, you'll receive more than a kick to your belly."

Joseph gulped as he stared up at Simon.

One of the men reached for a bucket sitting in the stall and threw cold water over Joseph, causing him to start shivering. The men used filthy rags to dry Joseph off roughly, then they slathered grease all over him.

As tears poured down Joseph's face, he begged, "Please let me go back to Cherokee territory, to my family."

One of the men slapped Joseph. "What makes you think you have rights here, boy?" he asked.

"I just want to go home to my mommy. I want to go back to Indian Territory."

The men scoffed and told Joseph to put his clothes on. One of the men put shackles on the boy's wrists. Grabbing the chain they attached to the shackles, Simon tugged Joseph to the stable door and walked him past a bunch of White men as they watched him.

Joseph's heart raced, and his body began to tremble. As Simon pulled him along, Joseph noticed Black and brown people with sad faces standing in place against a wall adjacent to the large podium.

"Stand over here, boy, and don't move or you will be shot," Simon threatened.

Joseph stood still next to a much older Black man with wide eyes and sweat running down his face. He looked at the White men wearing their frock coats and top hats.

Mr. Waters came up to the men and asked them to be quiet. "Gentlemen, it is my pleasure to introduce to you these fine specimens," he said. "These slaves have been brought from all over the country and are ready to serve, whether it be out in your fields or in your homes. Now, may the bidding begin!"

A young woman was pushed onto a short podium by a White man. She was stripped down, and the men approached and inspected her. Mr. Waters called for the bidding to begin, and the men shouted for $500, then $600, until the winning bid was given at $1,100. Then the woman was pulled away, tears running down her face.

The bidding continued with several men and women being sold before Joseph's eyes. Then a woman with two children younger than Joseph was put before the slave owners. The children held onto their mother, wide-eyed and crying. Two final bids were accepted as one of the woman's children was bought by a different man than her and her other son. The woman fell on her knees and begged the White man who'd bought her to buy her other child as well. Seeming sympathetic to the woman's plea, he made offers to the other man, but the older man rejected the offers. The older man and his assistant approached the Negro woman and her children. The woman grabbed both of her children and tried to put them behind the man who had bought her. The older man who had bought her son became upset and began to hit her with a small whip. The younger White man who'd bought the woman grabbed the older man's arm and the two men argued. As they argued, the son bought by the older man was grabbed by his assistant. The boy screamed for his mother as the man dragged him away. She went to go grab her son, but Mr. Waters blocked her path.

The two men who had greased Joseph up grabbed her and put shackles on her. After the women was forced onto a wagon along with her other son, her cries could be heard as the wagon took them away.

Joseph began to cry, drawing the attention of the older man standing next to him. He looked down at Joseph and asked, "You not one of us, is you, boy?"

Joseph replied, "No, I'm not. I was never a slave."

The older man huffed and shook his head. "Boy, you was a slave the day you was born in this land. The masters control all."

"I'm a Cherokee. Not a slave."

The man shrugged his shoulders. "The White man still tell you Indians what to do, so you still slaves too. Just don't have chains on you like we does. Now you do have chains. This God's order. We work for the masters, and they feed us."

"This isn't God's way. My momma taught me the White man lies."

"*All* men lie, boy."

Joseph sneered and looked up at the older man.

Soon the older Negro was taken to the podium and sold for $800. Joseph was the second to last slave remaining, the other being a woman close to his mother's age who stood motionless and speechless next to him.

Simon approached Joseph as Mr. Waters announced he was a nine-year-old Negro child. He tugged Joseph by his shackled wrists and placed him on the podium. The men walked up to

Joseph and inspected him. They decided the boy looked well fed and strong, but one man remarked that he didn't like the way Joseph looked at him, said the boy would most likely run away or be a bigger problem. Simon and Mr. Waters both assured the man that Joseph would be a great slave and future breeder.

The men stood before Joseph and began bidding.

Joseph's eyes shifted toward the exit as he bit his lip. Then he yelled at them, "I'm a Cherokee child. I'm not a slave." Then, in his native language, he yelled out, "I'm Cherokee!"

Mr. Waters struck Joseph, knocking him down, then he turned to the bidders and said, "My apologies, gentlemen. This one is still learning when to be silent."

Joseph looked back at Mr. Waters with fire in his eyes as he stood back up.

The bidders' eyes grew wider. "The boy can take a hit," one man said. "It's easy to see he's in good health."

Another man replied, "I agree. He'll do well on a plantation. Definitely a half-breed."

"Well, gentlemen, don't let this half-breed's outburst scare you now," Mr. Waters said. "Please continue your bids."

The men anxiously threw out competing bids, increasing from $600 to $650 to $800 to $900. One man shouted, "$1,130 for the boy." The other men looked at the man bitterly as he walked forward silently.

Mr. Waters replied, "Going once, going twice…sold to Mr. Plecker for $1,130. I'm sure this half-breed boy will do you a lot of good, Mr. Plecker."

Mr. Plecker confidently stepped up to Mr. Waters with a black cane in his left hand. "I'm sure he will," he said. "I see he has those Indian eyes, and his speech shows appropriate intelligence."

"These breeds are difficult to find now, Mr. Plecker. The Indians have gotten smarter, and it even cost a man his life taking this profit."

"Well…then this boy must be promising for the Indians to fight for him that hard. I'm sure he'll get along with the others on my plantation." Turning to a bearded, slightly stocky man who had followed behind him, he said, "Wade, please take the boy to the wagon. I would like to make it to one of the inns in Mississippi instead of being stuck out in the wilderness for a night."

"I think we can make it to a nice town, Mr. Plecker," Wade said as he approached Joseph.

Joseph saw his chance and bolted for the exit.

Simon quickly grabbed the boy by his shackles, dropping him to the ground.

"He is a quick one," Mr. Plecker said as he rubbed his blond beard.

"He will certainly serve you well, Mr. Plecker," Mr. Waters said.

Wade replied, "This boy is going to need some breaking. He's been free for too long."

Mr. Plecker replied, "That has never stopped us with the others. Now take the boy to the wagon, and don't underestimate him."

Wade nodded and reached for the boy again. Simon lifted up Joseph's shackles, and Wade grabbed them.

"Let me go!" Joseph shouted. "My family will find me, you ugly man!"

The other men began to cackle, making Wade's eyes widen. Wade punched Joseph in his stomach. The child collapsed, and Wade dragged him out to the wagon as he cried.

"So long, kid. I'll be sure to give your family a proper greeting if I ever run into them," Simon said with a leer.

"You had a run-in with the boy's family?" Mr. Plecker asked.

Simon replied, "Not personally, but two of the men who help keep the Indians in line did. I'm sure that one was killed because the other one completely panicked."

"Those grass niggers certainly make things interesting. I must admit, I enjoy breaking their spirit. Such a shame our forefathers decided to try to make them allies. Civilizing is one thing, but as my father told me, we've done a great misdeed against ourselves by giving them land. We should've crushed them when we had the chance decades ago."

"I agree, but little can be done about it now. The abolitionist movement is the greatest threat right now. The north and these missionaries keep pushing for more and more change that isn't in our economic favor."

"You're right, Simon. Well, I must be leaving. I do want to make it to one of the inns in Mississippi." Mr. Plecker came out to the wagon and leered. "Let's be on our way, Wade."

Wade drove the wagon to Mississippi with Joseph shackled down in the back, lying in a heap and moaning in pain.

CHAPTER 3

Searching

IN TAHLEQUAH, THE LIGHTNING-STRONGMAN FAMILY struggled to get through each day with no news about Joseph's safe return forthcoming. After four days since he'd been taken, Annabelle and her children were exhausted from the stress and shared tears. The days blurred, and she forced herself to eat to avoid headaches and be able to care for David, the girls, and eleven-month-old Jonathan. Each night, the girls slept with her since John was away. She caressed her daughters' wavy long hair and longed to give Joseph another hug. She now spent more time praying as she attempted to fall asleep.

Over a four-day period, the family processed their grief, and Lizzie nursed Michael's wounds. On the fourth day, after tending to Michael, Lizzie suddenly left the boys' room and looked at the supper table, where Annabelle had embraced David. She looked at a distraught Tsula and Maria while they sat in the rocking chairs.

"Where is Grace?" Lizzie asked in Cherokee.

Tsula replied in their native tongue, "She went back to the store so Lisa wasn't alone."

"I'll be back. I have something to do." Lizzie angrily marched to the front door and picked up her bow and quiver.

"Where are you going? Lizzie!" Tsula slowly stood up and

looked at Maria, then threw up her hands. "Forget it. I'm too fat for this. This child needs to come out."

"Where do you think she went?" Maria asked in Cherokee.

Tsula replied, "Hopefully *away* from people."

Lizzie hurried to the large green barn and took Queen out of her stable.

George and Jacob returned to the barn just as she rode off. "Where is she going?" George asked in Cherokee. Jacob shrugged. The two men took Cari and went back out into the fields.

Lizzie rode Queen through Tahlequah and beyond, to the outskirts of the town. She arrived at a wooden house with smoke coming out of the chimney, on a small hill overlooking a part of Tahlequah. She got off Queen and approached the house, holding her bow at the ready. She moved around to the side of the structure, quietly clicking to signal Queen to follow her. She saw Brock's horse in its pen, then waited several minutes for Brock to come out of the house. When he came outside and approached the horse pen, Lizzie drew her bow back as she aimed at him.

The thought of what Jesus would think echoed in her mind.

Lizzie reluctantly lowered her bow and walked toward Brock. "Mr. Jackson, we need to talk," she yelled.

Brock froze next to the pen gate and swung his gaze to her.

Seeing the fear in his widening blue eyes, Lizzie said, "It would be unwise for you to run."

Scowling, Brock watched as Lizzie came closer. "What do you want, Lizzie Lightning? You're on my land."

"You're on *Cherokee* land. I think it's good for you to remember that."

Brock sneered. "What do you want?"

"I know you know about my nephew's kidnapping. Here you are hiding instead of in the other parts of Tahlequah, or in the other Cherokee towns. Why is that?"

"It is no business of yours, woman. Now, I think it is time for you to leave."

"My nephew was kidnapped four days ago. My little Joseph

was taken from our farm by two White men. I heard him scream for Annabelle. In his entire life, I have never heard him scream like that."

"Why would I care, Miss Lightning?"

"You swore you would have my nephew sold into slavery, and now he's missing. We were able to capture one of the men who helped take Joseph. Mr. Sawyer is alive, and the Cherokee council now has him." Lizzie noticed sweat had started to run down the side of Brock's face. "You accuse me of being unable to be a lady, but here I am talking to you. Not fighting you."

"How can you call yourself a lady with that bow in your hand? I think it's clear what you came here to do."

"The truth is that I don't trust you. You alone have caused my family so much pain over the years. You raped Lisa and almost killed her spirit. Does it surprise you I came here with my weapons to protect myself?"

Brock's gaze shifted around the land, avoiding Lizzie.

"Where is my nephew, Mr. Jackson?"

Brock spit on the ground. "I have no idea where the boy is, and I had no involvement in his kidnapping. I suggest you look hard and fast for him. Indian children sell fast."

Lizzie scoffed. "You must think we're fools. You know something. God doesn't like ugly, and I'm sure your spirit is darker than any Negro's skin. Be grateful my sister spared Mr. Sawyer's life." She mounted Queen and began slowing riding away.

Brock kicked one of the wooden poles of the horse's pen. "You remember this day, Lizzie Lightning! I'll make sure you know your place if you ever come out here again unannounced! I'll—"

Lizzie stopped Queen, turned, and stared down at Brock. "I believe you really don't understand the pain of losing someone. I'm in a lot of pain. My family is in a lot of pain. You keep telling me how uncivilized I am, but I see why your wife left you."

Brock stepped forward and made a fist.

"If you have problems with me, come after me. Leave my family out of it, because if you come to our farm ever again, I will kill you as Lisa promised she would do."

Lizzie rode away while Brock watched, clenching his teeth.

He screamed and kicked a bucket sitting next to his house. "Curse that woman! Now I have to go make sure Hunter didn't tell those Indians everything." He rode off to the Cherokee courthouse with a tight grip on his horse's reins.

Mr. Plecker and Wade arrived in Hernando, Mississippi, with Joseph sitting in the wagon. As they rode through the town, Joseph remained silent. Arriving at an inn, the men forced Joseph off the wagon and inside, making him sit on the floor as they talked between themselves and ate their evening meal.

A thunderstorm quickly arrived, the thundering clouds giving Joseph hope that God was angry. He thought, *Maybe the Father is going to punish them. I want my momma. Father, please break these chains.* The storm raged on for the rest of the day and half into the night, keeping Joseph awake.

The next day, the men forced Joseph into the wagon again. When Wade pushed him farther back into the wagon, Joseph glared at him.

"Keep giving me that look, nigger. I promise I'll beat you so hard that your face stays stuck like that," Wade snarled.

Joseph murmured, "I'm not a nigger."

Wade stopped and stared at Joseph. "You say something?"

Joseph looked down at his hands.

Wade scoffed and got into the wagon, then drove it away from the inn and on through Mississippi.

Through the window of their home, Tsula watched Lizzie return on Queen. She exhaled while rubbing her pregnant belly. She went outside the moment Lizzie took Queen inside the barn, and when Lizzie left the barn carrying her bow, the two cousins locked eyes on each other. Lizzie walked toward her cousin, stopping a few feet from her.

Tsula's mouth curved downward in a frown, and she took a deep breath. "Where did you go?" she asked, her voice slightly breaking with concern.

Looking at her slightly taller cousin, Lizzie curled her lower lip and shrugged. Clearing her throat, she said, "Where do you think?"

Tsula's brow lowered, and she shook her head. "Please tell me you didn't."

Lizzie's unremorseful nature shone through as her eyes narrowed, the smooth skin of her face crinkled, and her lips tightened.

"Please...tell me you didn't go to that man!"

"I needed to do *some*thing. I couldn't sit here anymore, knowing he was involved."

Tsula placed her hand on her pregnant belly. "Please don't tell me you killed that man." Her voice began to break. "Please tell me you didn't do it. We can't handle any more craziness. We've already lost too much!"

Lizzie's lips began to quiver, and her eyes narrowed. "I didn't kill him, but I can still feel the strength in my arm needed to draw my bow. I want to send that animal to hell for what he did to Lisa." Her eyes welled up, and she clenched her teeth. "And I can't get Joseph's screams out of my head. I want Brock to suffer. I'd never give him a quick death." She shook her head. "I'd make sure every drop of his blood stains the grass before he dies."

Tsula began to cry. "Don't say that! You're not a killer! You're my blood...more like my sister than just a cousin! You're not like those White men out there." Her voice rose. "You're not like them!"

Lizzie wiped away the one tear that had escaped from her eye before it could coat her unremorseful face.

"Promise me you won't go after him."

Lizzie's gaze shifted off Tsula, and her grip tightened on her bow.

"Lizzie, please! I'm hurting just like you! You want the truth? I want him dead too, but it will cost us more."

Lizzie's eyes fixed onto Tsula's pregnant belly and moved up to her face, tortured and drenched in tears. She inhaled and exhaled deeply. "I won't go after him, but I will kill him if he returns to our home." She approached Tsula and hugged her with her left arm, still holding onto her bow with her right hand. Then she moved around Tsula and walked away.

Tsula rubbed her forehead and watched Lizzie go to the practice grounds. "Jesus, please help us. I feel like we're running out of time. I'm afraid." She walked back to the family house no less worried and began thinking about what to cook for dinner.

———◆———

John, Luke, and Samuel arrived in Tennessee four days after Joseph's kidnapping. Upon entering a small town, they came across an old White man slowly riding along in his wagon. The old man was surprisingly kind to them, telling them several slave auctions were going on in Memphis.

The trio rode hard to reach Memphis a few hours later, arriving hungry and exhausted. As they passed a supply store, Samuel convinced John to stop so they could buy something to eat. Though impatient to find Joseph, John realized he would be no good if he was weak from hunger. They bought bread and shared it as they slowly rode through the town, keeping an eye out for any sign of Joseph.

As the three men traveled through the town, they noticed uncomfortable looks some of the townspeople were giving them. One White woman even moved her young son to her left, away from the men.

Samuel scoffed and said, "We really are away from home now. How do you think we're going to find these auctions?"

Luke pointed to a flier on a brown-bricked building. "We'll find him by following these."

And so they traveled through Memphis, following the paper trail until they found one of the auction sites. The auction was held outside with a crowd of White men standing before a wooden podium. A skinny, black-haired White man wearing a blue high-collared shirt covered by a brown vest and complementing brown trousers walked onto the stage. The pepper-bearded man pulled a gold pocket watch out of his brown vest and announced the beginning of the auction. The three Cherokee men's gazes fixed on the green-eyed man.

Luke tapped John on his shoulder and pointed to a line of Negros standing at the bottom of the podium. The line went around the tall podium, making it difficult to see who was standing behind it. The three men immediately marched toward the front. Some of the White men scowled at them, some whispered among themselves, and a few even scoffed at their presence.

The men reached the front as a young Negro woman stood on the podium and the auctioneer shouted, "Sold for $800!"

John exhaled, and his hand tightened into a fist as a few men cheered for the selling of a young woman. He kept his eyes locked on the line of Negros while moving around to see the others standing behind the podium. John stomped his foot once he saw Joseph wasn't there. "We'll have to ask these men where the other auctions are," he said.

The Cherokee men approached several White men after the slave auction ended. They were ignored by most of the men they asked, with a few even threatening them. One man told them to keep following the posted signs. Several were held each day, and he pointed to a wood post that had several auctions listed. John and the others quickly searched for Joseph.

After desperately looking for the boy at three different auction sites, they came across another auction that was about to begin in a red-bricked building called Waters' Auction & Negro Sales. John, Luke, and Samuel got off their horses and tied them to a post, then walked into the low-lit building. The funk of the air became stronger as the men approached the large wooden podium surrounded by wooden chairs and White men. The White men looked back at them with wide eyes and raised eyebrows.

"Good evening, gentlemen. Is there something I can do for you?" a chubby man asked.

"We are looking for a Cherokee child that was taken away from his home four days ago," John said. "We've checked other auctions in this city and wanted to see who you were trying to sell today."

The chubby man replied, "We have no Indian children here, and we don't sell them."

Samuel replied, "What about half-breed Indian children?"

"As I said, we sell no Indian children here. Now, if that's all you men have come here for, then you can leave. I have an auction to run."

John replied, "No, I think we will stay. What is your name?"

"My name is Mr. Waters, and yours?"

"I'm John, and these are my cousins, Luke and Samuel. Are those all of the Negroes you're selling today?"

"Why, yes. There are twenty being sold today. All of them in good health and well behaved."

John, Luke, and Samuel walked past Mr. Waters to get a closer look at the men and women being sold. A little girl around Joseph's age standing next to a Negro woman caught John's eye because she had a copper complexion and two long braids. She wore a plaid blue and red dress and had big brown eyes.

"That girl, is she one of ours?" John asked Mr. Waters, pointing to the child.

Samuel said to John in Cherokee, "She's an Indian child. We need to ask her where she is from."

Before Waters could reply, the three men approached the Negro woman and the little girl. John asked the woman, "Is this your daughter?"

The Negro woman replied, "No, she ain't mine. I ain't never had a child. I tried to comfort her, sir."

"What are you doing?" Mr. Waters shouted.

John, Luke, and Samuel looked at Mr. Waters as he quickly walked over to them. "Where are you from?" John asked in Cherokee.

The anxious girl looked confused by his question.

"Where are you from?" he tried in English this time.

"I'm from Illinois. I was with my daddy when some bad men took me," the girl said.

"Are you Cherokee?" Samuel asked.

"No, I'm Shawnee. My momma is Shawnee, and my daddy is N—"

"Enough of this!" Mr. Waters yelled. "Unless you gentlemen are interested in purchasing this girl, I suggest you stand with the other men."

John angrily replied, "You liar! You said that this auction doesn't sell Indian children, but here is an Indian girl."

"She is a half-breed, and it's perfectly legal to sell her! I think it's time for you to leave."

"Little girl, what is your name?" Luke asked.

"My name is Deanna Freeman."

"Deanna, was your mother a slave?"

"No, she is Shawnee and was born in Indiana."

Mr. Waters callously replied, "She is here for a debt, and that debt will be paid. She is not full blood, and she isn't your kin, so it is none of your business."

Brow furrowing, John clenched his fist.

Suddenly, Samuel placed his hand on John's shoulder. "We can't, John. We are outnumbered here," Samuel whispered.

John exhaled as he stared down Mr. Waters, then he spun on his heel and stomped toward the exit.

"I suggest you let the girl go, Mr. Waters," Samuel said before he and Luke turned to follow John.

The other men waiting to bid began to heckle the three Cherokee men as they walked across the auction hall.

Mr. Waters angrily walked after them, becoming bolder. "Unless you three savages are interested in buying some slaves, don't come back here! Did you hear what I said?" He moved faster, catching up to John, Luke, and Samuel and pushing John just before they reached the exit.

John spun around and narrowed his eyes in a determined, angry glare at Mr. Waters but kept walking with the others. They stopped by the exit door.

"I think we should take the girl," Luke said.

"So do I," John said. "We'll wait for the auction to end and wait for whoever brings her out. Then we'll take her. Luke, maybe you should take the girl to the outskirts of Memphis."

Luke asked, "What will the two of you do?"

John answered, "If it's two of us, the White men will have a harder time finding us once we take the girl."

"All right, I'll take the girl and keep her safe."

Like statues on either side of the exit, the three men watched Mr. Waters auction off men, women, and children for over two hours. Once the little girl was sold, John and Luke quietly left the auction and stopped on the right side, just inside the entrance. Samuel took up position on the left side, in front of the large dirty square window, as men exited the building. The Cherokee men waited for the man who'd bought the girl to finish the paperwork. While he was going toward the exit with his black walking cane, he tugged the girl's chain with his right hand. Samuel clicked his tongue. Luke quietly whistled back.

Samuel walked forward, paused, smiled at the brown-haired man, and casually said, "I'm sorry I'm in your way."

Luke came from behind Samuel, abruptly snatched the chain out of the man's hand, and picked up the girl.

"What are you doing?" the man yelled.

"What needs to be done," Luke said.

The man pushed Samuel out of the way and reached for the chain on the shackles that restrained the girl. Samuel pushed the man back, and the man swung his walking cane at him. Samuel ducked the man's swing and tackled him to the ground. The White man dropped the walking stick, and Samuel punched him, but the man punched him back. The man kicked Samuel in his stomach, causing Samuel to fall back. The White man quickly reached for his revolver, but Samuel drew his faster. Both men were breathing heavily as Samuel slowly stepped toward the exit. His eyes switched between the brown-haired man and the few White men standing by the podium.

Luke ran outside with the little girl toward the horses and put her up on his saddle before getting on behind her.

"What is this?" Mr. Waters yelled.

"Let's go, Samuel!" John said as he reentered the red-bricked building and tugged Samuel's arm.

The two men ran toward the exit with Mr. Waters and a few men pursing them.

Samuel tripped and fell but kept his revolver aimed at the armed brown-haired man. As the yelling White men advanced, John helped Samuel stand, and they left the building. Hearing running footsteps behind him, John turned around and punched Mr. Waters, knocking him down.

Eyes bulging, Mr. Waters yelled out, "Did y'all see?! This savage assaulted me!"

John and Samuel quickly got on their horses while some of the men chasing them hurried over to help the chubby Mr. Waters gather himself.

A few other men tried to pursue John, but their horses were roaming the streets. "These crazy redskins let our horses loose!" a man shouted.

"That felt good," John said.

"You and Lizzie are great at making new friends," Samuel joked.

The men rode through another part of Memphis in search of Joseph. As a few hours went by, John became more impatient and more desperate as the two men continued riding and avoiding confrontation. Samuel could see the growing distress in John, and when sunset began, Samuel stopped his horse.

"Samuel, what are you doing?" John complained in Cherokee. "We have to keep looking."

Samuel exhaled and looked over at John. "John, he's not here. He may have been here yesterday, but he's gone now. I'm sorry, but we need to meet with Luke before it's completely dark."

John reluctantly rode with Samuel past several houses in the more residential areas of Memphis to leave the city and reunite with Luke. The men constantly looked back while traveling down the dirt trail that led into a sparse forest. The men went deeper into the wilderness while the setting sun pierced through the trees. John whistled, and Luke whistled back. Arriving at Luke's location, the men got off their horses and calmly approached Luke and Deanna.

"How did you guys get through the town without a fight?" Luke asked.

"We went to another part of the town and waited to make it look like we had left," Samuel said. "The problem is that Joseph isn't here."

"If you want to go home, go home!" John snarled. "I'm not leaving my son behind. I can't go home like this again. I refuse to see that look on Annabelle's face. I promised her nothing would happen to Joseph. I failed our family…I failed them."

Luke replied, "There was no way we could've known."

John shook his head. "Our family was threatened. We never believed they would try."

"Mr. Marshall, when can I go home?" Deanna asked.

Luke kneeled down and put his hand on Deanna's shoulder. "Very soon. Do your wrists still hurt?"

Deanna's lips puckered into a pout. "They hurt a little."

"Are you hungry?" John asked.

Deanna nodded and replied, "Yes, sir."

John took a piece of bread from a sack and gave it to the girl. "I promise we will get you home, okay?" He playfully pinched Deanna's cheek. "You remind me of my daughters. You're a strong one."

The edges of Deanna's mouth curved upward to form a small smile. "Thank you."

John looked at Luke and Samuel. "I can't go home to the girls with nothing."

Luke and Samuel frowned. "I say we go back to the liar that told us they don't sell Indian children," Samuel said. "It's sunset, and people are going home if they're not already home. We can try to catch him alone."

Luke replied, "I agree. Let's give it a try. Samuel, stay here with Deanna. I'm better at negotiating than you."

John and Luke rode through Memphis calmly so the towns-people would ignore them. When they arrived back at Waters' Auction & Negro Sales, they saw only a few townspeople moving around. John and Luke got off their horses and tied them to a post. A few quiet steps inside the red-bricked auction building and they could hear paper rustling. They moved farther inside, finding Mr. Waters standing at a tall table to the right of the podium, putting papers into a satchel.

Mr. Waters suddenly noticed John and Luke standing behind him, their rifles aimed at him. "What…what are you doing here?" he shouted. "Get out!"

"Mr. Waters, no one is here, meaning there's no one here to help you," John said. "All we want is information. Did you sell another Indian child a few days ago?"

"I have nothing to say to either of you redskins. Now, get out!"

"Mr. Waters, my son was taken from his home. His mother and his siblings are heartbroken. Please tell us if you know anything."

Mr. Waters pouted. "Why would I tell a bunch of prairie niggers anything? You stole a man's property from my auction today in front of my other customers. I'll have both of you hanged. You have no idea what you're doing. You're not going to get that boy back."

"So you know who my son was sold to." John said, glaring at the man.

Mr. Waters suddenly gulped and closed up his satchel.

John pointed at Mr. Waters. "It's best you tell us, or there will be problems. I'm not going home without my boy, or at least with information that will help us find him."

"I don't know what you redskins want."

"Tell us who Joseph was sold to!" Luke stepped up to Mr. Waters and slammed him against a wall. "You're going to tell us, or we will hang *you*. I'm sure you've made some enemies in this town, enough enemies that it wouldn't surprise the people of this town if you were found hanging from a rope."

Mr. Waters gulped as he looked into Luke's eyes. "All right, all right, but you never heard any of this from me. The boy was brought here and sold to a Mr. Plecker or Decker. I don't remember exactly."

John's eyes burned with rage as they dilated, his teeth gritted, and his voice bellowed, "What do you mean you don't remember?!"

Mr. Waters's shoulders began to tremble. "Okay! It was Plecker. It was Plecker."

Luke's grip tightened on Mr. Waters. "Where is he taking him?"

Mr. Waters shrugged. "I don't know."

"How do you not know?" John yelled. "I know there are records! Where are the records?"

"What do you think you're going to do if you find him? What could three Indians do out here?"

"I'm going to take my boy home. Now, where was he taken?"

Suddenly, John and Luke heard footsteps coming toward them. They spun around and aimed their rifles toward the sound as a White man slowly walked around corner with his revolver drawn.

"Mr. Waters, what is going on in here?" the man asked.

"Lower your weapon," Luke said.

"An Injun telling me what to do? I think these fools forgot where they are. Mr. Waters, are you all right?"

Mr. Waters answered, "I'm all right, Ace, just terrified by these aggressive men."

"All we want is information on an Indian child wrongfully sold as a slave," Luke said.

"So, you going to buy the child back?" Ace asked.

John replied, "No, we are not buying him back. We are taking him home to where he belongs. He wasn't born a slave. He was kidnapped from his home."

"The man who bought the boy needs some type of payment. It's wrong to believe the man will give up his property without something to make up for his loss."

John's eyes narrowed. "My son isn't that man's property."

Ace tilted his head. "Well, then I think we do have a problem."

Luke pressed Mr. Waters against the wall again.

"Now, gentlemen, this can all be settled peacefully," Mr. Waters said nervously. "I only know the boy was taken to Mississippi or Louisiana. Ace, lower your revolver, please."

Ace reluctantly lowered his revolver while glaring at John and Luke.

"We'll be going now," John said. "Thank you for your cooperation, Mr. Waters."

Luke released Mr. Waters and quickly walked toward the exit with John following him, his rifle still drawn on Ace.

Luke left the building, but John stayed at the exit with his rifle aimed at Ace.

Luke quickly untied the horses and brought them closer to the exit. "John, let's go!" he shouted.

John kept the rifle fixed on Ace as he backed out of the auction building. Then he quickly got on the horse, and the men rode off.

"I can't let those redskins get away with this!" Mr. Waters shouted. "The information they have can fall back on me." He turned to look at the taller Ace. "Bring them back or kill them… and I'll make sure you're rewarded."

"Those savages mean business. I'm not wasting my time with that," Ace said. "I've already tried to help you, sir."

Mr. Waters stomped his foot. "But they're getting away! Okay, my niece. I've seen you watching her. Now, I can talk with my brother, and an arrangement can be made."

Ace's lips tightened, and he side-eyed Mr. Waters. "I don't like playing games, Mr. Waters."

"This is no game! Those savages are getting away! Now, do you want a chance with my niece or not?"

"You have a deal, Mr. Waters," Ace said as he got onto his horse.

Mr. Waters nodded, and Ace galloped after the Cherokee.

John and Luke quickly rode down the brick streets of Memphis on their horses. The few townsfolk on the street watched with wide eyes. The men came across a four-way intersection when a wagon filled with produce crossed. The Cherokee men halted their horses, seeing that too many people were on the sidewalk for them to bypass the wagon. John noticed Ace approaching on his horse. The men snapped the reins of their horses and went around the end of the wagon, causing a few people on the sidewalk to yell at them.

"You were right, Luke," John said. "He's coming up fast."

The two men flinched in their saddles as a gunshot from Ace's revolver whizzed between them.

"Great, more trouble," Luke said.

John yelled, "Move around that building!"

The high-speed chase continued as Ace took another shot at them.

The men made a quick right turn around a red-bricked building and waited. Ace rushed around the corner only to come across John and Luke with their rifles drawn. The sound of two rifles firing echoed in Memphis, and Ace fell off his horse.

Ace crawled on the ground as the Cherokee looked down at him.

A few townspeople saw the incident and began to scream.

The Cherokee spurred their horses into a gallop, heading toward the edge of the city to meet with Samuel and Deanna.

"John, we have no choice but to go home now," Luke said in Cherokee. "It would be wise for us to get more food from home. We don't know how hard these White men will look for us after this."

John frowned. "This ruined all that we came here for. I don't know how to tell Annabelle we missed him."

"We know which state he's in. If we found Jacob, we can find Joseph, and we will."

"It's different, Luke. Jacob is a strong, grown man. Joseph is a child. He's not even ten years old."

"I know, but we're no good to our family if we get caught. On our next trip, we won't need to go through Tennessee and can focus on finding the plantations in Louisiana and Mississippi. The next thing we need to do is return Deanna to her family. That'll take us a few days. Then we have to return back to Indian Territory."

"Yeah, we can at least heal one family."

John and Luke met up with Samuel in the sparse forest, and the men quickly rode away with Deanna toward Illinois. A few days later, the three men successfully took Deanna back to her home and were thanked with food and blessings. The men con-tinued to ride into the plains toward Tahlequah, holding onto hope. It was breaking John's heart that he was being forced to return home almost empty-handed.

CHAPTER 4

A Desperate Return

BY JUNE 7, 1860, ANNABELLE had secluded herself, sitting by the old redbud tree and praying. When a herd of bison passing by in the distance caught her eye, she was shocked to see only several dozen of the majestic animals. She refocused and resumed praying, but feeling she wasn't getting any answer, she began to cry.

Then she heard a small voice call her name.

Annabelle looked around, seeing nothing.

The voice came again, this time saying, "Go to Rebecca."

Heart racing, she was convinced it was the Holy Spirit. She went to the house and spoke with the women about it. Grace objected to the idea of Annabelle going back to Mercy to find Rebecca.

"You're sure it was by the spirit you heard?" Maria asked.

"I know it was," Annabelle answered.

"If you're sure this was the Holy Spirit and not from your head, we should follow," Lizzie said.

Grace wanted to pray on the decision before she would agree Annabelle should go, fighting the fear this could endanger her family again. She left the family house and returned several minutes later. "It seems this is a walk of faith. I may be more scared to take it than any of you," she said. "I believe you, but

I also know this will be dangerous. I'll go with you, and Eli will join us."

"I should go too," Lizzie said.

"We need you here. Tsula is pregnant, Lisa has been watching the children, and Uncle George, Jacob, and David are working the fields. We need someone to watch Michael, the store, and be strong enough to protect our home."

"Uncle George and David can watch Michael, and the store isn't important right now. Finding Joseph is," Lizzie barked.

"I agree, finding Joseph is more important than the store, but we can't risk the supplies getting stolen. It would hurt us too much."

Lizzie's mouth curved downward, forming a slight frown. "I'll stay behind."

Grace gave a half-smile. "Thank you, Lizzie."

"I think it would be wise for Lisa and the children to come with me and my family for a few days," Maria said in Cherokee. "It'd be a safer house if Mr. Jackson or any other White men came to attack us. They don't know where my family lives. Tsula and Luke could go live with his mother for a few days."

"I'm not leaving," Tsula unapologetically said. "I want to watch Michael. And I don't want to see Luke's momma. That woman is part of the reason I'm as big as I am now. If I go over there for a few days, I'll look twice the size of Annabelle when she had the twins."

Lisa chuckled, putting her hand over her mouth.

"I'm not going to fight you," Grace said. "Make sure you stay aware, and keep your revolver and bow with you."

"I think something else will help too," Lizzie said. She walked into her room and then returned holding a green bonnet with an elongated hood. "We can put this bonnet on you, Annabelle. It'll make your face less visible, so people won't recognize you easily."

Lizzie put the bonnet on Annabelle's head and stepped back. The woman all watched her for a moment as she adjusted the fit and then looked around.

"This feels a little weird, but I think it will work," Annabelle said. "I can't see anything on my sides though."

"Where did you get that from, Lizzie?" Lisa asked.

"That would be one of her failed attempts to make a dress," Tsula blurted in Cherokee. "So she turned it into a cotton bonnet."

The others giggled, but Lizzie narrowed her eyes and stared down Tsula, who smiled at her with her hands on her hips.

"Enough, Tsula," Grace said. "You always have something to say."

Tsula smacked her lips, then picked up her sewing kit and a baby gown she was making. She walked past the others, sticking her tongue out at Lizzie, and sat down at the supper table, facing away from Grace, who said, "She'll stay mad at me for the next five minutes."

"Nope, *fifteen* minutes now!" Tsula snarled.

The other women sighed and looked at each other, knowing the cousins couldn't help but argue.

"Maria, you should take the children first thing in the morning," Annabelle said. She rubbed her forehead. "I will possibly miss Jonathan's first birthday."

Maria replied, "Two babies won't be a problem at my papa's home. There are enough women there. It will take Jonathan some time before he knows that you're not there. The last time I went there, I didn't get to hold Sky at all."

"I'll go get the carriage ready for y'all now so you can leave early in the morning," Lizzie said.

"Sounds like a plan," Grace said. "Let's start supper, and we'll explain the plan to Uncle George and the others when we eat. It wouldn't be right to make the final decision without hearing what they have to say."

The women marched toward the kitchen as Lizzie went outside to the barn.

Tsula stood up and stretched. "Be happy that I'm hungry," she said. "That's the only reason I'm going to help cook."

Annabelle and Maria chuckled and then smiled at Tsula as she followed them.

George, Jacob, and Eli later sat at the supper table with the children. Annabelle, Grace, Maria, Lisa, Lizzie, and Tsula placed their food on the table. George blessed the food, and the family began to eat. Grace introduced the plan to the men of the family.

"Grace, this is a dangerous plan," George said in their native tongue.

"I know, Uncle George, but I believe Annabelle did hear the Holy Spirit," Grace said. "I did pray on this seriously. I don't believe we're doing this outside of the Father's plans."

"Annabelle, I understand your worry and pain. But endangering yourself won't bring Joseph back sooner," Uncle George stated.

Annabelle replied, "I swear I wouldn't do this if I didn't believe I was guided. You're right. I'm in a lot of pain. I miss my baby, but I can't put myself in danger when the twins and Jonathan need me."

"John told me the White people are almost ready to go to war against themselves," Jacob said. "This will be dangerous. Are you sure you heard the Creator or Holy Spirit speak?"

Annabelle answered, "Yes."

Eli tapped his pointer finger on his chin. "I know John would disagree, but...I'll take Annabelle to Mercy and protect her," he said. "I believe her."

George sighed and rubbed his forehead. "This is risky," he said. "Lizzie should go with Annabelle and Eli."

"I should go instead," Grace insisted. "We need to do this as quickly as possible and without conflict."

"We don't know what's to come, and Lizzie is better for this."

"I know my sister is skilled and stronger than me. To be completely honest, her strength is far beyond mine. But she still struggles with her temper. We need to do this with no drama."

George sat back in his chair and rubbed his chin. "Lizzie?"

Lizzie looked at George, then shifted to Annabelle and back to George. "She's right about me," she said. "I might lose control if the wrong White man approaches me."

George grunted as he tapped his fork on his plate.

"I'm sorry. I don't trust myself," Lizzy said.

"There's nothing to apologize for. You're right to be honest with yourself and us in this way. Time is against us. This must be done carefully. We'll stick with the plan y'all came up with. We'll make sure the children are gone in the morning."

Annabelle was pleased with the family meeting but could feel her heartbeat pick up when she thought about returning to Mercy.

The plan had been solidified and prayers made before the family went to sleep. That night in Jacob and Lisa's house, Grace lay in bed next to Eli. She stared up at the dark ceiling and noticed Eli's arm stretch out.

"Eli, am I keeping you awake?" Grace asked in Cherokee.

"No. I keep trying to think of other ways of going to Mercy without Annabelle coming," Eli said. "I know John wouldn't be happy with this plan. But the truth is, there's no other way. The longer Joseph is enslaved, the harder it'll probably be to find him."

"My brother has always done things that felt right in his heart. He lets fear blind him sometimes, and he wouldn't approve of this plan. But John has no say in this, and as you said, the more time that goes by the harder it will be to bring Joseph home."

"What answers do you think we'll find in Mercy?"

"I don't know, but the White people have more power than us and will be able to get answers we'd struggle to get."

"I heard Mercy is a city that's really divided on slavery. That makes it more dangerous for Annabelle."

Grace turned over on her side and looked at Eli. "That isn't the real reason why it is so dangerous for her to go to Mercy. It's dangerous for her because she escaped from Mercy. Annabelle was rescued from Mercy by John and Samuel years ago, after her first husband was murdered and she was threatened to be put back into slavery."

Wide-eyed, Eli turned his head to look at Grace. "How long have you known this?"

"I always knew. John and Samuel brought her to me when they rescued her. The woman we're going to see is one of the women who protected Annabelle years ago. You can't tell my uncle, or Jacob, or Michael, or Luke, and *especially* not David. Learning his mother was a slave will only make him worry more. He doesn't even know Annabelle's first husband was murdered by a White man in Mercy."

"Great, so we are returning her back to the town she escaped from. That's why Lizzie made that bonnet for her. Are there any more crazy secrets before I go to sleep?"

"Just one more. I love you, Eli Five Killer."

Eli attempted to keep a straight face, but his mouth curved into a smile and then he chuckled. The two kissed each other and went to sleep.

<hr>

Two roosters crowed in the early morning, announcing the beginning of a journey Annabelle was not prepared for. During breakfast, she stared at the boys' door, drawing more motivation to rely on her faith.

The family went forward with the plan after one final discussion while they ate breakfast together. When everyone finished their breakfast, they held hands around the table and George prayed. The girls ran outside, waiting for Annabelle, Eli, and Grace to leave. An injured Michael gave Annabelle and Grace each a hug and a kiss on the cheek before Lisa escorted him back to bed. George gave Annabelle a hug and calmly let her go. "May the Father continue to guide you, daughter," he said.

Annabelle's eyes welled up, and she gave George a tight hug. "Thank you, Papa." After David hugged Grace, he approached Annabelle and gave his mother a hug. Annabelle gave David a kiss on the cheek. "Protect the family and listen to what you are told."

"I promise, Momma," David said.

The rest of the family left the house, and George put his hand on Eli's shoulder as they walked. "Eli, by now you know, I have no nieces," he said. "When Cliff walked on, it became my responsibility to be Grace and Lizzie's father. I was not a great father, but they are my daughters. Protect my daughters as you travel. It's all I ask."

"I promise to bring them both back safely," Eli said.

"Let's get to these crops," George said.

Jacob said his goodbyes to Annabelle, Eli, and Grace while David walked to the fields, looking back at his family. Tsula spoke with her family before giving them hugs and kisses. She went to the family house and sat down in a wooden chair next to the house steps. Lizzie got Queen while Eli had Ray fitted for the carriage. Annabelle, Grace, Maria, and Lisa got into the carriage along with the young children. Eli drove the carriage out to Maria's family first, to leave Lisa, Maria, and the children with them. Lizzie rode beside the carriage with her bow and arrows. Traveling through the long grass prairies, the children pointed at a family of prairie dogs playing. An hour later, the carriage stopped in front of a brown wooden house with a small fenced-in garden on the right side and a large brown barn further to the right. To the left of the house sat a water well and a tiny stream zigzagged several feet behind it. The women and children got out of the carriage and were greeted by Maria's family. The girls gave Eli hugs and kisses once he put down their luggage. He returned to the carriage while Lisa and Maria greeted Maria's family.

Carrying Jonathan, Annabelle approached a raven-haired young woman with a cinnamon skin tone. The woman stood as tall as Annabelle. "Good morning, Antoinette," she said.

Maria's sister brushed back her long straight hair, replying with a Spanish accent, "Good morning, Annabelle, and hello, Jonathan, you handsome little man."

Jonathan bounced in Annabelle's arms. "He seems to remember you," she said.

"Yes, he does," Antoinette replied with a smile.

Annabelle spoke with Antoinette and gave Jonathan to her. Her dimpled smile fit her round face beautifully, and her cheerful round, light brown eyes made Jonathan smile. Annabelle's brow lowered as she looked at her smiling son. She exhaled to keep herself from frowning, gave the baby a kiss on his cheek, and ran her fingers through his soft, wavy hair.

"Thank you for taking in my children," Annabelle said.

"It's my pleasure. Hopefully you find the answers needed to end this nightmare."

"We will see each other again, my sweet boy," Annabelle said in Cherokee as she held Jonathan's small hand.

"May God bless you with safe travels, Annabelle."

"Thank you, Antoinette." Annabelle turned to the girls and took a deep inhale. She walked over and gave the twins and Rosita big hugs. Rosita then walked up to Antoinette.

"Momma, are we going to see you again?" Rain asked in her native tongue.

Annabelle's brow lowered. "What would make you ask such a thing?"

Rain frowned. "They took Joseph from us. You're Negro. Won't they try to take you too?"

"Oh, baby, I promise I'll be safe. I'm going to see my good White friends, and I have Uncle Eli and Auntie Grace with me. I have to see them to get help for Joseph. I promise both of you, I'll return." Annabelle turned her head to Jannie and could see her eyes shimmering with tears. She put her arms out. "Come on, Jannie."

Jannie hugged Annabelle tightly.

"Come on, Rain," Annabelle invited with one arm still open wide to receive her.

The child stepped into the embrace and gave her mother a tight hug.

Annabella leaned back to look at each of them as she said, "The two of you be big girls now. You have Auntie Lisa and Auntie Maria, and Auntie Lizzie isn't far away."

"Is she going with you?"

Annabelle let go of the girls. "No, Auntie Lizzie is staying here."

Rain's brow drew together. "Why? She's so strong she can fight a man!"

"Yeah! Cut their throats and heads off!" Jannie boldly said.

Annabelle's and Grace's eyes bulged. "Who said anything about cutting throats?" Grace asked with a stern tone.

"Nobody, I was just—"

"Never wish such a thing out of your auntie…ever!" Annabelle sternly commanded. "She never killed anyone!"

Jannie gulped. "Yes, Mommy."

Annabelle sighed. "Behave yourselves. I promise I'll return." She gave the girls each a kiss on their cheeks. "Love y'all so much."

"Love you, Mommy," the girls said.

Grace approached the girls and gave them hugs and kisses. "Love you both," she said.

"Love you, Auntie," the girls said.

The girls frowned as they watched the women go to the carriage and be helped up by Eli. The inside was brightened by the sunrays piercing through the carriage's windows.

Annabelle sat down and looked at Grace. "Lord Jesus, I just lied to my babies about Lizzie killing," she said.

Eli signaled the horse to move along and then turned to the women. "Killed who?" he asked.

"Nobody," the women growled.

Eli turned back around wide-eyed, and the women exhaled the breaths they'd been holding without even realizing it.

Two days passed as Annabelle, Grace, and Eli rode to Mercy. The separation from Jonathan made Annabelle nervous. She often tapped her finger on her thigh as she talked with Grace. Her only comfort was in knowing God was with them and that there had to be a reason for her to return to Mercy. The family arrived in Mercy on the third day, riding among townspeople along the main roadway slowly. Annabelle directed Eli and put on the green bonnet.

Looking around while they passed through the town, Annabelle murmured, "Wow, this brings back some memories."

The family arrived at the Keys' brown-bricked home. Annabelle anxiously got down from the carriage, looked at the home, and then took a deep breath.

"It feels good to stretch the legs," Eli said. "We did good with time."

"So, this is it," Grace said.

"Yeah, this is it," Annabelle said, then she walked up the pathway, past the hammock, and onto the porch.

Eli and Grace followed a few steps behind her. Annabelle raised her hand to knock on the white door, but paused a moment first.

After hurried footsteps could be heard beyond the door, it was opened and a teenage brunette girl stood in the entryway. The girl's brown eyes widened when she recognized Annabelle. "Mrs. Annabelle?" the girl asked.

Annabelle gasped. "Ashley? Ashley, sweetie, is that you?"

The teenager nodded yes, and Annabelle embraced her.

"Look at you! Look how much you've grown! Oh, how you look like your mother."

Ashely blushed as Annabelle rubbed her shoulders.

"Such a beautiful young woman now. Ashley, this is Mrs. Grace, my sister-in-law, and her husband, Mr. Eli."

"It's a pleasure to meet you both," Ashley said.

"It is nice to meet you too, Ashley," Grace said.

"Nice to meet you," Eli said.

Ashley replied, "Please come in. My mother is going to be so pleased." She stepped aside to let them in and called out, "Mother, please come to the door."

"Ashley, I need to start preparing supper for your siblings. I'd appreciate it if you helped, dear," Rebecca called back from somewhere in the house.

"Mother, please come here," Ashley pleaded.

Rebecca grunted, then started toward the front of the house. Her footsteps announced her before she appeared around a corner in a green-and-white Victorian dress with a plate in her hand. When she saw Annabelle, she dropped the plate. As the plate shattered on the floor, she ran toward Annabelle and gave her a hug. After letting her go, she asked, "Annabelle, what would bring you back here?"

Annabelle's eyes welled up as she replied, "They took my

baby boy. They kidnapped Joseph." Her tears fell, streaming through the trail dust clinging to her cheeks.

Rebecca embraced Annabelle and began to cry with her.

Ashley put her hand on her heart and looked at Grace and Eli, seeing the pain in their eyes. Struggling not to cry, she mumbled, "I feel so powerless."

Rebecca sat Annabelle down and introduced herself to Grace and Eli. Grace told the entire story of Joseph's kidnapping while Rebecca and Ashley listened. Rebecca was infuriated when hearing how the tribe considered Joseph's rescue unimportant.

"You know I have been involved with this Underground Railroad, and we even get help from some of the Indians," Rebecca said. "Two years ago, some runaway slaves came to one of the hidden areas, and with them were three Indian children from the Shawnee. It was hard to believe these children had no Negro blood, but they didn't. We were able to find their families again, but it took months. One of them even stayed with us for two months until we found her family in Indiana."

"The United States has been of no help to us getting back the children that were taken away from their families," Grace said. "To my knowledge, fifty children have been reported missing, and only five of them have been brought home. Only two of the children came from the same plantation in Tennessee. We are running out of time to find Joseph."

"You're right. The more time that goes by, the harder it will be to find him if records were to be changed or destroyed."

"Can you tell us which plantations we should check to see if they have Joseph?" Eli asked.

Rebecca replied, "Abolitionists have created hidden records of slave owners known to have a high number of mixed-blood slaves and even a few mentions of them having Indian slaves still. The real problem is that most slaves are marked as Negro even when they have no Negro blood. Most owners won't even answer such questions. What does he look like?"

"He's a little taller than my waist," Annabelle said. "He has curly hair, but it is not as rough as mine. He is a lighter color than me, and he has John's eyes. He speaks good English and

Cherokee. He's not even ten years old yet. He only knows how to be Cherokee. I know they're going to try to break him."

Rebecca placed her hand on Annabelle's hand. "We have to pray Joseph remains strong through this. At least what you've told me can help us look for him. These men are animals and will certainly claim Joseph was bought legally. How much money does the family have to buy him back?"

"We have no plans of buying him back. We're taking him home," Grace said with an authoritative tone.

Rebecca smiled at Grace. "I like your thinking. I won't be able to get the records until Allen returns. In the meantime, I believe it is long overdue for some old friends to see you. Ashley, I want you to go see Mrs. Pots first and tell her Annabelle is here, and tell Mrs. Avail, Mrs. Wilson, and, if you see her, Mrs. Heinz."

Ashley nodded. "Yes, mother." She gave Annabelle a tight hug and left the house immediately.

Annabelle looked at Rebecca with a skewed frown. "Mrs. Heinz…who is Mrs. Heinz?" she asked.

"Your old enemy turned friend," Rebecca said with the corner of her cheek pinching into a smirk.

"You mean Sierra Nicole? Wait, her last name was Deeds, not Heinz."

"Well, yes. I may have forgotten to mention she married five years ago and has a five-year-old daughter, and is expecting another. She has changed for the better and even gives us new information on political changes her husband talks about."

Annabelle replied, "The Lord does work in mysterious ways." She turned to Grace and Eli. "Sierra Nicole was almost like Nancy but way more physical."

"Well, let's be grateful she's changed," Eli said. "We have some difficult people in Tahlequah too."

Rebecca tilted her head. "I believe it."

An hour later, as Rebecca prepared food and talked with Annabelle and Grace, the front door opened. "Where is she?" Marilyn called out from the entryway.

Annabelle walked out of the kitchen, seeing Marilyn holding the hand of a beautiful toddler.

Marilyn rushed to Annabelle and gave her a hug, then she looked at Eli and smiled. "Who is this? This isn't John, but he is handsome."

Eli blushed while Annabelle smiled and lightly hit Marilyn on her shoulder. "He's my brother-in-law, and this is John's older sister Grace," Annabelle said.

Marilyn replied, "It's a pleasure to finally meet you. Annabelle has written about you, and John has spoken a lot about you."

Grace replied, "Nice to meet you finally, Marilyn. Annabelle has spoken well of you."

The toddler ran over to Marilyn, and she picked her up. "I want you to meet Naomi, my star. I now make dresses for little girls...hoping to put some nicer ones on her. Wait a moment! Where are they? Benjamin and Angel, come in here!"

A young boy and girl with hazel eyes ran into the house and stopped to stand on either side of their mother. Ashley immediately entered the house after the younger children and approached Rebecca.

"Look at them! Ruthanne wasn't joking. They're beautiful, and the girls look just like you," Annabelle said.

"I know they look like smaller versions of me with a little bit of color. Benjamin is a handsome cross between Daniel and me." Marilyn frowned. "So, what would bring you back here? This is dangerous, Annabelle."

Annabelle's grin faded, and the corners of her mouth curved downward while her brow lowered. She shook her head. "My son." She told Marilyn about Joseph's kidnapping.

Marilyn listened in disbelief as she held Naomi close to her while the other two children giggled and played with Ashley in the living room.

Soon a young brunette girl opened the front door and excitedly ran inside. "Ashley!" the green-eyed girl yelled.

Ashley stopped playing with Marilyn's children and gave the young girl a hug. Ruthanne stepped inside with a younger green-eyed girl while holding a sleeping toddler in her arms.

"Good afternoon, Mrs. Avail," Ashley said with a smile while resuming her play with Marilyn's children on the sandy-colored checkered couch.

"Good afternoon, Ashley," Ruthanne said as she took a step forward. She turned to her right, walked through the living room, and walked through the arch to enter the dining hall with her daughters following her. She looked directly at Rebecca and Marilyn, who were sitting at the center of the large cedar table.

The redhead looked to her right, seeing Annabelle, Eli, and Grace sitting at the large cedar table, and smiled. "You're a brave woman to return, Annabelle," she said in her southern tone. "I would like you to meet my children, Belle, Christina, and this handsome little man is Jonah Peter, since I refused for him to have the same first name as Peter."

"You haven't changed at all," Annabelle said.

"Well, a preacher's wife has to look good."

Annabelle stood up and gave Ruthanne a hug.

Ruthanne said, "Words can't express how much I miss seeing you. I like your hair. Four braids, that's different."

"When did you get a scar by your eye?" Annabelle asked.

"This beauty...I got that from doing my time, but I think it makes me look tough. I'm cute with it," Ruthanne said with a smile.

"I can see that."

Ruthanne sighed. "Well...there must be a serious reason for you to be here, and with more Cherokee. It's too dangerous right now for you to come back."

Annabelle frowned. "I wish there weren't a serious reason." She told Ruthanne about Joseph's kidnapping.

During the group's talk about other ways to help Annabelle, Catherine arrived with Esther and Elisha. Annabelle was excited to see Rebecca's twins and Catherine. Right after they entered, a pregnant Sierra Nicole arrived. It was a weird moment for Annabelle, seeing her old enemy now welcoming her with open arms. Daniel and Allen Keys later arrived at the Keys's home, both shocked and happy to see Annabelle. Mr. Keys's demeanor had even slightly changed from what Annabelle remembered. He was far more vocal about his position against slavery, and his tone echoed anger once he learned how Joseph had been kidnapped.

"I assure you, Annabelle. I will try to get some extra help for you and your family," Mr. Keys authoritatively said. "To steal a child in the early morning from his very home…it's sickening. I'm grateful you're at least safe and accompanied by good people."

"Thank you, Mr. Keys. It's rare we hear a White man speak like you," Grace said. "Reverend Hills is the only White man we've met recently that's strongly against slavery."

"The country is changing, and we will either see a successful awakening, or we will see a war like nothing the world has seen before. Evil is trying its hardest to keep its hold on the land."

"Would White men really fight so hard for slavery?" Eli asked. "Would it go so far as a war?"

Mr. Keys replied, "Men have fought for what they believed in aggressively for thousands of years. The Bible shows us this, and even our own history here in America shows us this truth. I hope we never see anything like that ever again."

Eli replied, "I hope that too. Indian Territory is affected by what happens in the land, and a war will bring destruction to us."

Mr. Keys nodded in agreement. "Annabelle, I must say it is a blessing you made it here safely. Despite such deplorable reasons that brought you back to us, of course."

"It's good to see you too, and I see Marilyn has been feeding you well, Daniel," Annabelle said.

Daniel chuckled. "Well, I have a hard time saying no to anything Marilyn cooks for me. Her chicken is so good, I'm sure it feeds my soul too."

Everyone laughed. After several minutes of conversation,, the women went into the kitchen and started preparing a meal. Eli, Daniel, and Mr. Keys remained at the cedar table, talking about current politics. Mr. Keys emphasized the consequences of not being able to save Joseph peacefully but supported any means to save him. A little over an hour later, Annabelle, Ashley,

Marilyn, Rebecca, and Ruthanne began to bring food platters into the sunlit dining hall and set them out on the table.

"Ah, Rebecca, you're going to make me fat too," Danielle said.

Rebecca chuckled while she set out freshly baked bread for everyone. "Daniel, I doubt that. I'm sure Marilyn will be the one to do that deed," she joked.

"Well, I must be off," Sierra Nicole said. "I have a husband to feed, but I'm glad to see you, Annabelle. I'm horrified with what has happened. I truly hope the next time I see you it will be for good reasons, and I will be able to meet your children."

"I hope that as well, Sierra Nicole," Annabelle said.

The two women hugged, and Sierra Nicole left for her home.

The other women finished bringing in the food, and Mr. Keys said the blessing. As the friends ate supper, there was a knock on the door.

Mr. Keys opened the door and smiled. "Ah, Pastor Avail, I was wondering when you would come," he said.

"Well, yes, my empty house prompted me to come here," Peter said. "And you know not to call me Pastor outside of the church."

"It took you long enough. Look who is here," Ruthanne said.

Peter walked into the dining hall and dropped his walking cane as his gaze found Annabelle looking back at him with a smile. "Annabelle, I never expected one of my prayers to be answered so quickly," he said.

Annabelle replied, "Pastor Avail, it is good to see you. Your children are adorable."

"Why, yes, they are, but Belle and Christina are clearly Ruthanne's children. I'm amazed I haven't grown any gray hair yet."

Everyone laughed as Peter took off his black frock coat and set it on a chair in the living room, then moved closer to the dining room.

"I saved you a seat, Peter. There's a lot we have to talk about," Ruthanne said.

Everyone had a blank expression, indicating the conversation was serious, as they waited for Peter to take his seat. He exhaled and drummed his fingers on the table as Ruthanne made him a plate. Then she told him why Annabelle had returned.

The dire news made Peter look at his daughters. His lips slowly pinched, his brow furrowed, and he slowly shook his head. "Annabelle, saying to you that I'm sorry to hear of this occurrence feels worthless. This truly is in God's hands, and it's worrisome, because we don't know the outcome. It's easy to say trust in Jesus, but usually the first thing we follow is emotions. Our emotions often betray us. For a lot of us, we do struggle to go to God first. We make the mistake of thinking we deserve the trouble or God won't do anything. We're shortsighted. With that, I encourage you not to lose faith. We're to move by faith, not by sight. With that said, I'll be praying every day for your son."

Annabelle smiled, withholding her tears. "Thank you, Pastor Avail," she said. "It is hard, not knowing how long I have to wait to hold my baby boy again."

"Put your hope in God. Not in your own strength. Never hold back on your prayers."

Annabelle nodded. "I won't hold back."

The supper continued with other topics being brought up to make some good memories of their reunion. After the meal, Mr. Keys left to get the records of plantations they were tracking in their efforts to help the Underground Railroad. When he returned, he placed the records on the wooden coffee table in the living room and sat down on a sandy-colored, checkered couch.

Eli entered the living room and rubbed his chin. "All of these records?" he asked.

Mr. Keys answered, "Yes. All of these plantations have records of Indian slaves or those who are certainly mixed blood. A lot of people put work into this. All of this is illegal."

Eli picked up some of the lists and started to read through them. His brow furrowed and his nose creased. "I never imagined there were so many of us in chains. It doesn't make sense. I thought we were more aware of what these White men were doing."

"Some of the original records listing Indian slaves were changed to Negro when laws were changed. It took a lot of work, but at least some of the Indians and those with Indian blood were traced."

Eli shook his head. "These generations have no idea who they are. How can we figure out who their people are? It's impossible."

Mr. Keys tightened his lips. "The only solution I can think of is the tribes adopting them, but would they?"

"In the old days, yes, but nowadays…the answer will depend on how brown their skin is."

While Eli read through the lists, Grace stood up and smiled as she watched Annabelle interacting with the other women. After a moment, she announced to the room, "I wanted to make it clear. We must leave immediately in the morning," she said. "We have to tell our family what we've gathered as soon as we can. It's people like you that turn into lifelong friends. I don't know how Annabelle feels, but I now feel a stronger hope that we will bring Joseph back home. Thank you for your kindness."

"I'm glad Annabelle has other strong women in her life, and a good husband," Ruthanne said. "I never imagined she was going to stay in Indian Territory, but after seeing John over the years and now meeting you and Eli, I understand why it became Annabelle's home. I want my children to grow up with no memory of these discussions. May God guide us in making the necessary changes."

Grace smiled and sat back down next to Eli. The loving atmosphere strengthened Annabelle, and as the sunset began to fade, it was decided that everyone needed to go home. Peter had everyone hold hands, and he prayed extensively for Annabelle and her family. Annabelle gave everyone hugs, and each hug made it harder for her to say goodbye.

"We'll be praying every day for Joseph," Daniel said.

"Thank you, Daniel," Annabelle said. "It was good to see you."

"There will be better days." Daniel escorted his young children outside.

Marilyn stepped forward and hugged Annabelle. Her emotional hug was one of the hardest. "I miss you greatly, dear," she said, still hugging Annabelle. "I hope the next time we see each other, it'll be under far better circumstances. May every plantation burn to the ground."

"You're a great mother," Annabelle said. "I miss you too, and your perfume gives me strength."

The two friends giggled, then gave each other a kiss on the cheek. Marilyn said her goodbyes to the others before leaving.

"Annabelle, I know Rebecca would've wanted me to keep quiet about this because she'd want you to forget about him, but Mad Moe was shot dead two months ago," Ruthanne said. "That evil man broke into a family's home and attempted to rape the wife of the household."

Annabelle's eyes widened, and her jaw dropped a little.

"He must've believed he killed the husband because he was shot in the back by the husband. With his last breath, he saved his wife. If things really do change, you can return to Mercy freely. At least you'll never see Mad Moe again. I hope it's God's will that we find Joseph quickly."

Annabelle replied, "So do I." She and Ruthanne hugged, and the Avail family left the house.

Later that night, Annabelle, Grace, and Eli went upstairs to sleep in Annabelle's old room. Nostalgia hit her in the heart. Over the next few hours, the three created a copy of the plantation names and their locations. As Annabelle lay in her old bed in the early morning hours, she stared up at the ceiling, unable to sleep while hoping to be visited by the angel Constance. However, there was no appearance, and Annabelle finally fell asleep.

———◆———

In the early morning, Grace quietly got out of bed and quickly put on her shoes. She left the bedroom, and her eyes enlarged. She gagged but tightened her lips. She rapidly moved across the wooden floor, gagging again, and put her hand over her mouth. She aggressively reached for the front door and pulled it open. She tried to quickly go down the upper-quarters stairs with her hand still over her mouth. She then vomited on the side of the house while she stood on the stairs.

"I'd know that sound any day," Rebecca said, rocking in a hammock.

Grace slowly climbed down the stairs in her nightgown and looked at Rebecca. "What do you mean?" she asked.

Rebecca smiled. "I think you know what I mean. How long have you been having morning sickness?"

"It started last week, but this week makes it clear. I'm late…I haven't bled. This is terrible timing, and I don't know when I want to tell them. It was difficult hiding it from them on the way here. I've been telling them it's the stress."

"You're married. They'll be excited for you."

"I don't want this child to take away my family's focus on Joseph. I was beginning to feel scared I couldn't have a child because of my age. I'm happy I was wrong, but terrified. If we fail, this child will never meet my nephew."

"I understand how you feel. I think Annabelle has only remained strong because of God's grace and the strong bond she has with you now. She is a strong woman, but a person can only take so much."

"I lost my papa when I was a child not too long after I lost my momma. My younger sister was the one that found him. He drank so much it killed him, and I spent the rest of the day holding her as she cried, and at night, my Auntie Shay held her. Lizzie went everywhere with him, she learned how to hunt from him, and in some ways, I think she was closer to him than to me. When he died, she cried so hard she passed out. I'm tired of my family experiencing hard times."

Rebecca sighed. "I understand hard times. I lost my first child. I imagined the baby was a boy and gave him a name, Stanley. I thank God every day for helping me heal past that. Occasionally I wonder what he would look like now. I don't know how to explain it, but I feel in my spirit that Joseph will come home before he becomes a man."

"I hope for that too. We wouldn't have been able to find him alone. The Father spoke to Annabelle, and that's what gave us the courage to come here."

"He does work in mysterious ways. I hope that list is the key."

Grace nodded. "So do I. We don't need any more pain."

Later in the morning, Annabelle and the others said goodbyes to the Keys family. Still adjusting to seeing Ashley as a teenager, Annabelle gave her a long embrace. "Seeing you growing into a beautiful young woman brings so much joy to my heart," she said to the girl. "You make your parents so proud."

"I miss you so much, Miss Annabelle," Ashley said with a happy tone etched by sadness. "My mother read all your letters to me. I hope you bring Joseph home soon."

Annabelle pursed her lips. "So do I."

Annabelle and the others left Mercy with a copy of the plantation records. During their return to Tahlequah, she and Grace went through records again. Annabelle's heart dropped once she saw Columbus, Mississippi, listed next to one of the plantations, the town where she was born and had been raised as a slave before escaping. She said a silent prayer, hoping Joseph wasn't there, and continued to look through the other records.

CHAPTER 5
The Hierarchy

I T WAS JUNE 11, 1860, when a wagon stopped before a large white mansion with four pillars supporting the front of the roof. Rows of Carolina roses grew around the front of the mansion, and two large willow trees towered over the mansion on either side. A cookhouse to the left of the house had a short, attached pathway between it and the house, and a small white house sat across from the cookhouse. Apple and walnut trees stood fully grown adjacent to the small house.

Joseph had never seen a house that large, and he watched as a few slaves walked past carrying various supplies. Wade grabbed the shackles on Joseph's wrists and pulled him out of the wagon. Joseph pulled back on the chains and struggled to fight him off. Wade smacked Joseph, knocking him down on the ground.

"I think it's time for you to accept the truth, boy," Wade said. "This is your new home until the day you die."

"It will *never* be my home," Joseph growled.

Wade was about to hit Joseph when Mr. Plecker stepped up close to the boy. "I believe that's enough. I don't want him damaged," he said. "I want him taken around the rest of the property so he'll know where everything is. Then bring him inside to Mrs. Plecker and the others so they can have a look at him."

Wade replied, "I will get this done immediately."

Mr. Plecker smiled. "Welcome to Caledonia, Mississippi, Joseph. I own you, boy."

Wade pushed Joseph to start walking. As the man led him around, Joseph saw eight massive unevenly spaced willow trees that seemed to make a large, slanted line connecting the mansion and the slave houses. There were slaves working in the four large cotton fields, with two White men watching them. Joseph and Wade traveled down a large road to the slave houses. There were several slaves houses, all the same size and made out of wood, and they were in a worse condition than the small white house next to the cookhouse. Joseph noticed the slaves looking at him as he passed them, but he was too angry to acknowledge them.

At a large red barn, Wade stopped and called out, "Bo, you come out here. We got someone new for you to teach." Then he took off Joseph's shackles.

A brown-skinned Negro man wearing a straw hat came out of the barn, his white cotton shirt and beige trousers stained with sweat and dirt. "Good morning, Master Wade," Bo said.

"This boy here will be helping bring cotton over to this cotton gin, and he'll work there until I believe he's old enough for the fields. Make sure you teach this boy correctly, or I'll have your hide beat."

"I'm not touching none of that cotton," Joseph bickered in Cherokee. "I'm no slave. I'm a Cherokee child. You can't control me."

Nearby slaves paused in their work to stare at the boy with big eyes. One long-haired girl's eyes locked with Joseph's eyes while she stood behind a broken wagon several feet behind Wade.

Suddenly, Wade punched Joseph, knocking him down. "Pick him up, Bo!" he shouted.

Bo quickly went to pick Joseph up and whispered, "You need to keep your mouth shut, boy."

Joseph glared daggers at Wade as Bo helped him up.

"You ain't no Cherokee here, nigger," Wade said. "Like I said, this is your home now, and that's the last time I'm going to tell you."

"I got him, Master Wade. I go teach him now."

Wade crossed his arms. "No, Master Plecker wants the boy to be brought to the mansion so the family can see the boy." He grabbed Joseph by his arm and forced him to go with him. "I promise you, boy. You keep this up, and I'll beat that Indian blood out of you. Won't be no Cherokee-nothing left in you."

The two continued down the large dirt path while Bo and the other slaves watched. Bo turned to the long-haired girl and said, "Looks like you got someone else to talk to."

Back at the mansion, Wade escorted Joseph inside. Joseph stood in the foyer and stared up at the elegant front staircase, eyes bulging.

"Mr. Plecker, I've brought the boy in to be viewed," Wade called out.

To Joseph's right, a brunette woman with big round green eyes left the dining hall, followed by a hazel-eyed mulatto woman. The short, middle-aged White woman wore a green Victorian dress with yellow flowers embroidered on her sleeves and had her hair styled in two buns. The young mulatto woman wore a blue cotton dress and had her frizzy brown hair put into one bun. She was Tsula's height, but still slightly taller than the White woman. Joseph could tell the olive-skinned woman was close to his mother's age, if not a little younger.

"What a healthy-looking Negro child," said the woman with a heavy southern accent. "Didn't Master Plecker do a good job with this purchase, Dorothy?"

Dorothy replied in her southern smooth voice, "Yes, Mrs. Wilma. I do believe he did. Will he be working inside here?"

Wilma chuckled. "Don't be so naive, Dorothy. Look at him. He is a healthy Negro boy with no apparent ailments. He'll work well in the fields and father some impressive children. I'm sure of it."

"I'm a Cherokee child. I'm no slave to you or anyone else on this land," Joseph boldly said. "I want to go home to my family."

Wilma gasped at Joseph's outburst.

Wade forced Joseph down on his knees and smacked him, garnering a frown from Dorothy.

Wilma said, "Enough, Wade. It's obvious this child was not taken from any plantation around here. So, a Cherokee…well, I think you will find your place here. What is your name, child?"

"My name is Joseph."

Wade kicked Joseph. "You say 'Mrs. Wilma' after you finish speaking to her!" he said. "Do you understand?"

Holding his stomach, Joseph glared up at Wade.

"Hmm, enough of this. Riza, come here. I know you hear this commotion," Wilma said. "Help the boy up, Wade."

Wade grabbed Joseph's arm and forced him to stand as a long-haired girl came through a swinging double door leading to the cookhouse walkway on Joseph's left. The honey-skinned girl wore a blue cotton dress and had on a white bonnet.

Joseph looked into her brown eyes and almost began to cry. "Are you Cherokee?" he asked in his native tongue.

Wilma gasped when she heard Joseph speak the language.

"A half-breed. I guess Master Plecker is getting tired of me," Riza said with a New York accent.

Wilma angrily replied, "Watch your mouth, Riza! What did he say?"

Riza's left eye squinted as she replied, "I'm not Cherokee. I'm Mohawk." She turned to Joseph. "I only understood some of what you said because one of your people is also here. I'm sure she'll be interested in listening to what you have to say."

Wilma's tone became more authoritative. "Enough. There will be no speaking of those savage languages on this plantation. English is the proper language, and it will be the only language spoken! It doesn't matter how much Indian blood is running through your body. There will be no tolerance of any uncivilized tongue. Is that understood, Joseph?"

Joseph's eyes narrowed at Wilma. "Yes, ma'am," he replied.

Wade slapped the back of Joseph's head. "Yes, Mrs. Wilma."

Wilma smiled. "Ah, see, that's much better. Riza, you and Doris make sure the sheets are properly set on our beds. I was not pleased with how Kenneth's were not tightly tucked."

Riza replied, "Mrs. Wilma, Master Kenneth said he does not like them tucked tightly."

Wilma irritably replied, "He is a grown man and in some time will find a wife. He must let go of his childish ways. It's becoming quite annoying."

Kenneth came out of one of the upstairs hallways and stopped at the top of the stairs on the landing. "I don't find it annoying, Momma," he said, charm echoing from his tenor southern voice.

"What are you doing here?" Wilma asked. "I thought you were meeting with your sisters and their husbands today for lunch."

Kenneth strolled down the stairs in a blue vest that covered a high-collared white shirt and a blue cravat that highlighted his black trousers. "I'm meeting them. Pa wanted to speak to me about some future plans first." He pulled a gold pocket watch out of his blue vest and looked at it. "I won't be late and I won't be early, especially if Anthony insists on talking about politics today."

Wilma frowned. "It is proper to at least be on time, Kenneth, even when it is family. While you're here, take a look at our new slave, Joseph."

Kenneth finished walking down the majestic white stairs and stood before Joseph. "He is quite a healthy boy. I'm sure he'll do some good around here." He placed his hand on top of Joseph's head and rubbed his coarse curly hair. "Hmph, not as rough as I thought it would be." His light brown eyes fixed on Joseph's face again. "Another one with Indian blood, I'm guessing. What are you, boy?"

"Cherokee," Joseph said apprehensively.

"I do like being right about things." Kenneth turned away from Joseph and walked around his mother as she kept her eyes on Joseph. On his way into the dining room, he gave a small smirk to Dorothy and let his light brown eyes quickly glide up and down her body behind Wilma's back.

Dorothy's gaze shifted to Kenneth as she kept her head straight, rolled her lower lip into her mouth, and quietly exhaled.

Wilma looked up to the top of the stairs and called out,

"Calvin, you come down here to this carriage and make sure Kenneth leaves on time to see the girls. I like Joseph. I think he'll do quite well."

Master Plecker shouted back, "I told you I was getting a nice strong boy that will work well for us in the future. I'll be down in a moment. Little Susie is getting me a towel so I can wipe my face. The heat is growing strong today. Wade, take Joseph back to be taught how to work in that barn."

"Yes, sir," Wade said.

"Good, and I'll have Riza bring that boy some new clothes," Wilma said.

"You heard Mrs. Wilma. Riza, go get this boy some new clothes," Wade said.

"Yessir, Master Wade," Riza said.

A little girl giggled, and Joseph turned to his right at the sound. There at the doorpost of another room stood a hazel-eyed toddler. The light brown-haired girl wore a tiny white apron that covered her blue dress. "Hi, everyone," she said.

"Aw, hi, little Daisy," Kenneth said playfully.

Wilma turned toward the little girl, saying, "Why is that high yellow child in my dining hall?"

Kenneth replied, "Oh, Momma, she's only three."

"The girl needs to learn quickly."

"I agree with Kenneth," Master Plecker said as he calmly marched down the stairs with a confident smirk. "Oh, and there she is, my favorite little one. Come here, Daisy."

Wilma's brow furrowed while she watched Daisy run past Kenneth toward Master Plecker. "Yes...I wonder why she's your favorite, dear." Her green eyes shifted to Dorothy, and she crossed her arms. Her eyes then anchored on Master Plecker as he playfully pinched Daisy's chubby cheek. With her voice dripping with sarcasm, Wilma continued, "I truly wonder why."

The frizzy-haired toddler giggled while Master Plecker continued to pinch her cheeks.

Master Plecker answered his wife, "She's got the prettiest little smile and is already showing good progress. She made my pillow just right."

Joseph noticed Wilma's pointing finger tapping on her folded arms.

"If you say so. Dorothy, I want my piano polished…right now."

Dorothy nodded and replied, "Yes, Mrs. Wilma."

"Momma, it can wait. I was going to play a little," Kenneth said.

Wilma put her hands on her hips, her voice raised as she replied, "You need to go! Calvin, tell this boy!"

"All right, that's enough," Master Plecker said. "Kenneth, be on time to keep peace in this house. Dorothy, bring me a roll, and then you can go take care of the piano."

"Yessir, Master," Dorothy said.

Joseph watched her move past Riza quickly, but also noticed Wilma's thin lips tighten into a pout.

"Wade, go on with the boy," Master Plecker said.

With a frown, Wade turned around and lightly shoved Joseph. The two left the house, and Wade forced the boy to walk down a pathway. Riza stood at the double doors in the foyer and watched Joseph through the wide windows before heading off to get his clothes.

Back at the large red barn, Wade left him with Bo, who began to show Joseph what he would be doing. "I know it hard, Joseph," Bo said. "My momma was sold when I was seven years old, and I never forget."

Joseph replied, "Did you ever try to run away?"

"I was always too scared to try. I seen many try to run away, but few make it. The slave catchers, they bring them back beat up badly or dead. I don't want to die like that."

"I would rather fight for my freedom than die a coward."

"You think the scariest thing was being taken from your momma? You have much to learn out here. Them White men don't care you got Indian blood. They own you now, and they not gonna let you go."

Joseph scowled. "I'm going back home. I wasn't born a slave, and my Auntie Lizzie says the White men always take from us. White men have never kept their promises because they're greedy. I can't stay here with people like that. I'm running away tonight."

"You're a fool," said a young girl in a blue cloth dress. "The White men will send the dogs after you, and sometimes the dogs kill whoever runs away," she said in Cherokee with a southern accent. "My name is Susie Coleman. I belong to the Panther Clan."

"I'm Joseph Lightning from the Wolf Clan," Joseph replied in Cherokee.

Susie approached Joseph, holding some clothes. "So your mother is from the Wolf Clan?"

"No, my mother is Negro, but my father is from the Wolf Clan. My aunties claim me, so I belong to the Wolf Clan."

"In our ways, you're supposed to follow your mother's clan. You know that, so that makes you Negro."

"I'm still Cherokee by blood, and you know that."

"Still…you're supposed to follow our traditions. How long have they had you?"

"About a week ago, I was taken from Tahlequah. How long have you been here?"

"I've been here for two years. I was taken from a town outside of Tahlequah, at night. I'm ten years old now. How old are you?"

"I will be ten years old in October. Two years is a long time, but I know my family is coming for me. They killed a White man trying to save me."

Susie frowned. "I used to think my family would save me quickly too. Don't hope very hard. It will break your spirit, Joseph Lightning." She handed Joseph the clothes. "These clothes are from Riza, and she said she would like to talk to you."

Joseph sharply replied, "I don't need them."

"Your shirt is torn and dirty. You need the shirt, and keep the trousers so you have more than one pair. The White men will be very mad if you don't wear the shirt."

Joseph reluctantly took off the torn shirt and put on the new one. "Thank you, Susie."

"You're welcome. There is someone else like you here. His

name is Tom, and he is from the Natchez. I think you will like him."

Joseph's brows drew together. "What do you mean like me?"

"He has Negro blood like you, but his momma is Natchez. I have to leave now. I'm not supposed to be here. We will see each other again."

"We will see each other again," he replied as he watched Susie leave.

"I understand no words y'all just said," Bo said. "First time I ever heard little Susie speak them words like that. Maybe she'll make it easier for you to be here. Well, come on, boy. I still have to show you more."

Bo spent the rest of the day teaching Joseph how to work in the barn and help use the cotton gin. It became more agonizing for Joseph, seeing other slaves pass by in wagons full of baskets filled with cotton and knowing it meant there was more work ahead of him. He wiped sweat off his forehead while more sweat ran down his body. The Mississippi heat could be seen rising off the cotton fields and dirt paths. Some of the Negro men in the cotton fields wore straw hats, and some of the Negro women had on white bonnets. All of the women who were field slaves wore brown cotton dresses. Children around Joseph's age followed their mothers as they picked cotton. He had also seen one girl with a water bucket giving water to working slaves.

Joseph was about to leave the area with the cotton gin when the bellowing voice of an overseer heard in the distance made him jump. He backed up into the cotton gin and leaned against the wooden door to avoid being seen while his heart raced. He couldn't tell if the voice was Wade or not. Another wagon stopped in front of the cotton gin. Joseph grunted at the sight of the cotton baskets, but from a side glance he noticed Wade watching him. He pouted and picked up the baskets full of cotton, grimacing as his stomach growled.

As the day passed on, another wagon stopped in front of the cotton gin with an old man and two boys. Joseph and Bo worked inside at the cotton gin as the old man and two boys began to take the baskets of cotton off the wagon.

"Bo, we have more baskets," a young boy said with a chipper southern voice. The caramel-toned boy walked inside the barn, past the opened double doors, and put down a basket. He pointed at Joseph. "Who this?"

Bo replied, "This here Joseph. Master Wade bring him today."

Joseph looked at the wavy-haired boy and sighed. "Are you Tom?"

Tom replied, "Yes, I'm Tom Clearwater. How'd you know that?"

"Susie told me you're Natchez. Well, I'm Cherokee like Susie."

Tom slowly stepped up to Joseph and took a closer look at him. "So you're a half-breed like me? You remind me of my sister. She has hair like you."

"How long have you been here?"

Tom frowned. "I have been here for three years."

"How old are you?" Joseph asked.

"I'm eleven years old. How old are you?"

Joseph exhaled. "I'm nine years old. I will be ten in October. Have you tried to run away?"

"The White men will let the dogs go after us if we try to run. The last man that ran away, they caught him, and they beat him so much he didn't have skin on his back no more."

Joseph's gaze shifted downward.

"No more of this talk," Bo said. "Master Plecker does good to slaves that do good, so watch what you say."

"We're not slaves," Joseph snarled.

Bo pointed at Joseph. "You is now, Negro."

Joseph's and Tom's noses crinkled, and their lips tightened in angst as they glared back at Bo.

"Tom, you come on now. We must get more before Master Rice come look for us," the old slave man from the wagon said.

Tom grunted and walked toward the wagon. "I will see you when we bring back more cotton."

Joseph looked down at the big basket of cotton he had forgotten about, then looked up and watched Tom ride off in the wagon with the other slaves. "Who is Master Rice?" he asked.

"He an overseer, like Master Wade," Bo said, rubbing the

back of his neck. "You'll see him today. Come on, Joseph. Cotton can't carry itself. Use them strong little arms."

Joseph kicked the basket, causing it to move. "All of this is stupid," he yelled. Then he grabbed the basket, picked it up, and placed it in front of the cotton gin.

"Boy, you got much to learn. I wish I could get you home, but like Tom say, they probably kill you if you try to leave. Maybe yo family will find you."

"How long have you been here, Bo?"

"I was born here. Like I say, my momma gone."

"She died?"

"No, Master Plecker sell her to Master Anderson years ago. Sometimes Mrs. Wilma lets me go to Mr. Anderson's plantation to trade supplies with Mrs. Anderson. Sometimes I see my momma. So I understand how you feel, missing yo momma. I sorry you here."

"Thank you, Bo."

Joseph hung his head and focused on doing whatever Bo told him to do for the rest of the day. Mostly he moved baskets of cotton from wagons to the cotton gin. When no wagons were present and the remaining cotton had been put into the cotton gin, Bo had Joseph carry supplies with him to a broken wagon. On the way, Bo pointed to different areas of the plantation. The walk allowed Joseph to see more slaves struggling in the other cotton fields farther from the cotton gin. Suddenly, the sound of a hymn being sung by some of the slaves hit his ear. *Why are they singing?* he thought. *Are they happy?* He turned his gaze away from them and frowned. After Joseph and Bo put the supplies down by the broken wagon, they got water from a well and returned to the cotton gin barn. The work made Joseph's muscles hurt, as the movement of the sun indicated how much time was passing.

A few minutes after they'd returned to the cotton gin, a shy, coarse-haired slave girl who wore a beige cotton dress entered the barn. "Oh, you done in that cookhouse now. Okay, Maddie, you gonna help Joseph here with this cotton," Bo said with a smile.

Maddie smiled. "Hi, Joseph."

"Hi, Maddie," Joseph said with a half-smile.

"Now you and Maddie gonna work together a lot, Joseph," Bo said while pointing at the children, smiling. "I can tell y'all gonna like each other. Now let's get started so Master Plecker happy."

Joseph worked beside Maddie, attempting to keep himself from staring at her while he listened to her cheerful talk. He had never met someone with a darker complexion than his mother before. *How can she be happy here? She's a nice person,* he thought.

Later in the day, a wagon stopped in front of the barn and a White man commanded several slaves to carry more cotton baskets into the barn. The brown-haired man entered the barn and walked up to Joseph, then stared down at Joseph with his arms crossed over his brown vest.

"So this is the new nigger Mr. Plecker spoke about. I heard you have a mouth on you, boy," the southern man said, his tone instigative.

"Master Rice, he good learner," Bo said.

"Now, Bo, did I ask you for your opinion? I was asking this boy."

"I'm no nigger," Joseph said. "I'm a Cherokee, and my papa said not to answer to being called a nigger."

Master Rice cackled. "You half-breeds really think y'all something special. Boy, you ain't nothing but a nigger with Indian eyes. I guess Wade didn't give you a good enough beating, but I promise you I will. So don't test me. I have the power to break your spirit, boy." He chuckled, still staring down at Joseph.

A young woman slave came in and said, "Master Rice, we ready to go back to the fields now."

Master Rice's grin quickly turned into a frown as he turned his attention to the slave woman. "Felicia, do I need to remind you again not to tell me what to do? Do we need to have another talk?"

Felicia humbly replied, "No, Master Rice."

"I'll decide when y'all are ready. Now, go wait in that wagon."

The wide eyes and slanted eyebrows of the young woman reflected her fear, and then she quickly walked toward the wagon. "As I said, boy, I'll break whatever strength those Indians gave you. Tomorrow, you give the cattle corn with Bo, and it better be done right."

Joseph cautiously watched as Master Rice walked back out to the wagon.

"You need to do as they say, Joseph," Bo said. "You don't want Master Rice to notice you too much. One moment he nice, and then he pure evil. He enjoys seeing a Negro bleed."

Joseph replied, "He's not the first evil man I've met. My Auntie Lizzie says men like them deserve to go to hell. They're not sorry for nothing they do."

"Your auntie sound like a smart woman."

"She is. My Auntie Lizzie could even fight a man."

Bo chuckled. "Yeah, I hear them Indian women can be mean. After what White men do to them, I understand why. Well, the sun now leaving us, so come on, I show you where you sleep. Maddie, come on, girl, it time to eat and sleep."

Bo walked Joseph to the slave houses, the other slaves they passed taking notice of the new kid on their plantation. Their stares made Joseph's throat tighten, but then a welcoming young woman strolled up to Joseph and Bo.

"Bo, who is this boy?" the woman calmly asked.

Bo answered, "This here is Joseph. Joseph this is Stella."

Stella smiled at Joseph. "It's nice to meet you, Joseph."

Joseph quietly replied, "Nice to meet you, Stella."

"Where are you from?" she asked.

"I'm from Cherokee territory. I'm a Cherokee."

Looking up at Stella and hearing her soothing voice, Joseph couldn't contain his grief any longer and suddenly started to sniffle. Her smile and dark brown skin reminded him of his mother.

Stella hugged Joseph. "It's gonna be all right. You was taken from your family, wasn't you?"

Joseph nodded yes and continued to sob in her arms.

"You come with Stella, and I get you some food." She took Joseph's hand and frowned at Bo.

Bo murmured. "I know, Stella, but we can't do nothing for him."

Stella said to Joseph as they strolled to her slave house, "Now you will get to sleep here with me and some other childrens, and we make the best of this we can. You such a handsome boy, I bet all the Indian girls out there like you."

Joseph struggled to rein in his emotions and stop crying while Stella wiped the tears off his face.

"I was about your age when I was sold from my momma, so I understand those tears. Now let's get you fed." Stella put a kettle full of stew on an iron stove and began to heat it up.

A very young woman wearing a brown cloth dress entered and looked at Joseph. "Who is that, Stella?"

Stella answered, "He Master Plecker's newest slave. His name is Joseph, from those Cherokee Indians."

Pearl's southern voice now dripped with bitterness. "Another Indian child. I guess he couldn't stop after Riza."

"Enough, Pearl. You know what it like to lose family."

Pearl put her hand on her hip. "Yes, I do. Hello, Joseph. I wish we could've met somewhere else. Slave life ain't good for no soul." She stepped over to Joseph and put her hand on his shoulder. "You a handsome little boy. You listen to Master Plecker, and you be fine here."

"Tell the others to come eat before I give it all to this poor child," Stella calmly said.

Pearl playfully replied, "Okay, Momma, but I tell the others before Clint come and eat it all."

"Oh, leave that boy alone. He growing into a man."

"I noticed, Momma." Pearl opened the front door.

Stella pointed a wooden spoon at Pearl. "Keep on calling me Momma, Pearl. I use this spoon like a whip on you."

Pearl looked back at Stella, and the two young women began to laugh as Pearl went outside.

Stella handed Joseph a tin plate with stew on it. "Go on now. Sit down and eat. We blessed here. Mrs. Wilma the reason we have a wood floor now. It was all dirt last year."

Joseph replied, "She seems different from Mr. Plecker."

"In some ways, yes, she is, but you still a Negro child to her. Don't hope too much. I think she just got tired of coming in here and seeing the dirt."

Joseph began to eat the stew, but some of his bites of the stew made him grimace. He forced himself to swallow and frowned. "What is in this?"

"Some potatoes, some turnips, some corn, and pork, is what that is. If Master Plecker feeling real good, we get some beef."

Joseph didn't like the food but kept eating it because he was starving and wanted to show his appreciation toward Stella. Suddenly, the door opened and two children walked inside.

"Joseph, are you sleeping here?" Tom asked.

Joseph replied, "Stella said I was."

Tom looked at Stella, and she nodded yes. He smiled and approached Joseph, a young girl following close behind him.

"Hi, my name is Mary," the little girl said, stepping around Tom.

"Hi, I'm Joseph."

"So, Tom said you're Indian too. I think that's nice." Mary smiled. "You meet Riza and Susie?"

"Yes, I met them. Riza told Susie she wanted to speak to me."

Mary's eyes widened. "She will probably come soon after Master's supper."

"Well, if she comes tonight, she comes tonight," Stella said.

"Where does she sleep?" Joseph asked.

Stella answered, "In the white slave house for the house slaves. Riza and Susie is blessed girls. Come now, get some stew so y'all don't sleep hungry."

Tom and Mary went to the kettle, and Stella fed them. As they ate, Pearl returned with a tall teenager who had a stocky build.

"So you Joseph. Pearl tell me about you. I'm Clint," the teen said, his voice switching between a tenor and alto. "Nice to meet you, Joseph."

Joseph replied, "Nice to meet you too."

Clint fixed his round brown eyes on the hot stew and walked over to it.

"You can have the rest of what is in the kettle, Clint," Stella said. "Me and the childrens had already eaten what we need."

"I need to eat too," Pearl said.

Stella replied, "I never said you can't have some, Pearl. Now, both of y'all come on and eat. The sun almost gone."

Clint and Pearl sat down, and as they ate the others talked. Joseph remained mostly silent, thinking about his family.

Suddenly, the door opened, and Riza entered the slave house. "There you are," she said. She looked at Clint and smiled but subtly scoffed at Pearl. "I was able to take some of the extra biscuits left over from supper."

Pearl replied, "Well, good. You can leave now, before they start looking for you."

Riza arrogantly replied, "I'm not tied down like you. I hope you're enjoying the fields. It'll teach you some humility."

Pearl sneered. "You ain't nothing but a little redskin. You ain't got nothing different from us. Brown eyes and yo skin would be darker too if you was out there. Eating from Master's table like it something to be proud of. You ain't nothing but a slave like the rest of us."

Riza scowled. "Unlike you, I wasn't born a slave."

"Like it matter, Miss Mohawk. Up in there like you better than us. All you Indians, mulattos, and half-breeds ain't better!"

Riza smacked her lips and released her long wavy hair from her hair bun. "Careful, all that jealousy might prevent that nappy hair from actually growing to the bottom of your neck."

Pearl jumped to her feet. "I will beat you like a—"

"Pearl," Stella said with an authoritative voice. "Enough of this. She's a child. Why are you letting a thirteen-year-old girl bother you so much?"

Pearl angrily replied, "Did you forget, or are you blind? She got me sent out to the fields. I was a good house slave, and Master Plecker bought this...clever snake. I'll cut that hair off, make you look like a man."

"I doubt Master Plecker sent you out into the fields because of Riza. She was a little child when she first came here."

"I ain't no fool, Stella. She took my place. Maybe if she worked the fields, she get more brown in that skin of hers."

Riza snobbishly replied, "I wouldn't mind getting a little darker. It would look good with nice, long, good hair, unlike those nappy curls you have."

Pearl grabbed Riza, but Stella and Clint pulled her off. "Let me give her one good beating," Pearl bellowed.

Stella replied, "Go outside and calm yourself. You letting this child play with your mind."

Pearl angrily moved past Riza as the girl leered at her.

Stella said, "Riza, you had to come here more than to just give us extra bread."

Riza replied with a smile, "I did. I came to speak to Joseph quickly." She looked over at Joseph and Tom, both watching the girls with wide eyes. "Don't look so scared. Pearl has never liked me."

Joseph replied, "You're thirteen?"

"Yeah, my birthday is April fifteenth. Susie told me you're turning ten in October."

"I am, but I don't want to spend it here. Is Susie coming here?"

"No, she sleeps in the same slave house as me. I'll speak with you later. I have to go."

"Thank you for the bread," Joseph said.

"It was no problem. I steal almost anything from that mansion when Mrs. Wilma sits at the supper table drooling because she ate too much. Goodbye, everyone."

"Goodbye, Riza," everyone said.

<hr>

On her way back to the mansion, Riza saw Pearl standing by one of the slave houses next to two other slaves. She strutted past them with her chin up, avoiding eye contact with Pearl.

"Keep on walking, Riza," Pearl said.

Riza replied, "How about you go eat a rat, Pearl?"

The other slaves cackled.

"You ain't nothing. It a reason yo people called savages."

Riza side-eyed Pearl and pointed at her while she walked. "They call us savages because they fear us, but they see you Negroes as nothing but property."

Pearl shrieked, and Riza picked up her pace toward the mansion. She entered the mansion through the back door and walked toward the kitchen, down the short pathway, and casually entered the cookhouse.

"Riza, Master Kenneth wanted another slice of bread," Dorothy said, making Riza jolt. "Where is the rest of the bread? Please don't tell me you gave it all to the field slaves."

Riza sighed and walked to the cupboards. "I hid some in one of the cupboards," she said.

"The next time, you need to wait. You know the punishment for giving the field slaves leftovers."

Riza stopped moving and looked at Dorothy. "Where is Susie?"

"Susie has already walked back to the house. She said you went to speak with that new boy. How is he?"

"What do you think?"

Dorothy's brow lowered. "Watch your mouth, Riza."

Riza's gaze went downward. "Sorry. Well, he's not good. He was stolen from his family like me and the others. He wasn't born a slave. He has no idea how much pain he is about to experience."

Dorothy frowned, and Riza pulled a small loaf of bread from the cupboard that she then gave to Dorothy. Dorothy's daughters, Doris and Daisy, could be heard running down the pathway.

Dorothy marched over to the doorway and angrily stared at her daughters. "What have I told you about running through here? Mrs. Wilma doesn't like children running through here, and you will listen to these rules or you will be whipped. Is I clear?"

"Yes, Momma," Doris said.

"Now, Daisy is three years old. I expect her to run around, but you too old for this, Doris. You seven years old, so no more of this childish running in the house."

Doris nervously replied, "Yes, ma'am. May I go with Riza?"

Dorothy looked at Riza. "Riza, are you going to the house?"

Riza replied, "I am."

"All right, you can go with Riza and take your sister with you."

Doris skipped over to Riza with a smile while holding Daisy's hand, and the three girls went out to the house-slave house.

<hr />

Dorothy went upstairs to Kenneth's room and knocked on his door. When he opened it, she held out the platter of bread and told him, "Master Kenneth, I brought you the bread you requested."

"Dorothy, what took so long? I was beginning to think you were avoiding me," Kenneth said.

Dorothy walked inside and hastily replied, "No, Master Kenneth, I wasn't. I was making sure the girls were behaving. I sent them to the house with Riza."

"The Mohawk child...she's always been a faster learner. I often wonder if she is planning anything inappropriate."

Dorothy raised an eyebrow. "What do you mean?"

"I think my parents are blind to what that little girl is capable of, but I find it so entertaining to watch her."

"You think she gonna run away?"

Kenneth closed his door. "No, I don't think so. I'm absolutely sure she would try if she could. Her fear is limited, and I think sometime soon she's gonna get the learning lesson she needs."

Dorothy frowned. "Surely there must be another way. She's a good girl, a good house slave. She makes your bed how you like it."

Kenneth placed his hand on the back of Dorothy's neck and caressed it. "No, she got too much Indian in her. She been here a couple of years, but she has never stopped thinking of a way to get free. Unlike you, she hasn't accepted her place." He snapped his fingers, and Dorothy began to take off her dress.

Moving slowly, she tentatively asked, "Please forgive me, but with your permission, can this be done another time? The girls are waiting for me."

Kenneth caressed Dorothy's face. Both of his hands then rubbed down her sides. "After two children, you're still so firm. No man would ever believe you gave life to two beautiful girls. I think the girls can wait a little for their momma."

Dorothy's eyes locked with Kenneth's. "Kenneth, please tell me you will keep your word. That you'll make sure they not separated."

Kenneth pursed his lips. "Why would you bring that up now?"

"I know you gonna find you a pretty White woman soon to marry, and...and I ask that they remain with you if something happens to me. You're their papa, and I know you tell me not to tell them who you are, and I haven't, but I want to make sure they are safe."

Dorothy began to sniffle while Kenneth caressed her back. "I must admit them girls remind me of my sisters when we was children. I'll make sure they never sold to nobody. You continue to keep your word, and I may even set those girls free when they get old enough. They pretty like they momma, and that nice light skin of theirs will certainly help them get a White man from the north. They can't marry a White man, but they will be cared for. Now lay down, beautiful, so you can see those girls."

Dorothy lay down on the bed to fulfill her obligation, believing it strengthened her deal with him. When he'd finished and rolled off her, she sat up on the bed facing away from Kenneth and said, "I better go now."

Kenneth rubbed her bare back. "You are the sweetest. Now don't you worry about those girls. Dorothy, look at me."

Dorothy turned around.

"I'm a man of my word. I hope you didn't forget that." Kenneth charmingly cupped her chin with his hand. She fell into his charm as he kissed her, and she kissed him back.

"Go on now. Tomorrow is a long day."

Dorothy stood up and put her dress back on. As she was

about to walk to the door, Kenneth smacked her butt. "Nice and curvy."

Dorothy quietly sighed. "Thank you, Kenneth."

"You sleep good now."

Dorothy smiled. "You too." She left Kenneth's room and quickly went to the house-slave house. Entering, she saw her girls playing with Riza and Susie as the other slaves were talking to each other.

"I guess today was a good day," Emma said. "Even you came inside not long after the sun went down."

Dorothy replied, "Yeah, I guess today was a good day, Emma."

Dorothy approached the girls and sat down next to them while Riza and Susie continued to play with them. Dorothy looked at Riza, her mouth curving downward exposing her concern, but smiled when she ran her hand through Doris's hair.

CHAPTER 6
Daring Plans and Pride

O N June 15, 1860, Annabelle, Grace, and Eli arrived back in Tahlequah. As they got out of the carriage, the twins ran outside excitedly to see their mother, aunt, and uncle. Annabelle gave the girls hugs, then looked up and saw John scowling with his arms crossed.

"Girls, go tell your brother we are back," Grace said.

Rain and Jannie ran to the crops.

Marching angrily toward Annabelle, Grace, and Eli while shaking his head, John yelled, "How could you go back to that town? Why couldn't you wait for me to return?"

Annabelle's brow furrowed. "I couldn't, John. I know you're doing your best, but I miss my baby. He's out there all alone, surrounded by crazy White people on some plantation!"

"You took advantage of my trust!"

Annabelle's eyes dilated, and her voice deepened. "I couldn't do *nothing*! Every day the scars on my back remind me of what I survived. He's my baby, and we're at war for my baby! I can't lose another child!" She covered her mouth with her hand, and tears fell from her eyes.

John frowned. "And what if you were enslaved again?"

"I'd fight my way back. I'll always fight for my babies."

"This was too dangerous."

Annabelle wiped the tears off her face. "I would do it again." She shrugged. "We needed more answers. I'm sorry."

John uncrossed his arms. "I can't lose you too. I don't know how I could handle it."

"John, we had a safe trip, and we have good news," Eli said. He handed John the records showing which plantations had known Indian slaves and mixed children.

"Who gave this to you?" John asked in Cherokee.

Grace replied in Cherokee, "The Keyses. Thanks to their connections to the Underground Railroad, we were able to get this information. There are some Indians who have been helping with the freeing of slaves, and a large part of their focus has been to free Indian children."

"Well, I have good news too. We found the auction where Joseph was sold, and we know that he was sold to someone named Plecker in either Louisiana or Mississippi. I think Samuel and I will get everything together and leave again tomorrow since all of you are home now."

Grace replied, "A plan needs to be made first."

John's voice raised as he said, "I know, but the more time that goes by, the more likely something bad will happen to him. I don't want to wait! My boy needs to be home!"

"If the two of you leave too quickly, you could fail. You need the right amount of supplies and a strong plan so y'all don't get into trouble bringing Joseph home."

"I will go with you," Eli said. "The courthouse can wait on me to do minor things later. I don't want to know what they decided to do with Mr. Sawyer."

John replied, "All I know is that Mr. Jackson demanded his immediate release. I don't know if they did let Mr. Sawyer go."

Grace replied, "Then a plan needs to be made so y'all can come home safely and with Joseph."

"Can I help?" David asked. The others looked at David, but with slight frowns. "I want him home too," he angrily said.

"Sweetie, we don't even have a plan yet," Annabelle said.

David frowned and then stomped off to the fields.

"I forget how old he is now," John said. "I will talk with him." He kissed Annabelle on the cheek and then went after David.

"He's a brave young man, but it's better for him to stay here and protect the family," Eli said.

Annabelle replied in Cherokee, "I agree. He is a brave boy. But I'm not losing another son to these White people."

Later the family made a plan to bring Joseph home. They only had enough rations for the men to be gone for a little over a month.

Over supper, Annabelle's gaze kept shifting to the boys' room. She forced herself to eat so she had energy for the other children. Later that night, she cuddled next to John and held onto his hand as she stared at the shadows the moonlight created.

***

The next day, John, Eli, and Samuel checked their supplies in the carriage and checked their weapons. John hugged his children and gave Annabelle a kiss. Eli and Samuel did the same with their wives.

As Eli turned to leave, Grace grabbed his hand and placed it on her belly. "You have more than one reason to return home," she said. "I'm sorry. I've struggled to decide when to tell you, but I know I couldn't let you leave without telling you."

Eli gave Grace a hug and kissed her. "Thank you for giving me more than one reason," he said, smiling. "Joseph has a new cousin to meet."

John smiled at Grace and gave her a hug, and the women watched as the three men rode away.

"So...to Louisiana first?" Samuel asked in Cherokee.

Eli replied in Cherokee, "Yeah, let's start with the Louisiana plantations because it looks like they have more with Indian children than the ones in Mississippi. Hopefully this path is the right one."

As the men rode through the plains filled with wildflowers. John saw a cougar playing with her cubs. The innocence of the cubs made him smile and reminded him of how Joseph would try to scare him by hiding behind trees when he was younger. His mind drifted through memory after memory of watching Joseph grow up, strengthening his determination and hope.

⸺◆⸺

After having been on the plantation for six days, Joseph was forced to work in the fields and struggled to put the heavy cotton baskets on the wagon, exhausted from the long hours of hard labor and the long nights of restless sleep.

"You should have ate more cornbread this morning, Joseph," Tom said.

Joseph replied, "The cornbread is nasty. It doesn't taste like what my momma or aunties make. And I'm not used to sleeping on a floor."

"You ain't got much choice, and you have to eat or you get weak. The masters don't care if you weak or not. They want you to work."

"What are you fools doing?" an overseer yelled.

"Master Kit, we're putting the cotton baskets on the wagon," Tom said.

Master Kit's nasally southern voice bellowed, "See now, it don't look that way to me. I hear too much talking, boy. Now you and that new nigger there get to that cotton gin, or we gone have problems."

Joseph stared at the fat bearded overseer, then grabbed one end of the last cotton basket to be loaded. Tom quickly grabbed the other side, and they placed it on the wagon. They got onto the wagon and were driven to the cotton gin.

"I hate that fat man," Joseph said. "He's always looking for a reason to yell at us."

Tom replied, "Master Kit isn't as bad as Master Rice. I would take him yelling at me any day. Master Rice is crazy."

Joseph's brow lowered. "Why are you so scared?"

"Because they will beat us if we don't do what they say, and I saw them kill a man. Master Rice shot him after the man hit him. I didn't even know his name because he was only here for two days, and I know he was someone else's slave before he came here."

"How do you know that?"

"Because of the scars he had all over his body. Master Rice shot him like he was nothing."

Joseph stared, speechless at the seriousness and fear etched on Tom's frowning face.

While the boys finished off-loading the cotton baskets, Master Rice rode up on his horse and started yelling for the slaves to go to the old cookhouse. Joseph and Tom traveled to the cookhouse to be given lunch, a stew of beans, peas, potatoes, and beef. Joseph was glad it was beef because when he was forced to eat pork it gave him severe stomachaches. After eating quickly, Joseph stood up to leave.

"Where are you going so fast?" Tom asked.

"I'm just going to walk a little. It's not like I can go anywhere else," Joseph said.

"Don't go near the woods or they will think you about to make a run for it."

"I won't." Joseph walked out of the cookhouse and looked around to see if anyone was watching him. He went around to the back of the house and sat down, then began to pray, asking God to save him from the plantation, to show him a way to escape.

"What are you doing?" Riza asked, startling Joseph.

"Riza...I was praying, asking Jesus to help me get out," he replied. "I know my family is coming for me."

Riza sarcastically replied, "How cute you look praying to the Jesus. Don't waste your words. I prayed for years to be set free, but here I am. Jesus isn't going to help us. He's watching all of this happen. He's probably sick of us and the White people, so why would he stop any of this?"

"You're wrong. My momma said Jesus loves all of us. I know if I keep praying, we will get set free."

"You're wasting your time. If we want out, we have to make a way out. Are we supposed to wait until Jesus comes back? When will that be? When we are old? It's time to stop being a child and have some faith in yourself instead of Jesus. The only good he's for is forgiveness and salvation."

Joseph scowled. "How can you say that?"

Riza huffed and side-eyed Joseph. "How can I say that? I've been here since I was seven years old. I watched my daddy get shot dead by two White men. Then they took me because my daddy owed them money. I wonder why you were taken. White people always attack the family."

"My family killed a White man, but that was when they were taking me."

Riza's voice softened as she replied, "I hope your family is doing well. White men don't forgive. If you want to see your family again, you do as I say. Do you understand?"

Joseph nodded yes as Riza looked at him with a furrowed brow. "What do you want me to do?" he asked.

"I'll tell you when the time is right."

"What about the others?"

"We can't do nothing for the Negroes, but I do want the other Indians with us. We have homes to return to. They don't."

"How can you say something so mean?"

"I do care! But they'll slow us down, and they don't have any home or family to return to. This life is all they know. Do you think they can follow us and the White people won't notice? The more who try to escape, the quicker they will notice." Riza frowned. "I do wish we could free everyone."

"When do you want us to run away?"

"It'll be soon, but be patient and stay away from Master Rice and Master Wade."

"Okay, and I'll be ready."

Riza began to leave but turned around. "Maybe you should say one more prayer. Maybe this one will actually be heard."

"You're still loved, Riza."

Riza's eyes widened. "What made you say that?"

Joseph shrugged, saying, "I don't know. I...I felt it in my spirit."

Riza's nose crinkled. "I know I'm loved, but almost every week I have a nightmare about my momma." A tear shimmered in her left eye, and she bobbed her head as she continued, "My siblings don't even know how I am." Her eyes shifted to her right and then back to Joseph as she exhaled. "I'm sorry. I know I sounded mean. Thank you, Joseph. Good night." She hurried away.

Joseph struggled to remove the doubt he'd started to feel and to remain positive through the rest of the day. He remained mostly silent as he and Tom waited for more cotton baskets to be filled up. Riza's lack of faith had made Joseph question why God would allow him to be taken. Joseph remembered what his mother had told him about the world being filled with evil and being broken.

———◆———

During the night, Riza and Susie remained awake while the others slept. "Are you sure Joseph will leave with us?" Susie asked.

"I know he will," Riza said. "He doesn't belong here like we don't belong here. He's a little scared, but I can tell he's a fighter."

"Are you sure we can do this without anyone getting hurt badly?"

"You worry too much about these White people. Have you forgotten we're here because of them?" Riza scoffed. "No, none of them should get hurt at all even if they deserve it."

"It will make the Father happy if we do this right."

"I'm done with the Creator. Look how much the White people have taken from our families. The only good news we have is knowing that when we die, the White people will have no control over us, and we can join our ancestors in heaven and dance, knowing we're free."

"I think we'll be shown when to run away," Susie said.

"I already have a plan, and I know it will work. Be patient. These White people will have no idea what to think."

Susie drifted off to sleep, but Riza stayed awake, staring at the moon while her anger grew against the Creator. "You know all I want is to see my momma again...to see my brothers again.

I'm tired of waiting for an answer," she murmured. She felt like the stars were stuck in place no matter how brightly they shined.

Days passed as Joseph struggled to keep out of the way of Master Rice and adjust to the living conditions. Unwilling to tolerate being served cornbread and pork for breakfast every morning, he chose to eat some of the corn meant for the cattle while feeding them, to subdue his hunger pains.

On the afternoon of June 18, 1860, Tsula went into labor. Her labor was hard, but with Joyce's help, she gave birth to a beautiful baby girl. Luke sat speechless and filled with joy as he watched Tsula nestle their daughter.

"Look at her. I guess I can't call myself the most beautiful anymore," she said.

"What name have you chosen for the girl?" Joyce asked in Cherokee.

"I changed my mind. Will you give her a first name?"

Joyce smiled while she looked at the baby girl. "You surprise me...you seemed so certain. Are you sure?"

Tsula reassuringly nodded, and Joyce looked back at the baby. "I think she has the chance to live an even better life than we could imagine, so Katelyn, welcome to this world."

Tsula smiled in approval of the name. "My little angel, Katelyn Shay Fields. I think that sounds like a strong name."

"I know your momma is smiling down from heaven on this day." Joyce left Tsula's house with a smile.

As Joyce slowly walked to her wagon, Grace went after her. Stopping in front of her old wagon, Joyce watched Grace approach and asked, "What's on your mind?"

"I wanted to thank you, and I...I'm struggling to be happy," Grace said in Cherokee. "I'm having my first child, and I can't even find the strength to be happy about it."

"Grace, you can't allow your joy to be killed by evil. You are responsible for your own happiness. I know you're worried about Joseph, but we cast our cares to the Father. I know it's hard. Have faith and focus on taking care of the children that are here.

I'm so proud of you, child. You finally learned not to give so much of yourself that you miss out on life. Let your brother and the others focus on bringing Joseph home. Be careful. Sorrow can end the life of a baby. I've seen it before."

Joyce got into her wagon, but suddenly began to cough.

Grace frowned. "Elder Joyce, are you okay?"

"I'm fine. Don't worry. I just have a little cough. Not the first time I had a cough. I better hurry up. I'm sure Lea is at the house now. Who would've ever thought my youngest great-great-granddaughter would be the most interested in the old ways? Keep strong, child. A great change is coming."

"I will."

Joyce rode off as Grace watched, trying to hold onto Joyce's words. She walked back to Tsula's house wondering how John, Eli, and Samuel were doing on their long trip. She entered the sunlit house as Maria held Katelyn and showed her to the younger children. The happy voices of the children filled the home while she moved past the fireplace and stood next to the rectangular living room window.

Lizzie went up to Grace. "I should be a lot happier today, but I keep thinking about Joseph," Lizzie said. "I know Annabelle feels the same, but she chooses to distract herself with the other children."

Grace replied, "Do you blame her for her way of mourning?"

Lizzie leaned against the wall. "No, I'm jealous of how well she is dealing with it. What did Elder Joyce say?"

"She said for us to remain faithful and a great change is coming. She also told me to focus on the baby."

"Then do as she says. The boys are looking for him, and we need you here. I don't like being here while Joseph is at some White man's plantation, but I'm needed here. We have to stay on our guard, especially since Mr. Sawyer was released to Brock yesterday."

Grace sighed. "I think Mr. Jackson knows something."

Lizzie huffed. "I already spoke to him."

Grace crossed her arms, lifting one eyebrow. "When did you do that?"

"Days ago, and I'm sure he knew something, but he knows if he comes back to our farm, he'll die. If Lisa doesn't kill him first, I will."

"It's no surprise he's involved. Well, at least you didn't kill him."

"I could've. It was hard not to."

Grace shook her head as she rubbed her forehead. "His death would've brought us more drama. We're prisoners here even with all the buildings our people have built here in Tahlequah. We have to keep our family together. It's the only way we will survive."

"I remember watching the moon block the sun's rays and the sky turning black. That's what I feel is happening to the whole land. The sky has gone black, but we are too blind to see it."

"Then we have to make sure we stay prayerful for the sun to shine again. I'm proud of you."

"I wish I could say the same."

"You went out there and had enough self-control not to kill him. Would've been better if you stayed home, but I know you're trying. I know you're in pain too."

"It's hard doing nothing."

"It takes strength to let go and trust in what the Father is doing. I think we can do it," Maria said as she approached Grace and handed Katelyn to her. "The stronger we remain, the stronger this new generation will become."

Lizzie's eyes shifted to Katelyn, and she exhaled.

Over the passing days ahead, Grace prayed for her family and asked that her brother's first attempt to find Joseph would be a success.

* * *

With a week of serving the Pleckers' plantation behind him, Joseph was starting to become more acquainted with the other slaves. He met a bald-headed slave named Steven, a very humorous man. He became fond of Steven, who was kind and welcoming to him. As the boys were putting the cotton baskets on the wagon, the tall, skinny man in his beige cotton shirt and brown trousers walked up to them.

"Lord, the Indians are here," Steven said.

Joseph and Tom giggled and said, "Hi, Steven."

"Now, look, y'all have to limit how much y'all talk to the women. I keep my beautiful head shaved for the women. Y'all good-looking boys, so don't talk to them so much. I need to make my selection first."

Joseph and Tom cackled while they put more cotton baskets onto the wagon.

"I glad you boys having fun. Stay away from Master Rice today. Harry gone made him mad today, so stay away."

Tom replied, "We will, Steven."

The boys got on the wagon and rode off to the cotton gin barn.

"How were you taken?" Joseph asked.

Tom's mouth curved into a frown. "It was during a sunset. I was walking back to my grandma's home with two of my younger cousins. We had gone fishing. It was May, and it was a good day. We'd caught a few fish and were so happy. It was the first time I had caught a fish, and showing my pa what I did was the only thing on my mind. We got to the hill right before my grandma's house when these three White men came out of the woods. Two of them had ropes in their hands, and all had this evil look on their faces. It was like they didn't see us as children, and it made me scared. One of the men said, 'What you niggers doing out here?' I told that man, 'We're Natchez,' and then he said, 'A drop of nigger blood makes you a nigger.'

"I remember telling him that we were just going to my grand-ma's house over the hill, and he said, 'I don't see Grandma out here.' One of the men took a step toward my youngest cousin, Edward, and I told them both to run to Grandma's house. We all ran, and I screamed for her. Then I saw the man catching up and about to grab my cousin, so I grabbed his leg and made him fall. He cursed at me, and when I let him go to keep running, he grabbed my arm. I told him to let me go, but then he backhanded me. The other men ran up to him, and he yelled at them to get my cousins, but they got away to my grandma's house.

"He then yelled at me, 'Do you know how much money you just cost us, grass nigger?' He pulled me up close to his face and asked if I understood what he said, so I spit in his face and told him I didn't care. He let go of me and started to wipe my spit off his face. I tried to run to my grandma's house, but one of the men tripped me and then stepped on my upper back, pressing down on my back. I begged for my grandma and told the man I couldn't breathe."

Tom shook his head. "He didn't care. He was going to kill me because I spit in the other man's face. The other man told him to let me up, that they needed me alive and couldn't go back empty-handed. He took his foot off me, and then they tied my hands and put a piece of cloth over my mouth. I didn't eat for two days while they took me to the auction building.

"I remember seeing all of those people being sold to White men at different prices. I saw this one woman, she almost looked like Dorothy. She was very beautiful, and they stripped her naked on the stage. Those White men were making all types of bets on her as she covered herself with her arms. They sold her for more than $2,000, and the look in her eyes when she was taken off the stage made me cry. It didn't make her feel good some White man would pay so much for her. She knew her life was over, and she was now at the mercy of whoever bought her. I was sold right after her. I still remember the smile Master Plecker gave me. It still scares me."

"I'm sorry you went through that."

"You don't need to say you're sorry. I know it hurt you the same way when you were taken away from your family. My family didn't even get a chance to fight for me."

The wagon stopped in front of the cotton gin, and the old slave driving it looked back at the boys. "G'on, get this cotton in there," he said.

"Let's get this done before one of those crazy overseers gets mad at us," Tom said.

Joseph nodded, saying, "Okay."

The boys got off the wagon and started to put the cotton next to the cotton gin. Joseph thought, *He saved his cousins' lives. I hope we can get away from here and get back to our families. I miss everyone.* His brow lowered as he thought, *Momma, I miss you.* He then picked up another basket of cotton and carried it into the cotton gin room, forcing himself to keep a straight face.

Wilma Plecker watched the slaves with her friend as they drank tea at a small, round cedar table on the front porch of the mansion.

"I see your slaves are as fruitful as always, Wilma," the skinny woman said.

"Daphne, darling, you know I won't accept anything less than perfection," Wilma said. "I mean, my house slaves work with absolute obedience and even now we haven't had a slave try to escape in four years. Mr. Wade's competence has been a great contribution to our peaceful household."

"You're such a blessed woman, as always," Daphne cheerfully said.

While they continued watching the slaves work the fields and drank their tea, Daphne played with a blonde ringlet of her hair that hung down to her shoulder. She looked over to Wilma and sighed. "I feel a bit embarrassed to ask this, but would you be willing to sell me two of your slaves?"

"What for? I like the ones we have now, and I even enjoy that new half-breed nigger. He has the eyes of an Indian and the hair of a Negro. I'd even say he's almost a cute little worker."

"To my embarrassment, I recently found out my uncle had been forcing himself on one of my house slaves. She produced an adorable mulatto child, but of course my aunt won't tolerate this inexcusable behavior. I was forced to sell the toddler to the Abbott family plantation in Tennessee."

"What a shame, but you did the right thing to keep peace in your family. The Abbott family is unusually nice to their slaves. It challenges my mind how they control them."

"I had Thaddeus sell Gail to them as well. The cries of that toddler reminded me so much of my own children. I couldn't even separate them. Though I'm still furious with Gail. I'm glad I didn't have to beg Thaddeus to have them sold together. Embarrassing my family, she should've spoken up to me about my uncle's deeds. She had already been given lashes for the act, or I should say, acts."

"Well, then, you truly did the right thing. Your aunt will have nothing to say when she learns this matter has been dealt with."

"My aunt wanted Gail, but I had my suspicions that she was either going to have her shot dead or hanged. My aunt holds her slaves in an iron fist."

"I hope she holds such strong holdings on your uncle, though he is the man of the household. Some respect should be given. Especially since he touched a nigger."

"Yes, I never expected it from him. Gail isn't even a mulatto, and yet he still…"

"Well, since Thaddeus agreed to this arrangement, what are you looking for, dear?"

"I need more house slaves now that Gail is gone, and her daughter would have followed in line." Daphne looked into the fields, saw a young girl picking cotton, and pointed at the girl. "That child right there. How old is she?"

"Why, show me again which one were you pointing at?" Wilma leaned over to see exactly where Daphne was pointing. "Ah, that's Roberta, and she is thirteen years old. Why don't I give you two of my house slaves? You don't want that dirty thing in your home."

"I'd prefer one of the slaves that truly looks like a Negro. I want no chance of temptation with Thaddeus. He's a good husband, but he is a man with eyes. I don't want to be my aunt, and besides, the poor thing isn't that hideous. I'm sure she'll be placed with one of our male slaves easily when Thaddeus sees fit. He's given me the money since he and Mr. Calvin Plecker wanted to take their walk."

"All right, but this next one I'll offer and she'll certainly work for you. She is young but has been a fast learner. I'll go speak with Calvin quickly. Anything for a friend." Wilma went inside and commanded Dorothy to bring them more tea.

Dorothy placed down a full teapot as Wilma returned outside grinning and sat down next to Daphne. As Dorothy went back inside, Wilma took a sip of tea and said, "We've made an agreement."

"Oh, good," Daphne said.

"Dorothy, come here," Wilma commanded loudly enough for the slave to hear her before she got too far.

Dorothy came out of the mansion with a feather brush in hand and quickly stood before Wilma and Daphne. "Yes, Mrs. Wilma? What is it that you need?"

Wilma replied, "Bring Daisy to me. It has been a while since Daphne has seen her."

"Yes, ma'am." Dorothy went back into the mansion and quickly returned holding Daisy's hand.

Daisy stood before Wilma and Daphne in a blue cotton dress. "Hi, Mrs. Wilma and Mrs. Daphne," the girl said.

Daphne replied, "My word, she is always adorable, such a beautiful mulatto child, I must say."

Dorothy replied, "Why thank you, Mrs. Daphne."

"She is such a rare beauty."

"That's what I thought as well when I first laid eyes on her when she was born," Wilma said. "Now, Daphne, you can have Roberta for $600 as agreed earlier by Thaddeus, and this sweet little angel, you can have her for $100."

Dorothy's heart dropped, her eyes widened, and she pulled Daisy to her apron. "Mrs. Wilma, you can't be serious," she said.

"What did you say, Dorothy?" Wilma said with a raised tone.

Dorothy softly replied, "I sorry, Mrs. Wilma. I don't know what I said."

Wilma's voice deepened. "I heard you clearly, and I won't tolerate such a thing from you!" She stood up and slammed her teacup on the table, shattering it. "You walking around my home all happy with this high yellow child! Following anyone she pleases. Did you really think it would take me so long to figure out who this bastard child's father is?"

Dorothy's eyes widened. "Mrs. Wilma, I don't know what you talking about."

"Now, you see here. She sold a harlot and her child together out of superior kindness," Wilma said while pointing at Daphne. "But me…oh, no, no, no. You won't disrespect me in my house. His observation of you this morning is the last straw. I know she Master Plecker's child, and I won't have that high yellow thing running around here reminding me of my husband's activities anymore."

Dorothy shook her head. "I swear to you she isn't Master Plecker's child. He's never touched me! I promise you."

"Lies, all lies. You see this, Daphne? Such disrespect. I should have you beat, but I think seeing the look on your face when this child rides away today on that carriage will be fulfilling enough."

Dorothy got on her knees and held Daisy. "I swear to you she isn't a child of Master Plecker."

Wilma screamed, "Riza, you come out here right now!"

Riza ran out the front door and stopped at the sight of Dorothy on her knees, crying as she held Daisy.

Wilma yelled at her, "You go and get Mr. Wade right now and tell him to bring Roberta here now. Now move!"

Riza dashed away to do as she'd been told.

⎯⎯◆⎯⎯

Joseph and Tom heard screaming and crying and ran out of the barn to see what all the commotion was. They stopped and took a step back when they saw Wade dragging Roberta as she begged not to be taken. Bo walked up behind the boys, and they watched together. Suddenly Roberta's mother came running to her and gave her daughter a hug, temporarily halting Wade's progress. He broke up their hug and pulled Roberta away while she cried. The girl's mother watched helplessly, falling to her knees as she began to cry.

A tear fell down Joseph's face, and he wiped it away.

"Come on, boys. Nothing we can do but pray she given to nice masters," Bo said.

"What kind of hope is that?" Joseph angrily asked.

"The only kind we got as Negroes. Let's get this done so Master Rice ain't got nothing to say."

"I hate this place," Tom mumbled.

The boys went back to work, frowning with the thought of Roberta's abrupt departure on their minds.

Wade pulled Roberta as he marched up the dirt trail toward the mansion. Dorothy remained on her knees, holding Daisy and pleading with Wilma, but she stopped when she noticed Wade approaching with Roberta. Her hazel eyes bulged, and her arms began to shake. Roberta said something but was too far away to be heard. Wade stopped pulling the girl, backhanded her face, and she fell down. He grabbed the girl's arm and made her stand, then pushed the thirteen-year-old forward. She cried as she walked toward Daphne's carriage. Dorothy slowly stood while holding Daisy next to her hip.

When the two got to Daphne's carriage, Wilma shouted, "Mr. Wade, once you put Roberta in that carriage, you come here and take little Daisy too. She'll be a strong addition to Daphne's household."

"No!" Dorothy yelled in terror.

Wilma went to pull Daisy out of Dorothy's hands, but Dorothy slapped her.

Daphne gasped, and Wilma glared wide-eyed at Dorothy.

"You gone 'n done it now," Wade yelled.

Wilma lunged at Dorothy and tried to choke her, forcing her to let go of Daisy. The confused little girl stood on the steps and watched Dorothy and Wilma struggle against each other.

Wade grabbed Daisy and carried her to the carriage.

"Mommy!" Daisy cried.

Dorothy pushed Wilma off her and ran to Wade. "Please, Master Wade, please stop!" she begged.

Wade quickly turned around and punched Dorothy, knocking her to the ground. "Who do you think you are out here?" he growled. "You gettin' a beating for what you did to Mrs. Wilma."

Blood streamed down from Dorothy's nose. "Please, Master Wade, she thinks Master Plecker is Daisy's father!"

Wade looked at Dorothy with a skewed frown.

"I swear she isn't his! I swear she isn't," Dorothy cried.

"It don't matter what I think. You better count your blessings that you not being sold and Doris is still here."

Dorothy stood up and sprinted into the mansion's front door, passing Wilma as she tried to gather herself. "Master Kenneth! Master Kenneth, where are you!" Dorothy yelled. She ran into the family's living room, finding him sitting at the grand piano. "Kenneth," she cried.

Kenneth looked at Dorothy with raised eyebrows and wide eyes. "What in this world is going on?" he asked.

"She's taking our baby! Your mother is selling her!" Dorothy wailed. "She thinks I been with your daddy. Please stop her, please, Kenneth!"

Kenneth ran out the front door as Daphne climbed into the carriage. "Mrs. Daphne, now hold on a minute," he yelled.

Daphne replied, "Why, Kenneth, what has you so rushed?"

Kenneth continued to march toward the carriage. "I must apologize, but Daisy isn't for sale."

"Kenneth Plecker, what are you doing?" Wilma bellowed. "The existence of that child is an insult to me, you, and this entire household. I won't have that infidelity staring me down for my remaining years. Your papa wouldn't dare question my judgment."

"Momma, your accusations are false. I know this for certain," Kenneth said.

Wilma growled, "Then who is the father?"

"Geoffrey is the father of both of my girls, Mrs. Wilma!" Dorothy yelled. "I became pregnant right before Master Plecker sold him. The truth is he would force himself on me sometimes, and I never told anyone but Master Kenneth."

"Geoffrey…that high yellow weasel," Wilma said, each word deepening. Her hands tightened into fists. "You should've spoken up. I would've had him hanged for you! I've watched you grow into a fine slave since you were a child, but your latest outburst is inexcusable." She pointed at Dorothy. "Your punishment for putting your hands on me is the selling of that girl."

Dorothy looked at Kenneth and began to wail.

Kenneth's brow furrowed, and his face started to redden. He suddenly grabbed Daisy out of the carriage and carried her to the front door. "We're not selling her, Momma," he said. "I have a promise to keep, and I'm a man of my word as you raised me to be."

Wilma angrily replied, "What are you talking about?"

Kenneth kindly replied, "Momma, I promised Dorothy the girls would not be sold apart from each other for the rest of their lives. She was worried this day would come and begged me, and because she has served us faithfully for so many years, I agreed to her request."

Wilma grunted. "You always been a sweet child, even to Dorothy when you was a child and we first got her. But this agreement is an abomination." Seeing the seriousness in Kenneth's narrowed eyes, she said, "Very well, the girls won't ever be sold, but your father is gonna tear her hide up! Wade, take Dorothy to be whipped, and she doesn't get fed for two days. No slave on this plantation will ever lay their hands on me again after this!"

Kenneth looked at Dorothy, and she nodded, accepting her fate. "As you wish, Momma."

Wade moved past Kenneth and grabbed Dorothy by her arm. "Come on now, Dorothy," he said.

Dorothy submissively marched with Wade while Kenneth watched as he held Daisy.

"I love you, Mommy," Daisy said.

Dorothy smiled as tears fell down her face. "I love you too, my Daisy," she said.

Kenneth put Daisy down and held her hand. "You go inside now, Daisy. Your momma will return," he said.

Daisy ran to Wilma and gave her a hug, then ran into the mansion.

Wilma watched Daisy run inside and exhaled. "No more

promises, Kenneth," she said. "I'm sorry, Daphne. I think we will have to make another arrangement to help you."

Daphne casually replied, "That's quite all right. I think it is quite honorable for Kenneth to keep his word. Even to a mulatto."

Wilma handed her the $100 back. "I guess explaining the selling of one slave will be more acceptable for Calvin anyway."

"What a day this is."

"Yes, it is. The way he was looking at her rump this morning. Ugh, I was so tempted to pluck his eyes out."

"Men will be men."

"Mm-hmm, at least I know for certain now Calvin hasn't let his hands slide onto that one. I'm sure he has heard some of Dorothy's wailing." Wilma turned to look at Kenneth. "I can't believe this boy."

"We need more honorable men like him."

"Indeed…never thought I'd ever send Dorothy to get whipped." Wilma looked at Kenneth as he watched Wade escort Dorothy. "I wish he would hurry up and get a wife."

The two women chuckled, and Kenneth turned away and went inside the mansion.

Wade took Dorothy to an old stump with a nail in the middle of it and demanded her to take off her dress. She reluctantly took off her dress, and Wade tied her hands down on the old stump. She could feel her blood slowing down in her wrists.

"I guess that motherly instinct kicked in the moment you realized your little Daisy was about to get sold," Wade said. "I can't blame you for wanting to protect your young'un, but putting your hands on Mrs. Wilma is inexcusable."

"I couldn't lose my baby girl," Dorothy murmured.

Wade lifted up Dorothy's chin with the whip. "What makes you think you so special? That pretty face, or is it this nice smooth skin of yours?"

"I don't see myself as more special, Master Wade. My heart broke seeing my baby being taken from me."

Wade nodded, looking into Dorothy's hazel eyes. "You a bold one. I'll give you that. I'll tell you what. I won't mess up that pretty face of yours, but you not gonna forget this day," he said, his voice deepening. Then he cracked the whip, making Dorothy jump.

A tear trickled down her face, and she balled her hands into fists. Wade then cracked the whip across Dorothy's back, and she screamed in pain. The other slaves in the area briefly stopped working when they heard her screams. Wade continued cracking the whip, and Dorothy weakened with each new gash and trickle of blood running down her back.

"Heavenly Father, I ask for strength, and I thank you for protecting my girls," Dorothy murmured.

Wade squinted. "What did you say?" He scrunched up his face and cracked the whip again, causing her to howl in pain.

"That's enough, Wade," Master Plecker said, approaching them. "Wilma has told me everything." He knelt down next to an exhausted, bloody Dorothy. "You disappoint me, but I admire the bravery. Older women tend to sometimes act a little crazy. Wade, go ahead and have one of these niggers take Dorothy back to the house-slave house to be cleaned up."

"Mr. Plecker, she only got eight lashes."

"It's quite all right. I can see it in her eyes...a mother willing to do anything for her little chicks. I don't want my best house slave ruined by my wife's ridiculous accusations. I've already sold one slave today as a favor to family friends. Besides, I want to take a ride with you. We have to pay Geoffrey a visit." He lightly tapped his black cane on the hardpacked earth and rose to his feet. "I normally wouldn't care about a nigger raping another. But first it was my silver cufflinks he stole before he was sold and now a piece of my gut turns at knowing he fathered both of those girls without my permission. The audacity, to take advantage of my best house slave. He'll pay today."

"As you wish. I'll have Dorothy sent over to the house now." Wade untied Dorothy's hands and had one of the slaves help her to the house-slave house.

Riza was sent to the slave house to help clean up Dorothy's wounds. When she entered the wooden slave house, Emma had already begun to clean the wounds. As Riza saw the damage done to Dorothy's back, her eyes flooded with tears, and she rushed over to help stop the bleeding. Dorothy's screams echoed for almost an hour while they worked to clean her wounds.

"It's going to be okay, Dorothy," Riza said.

"Where are my girls?" Dorothy asked.

"They're upstairs cleaning. They don't know nothing."

Dorothy moaned, "Good. Nobody say nothing to them about this."

Riza looked at Dorothy's quivering wounded body and then met her gaze. Dorothy said, "It's okay, Riza. I promise."

"This isn't right."

"I broke the rules. I'd take another whipping for my girls if I had to. I'll try my hardest to make sure they never see a whip."

"You're always looking after everyone."

"Without love we're nothing. When you first came here, you reminded me so much of me. I'll always show you love, little Riza."

Riza's lips quivered as she replied, "You always did what you could to keep me out of trouble. I'm sorry for every time I made it difficult."

Dorothy grinned. "Don't talk like that. I'm not going to die. I only need some time to heal. After that, I'll boss you around again."

The three house slaves giggled.

Emma started to pick up the bloody rags. "Yes, you will heal. In Jesus name, you'll be standing strong right next to us again."

When Dorothy's wounds were finally taken care of, Riza left the slave house. She leaned against the house and began to cry. She thought, *None of us is nothing special to them. If they beat Dorothy, what would they do to me? I have to push forward with my plan.*

During the night, Riza fell into a deep dream of New York City when she was a young child. She saw five men gambling at a table.

"No…I can't live through this again. Why do I keep seeing this?" Riza said.

The men began to argue and one man threw his cards down. "No, not again, Daddy. Stay away from them!"

A gunshot echoed through the building, and tears began to run down Riza's face. She heard the men walking toward her and ran out of the building, into the busy streets of New York. She headed down an alley but it started to collapse behind her, so she panicked and jumped back onto the busy street to avoid being crushed. Then she looked back into the dark alley.

"Look, there she is," a man shouted.

A White man suddenly grabbed Riza, and she screamed for help.

Abruptly, she awakened breathing heavily and covered in sweat. She looked over to her right and saw Dorothy looking at her as she laid against the house wall.

"When did you start having the nightmares again?" Dorothy whispered.

Riza answered, "This was the first one in a long time."

"It's never easy losing a parent no matter how old you are. You're the bravest child I've met in a long time. Don't lose that spirit."

Riza lifted her head off the floor and frowned. "It still hurts, doesn't it?"

"I would've taken a hundred hits for my girls. I was sold away from my brothers and sisters. I'll do what I can to stop them from experiencing that kind of pain."

"Thank you for teaching me so much."

Dorothy quietly chuckled. "Oh, Riza, don't speak like that. You needed to learn how to survive out here, so I showed you. You became favored on your own, not because of me."

"I'm leaving this place for good. That's why I'm saying thank you now. I've been away from my momma and brothers for too long."

"Riza, please don't. I understand that you miss them. I really understand it, but they will catch you if you run. I've never known any slave from this plantation to get more than a day away from here."

"I have to try. This place breaks my spirit, and I don't like the way Master Rice looks at me. He's more evil than Master Plecker or Wade."

"If you plan to run away, tell me nothing, girl. Keep me in the dark so when they question me, I can say without hesitation I know nothing."

"Fine, I won't speak any more of it."

Dorothy smiled. "I hope you do succeed. We need more hope in this White man's land."

Dorothy and Riza fell asleep to the sound of crickets dominating the night.

CHAPTER 7
True Feelings

TWO DAYS LATER, DOROTHY STRUGGLED to work in the mansion with Wilma showing her no form of mercy. It was incredibly painful for her to be on her feet, moving about, as the slightest touch to her wounds made her cringe. She constantly exhaled deeply to help her cope with the pain and keep a straight face. After supper, Dorothy, Emma, Riza, Susie, and two other house slaves cleaned the dining room and the kitchen as they normally did.

Coming into the kitchen, Susie said, "Dorothy, Master Kenneth said he wants to speak with you in his room."

"All right, finish cleaning up here. I won't be long," Dorothy said. She moaned while she walked up the stairs to Kenneth's room, then she exhaled and knocked on the white door. "Master Kenneth, I'm here at your request."

Kenneth opened the door and frowned at her. "Come in, Dorothy," he said with his suave southern accent. He closed the door after she entered, leaving her standing there by the doorway of the candlelit room as he moved to sit on the edge of his bed. "You're a brave woman. I'm sorry for what you endured yesterday. I want you to know I will continue to keep my word about the girls."

Dorothy's eyebrows tilted upward, and she replied, "Thank you, Kenneth."

"Come sit down." He patted the bed next to him.

Dorothy sat down on next to Kenneth and said, "Kenneth, I'm sorry, but my body can't... I'm in so much pain."

"I guess I should expect you to think that's why I called for you." He pulled a plate from underneath his bed and placed it on Dorothy's lap. "The mother of my children should never go to sleep hungry."

Tears began to hit the plate as Dorothy cried and held onto the plate tightly.

"No need for tears, eat up," he said.

Dorothy quickly ate while Kenneth caressed her thigh as they talked about the girls. Afterward, she walked to the house-slave house and greeted everyone so none of them worried about her. She later thanked God for speaking to Kenneth's heart, and on the third day, Kenneth fed her again.

━━━━◆━━━━

On July 4, 1860, as Joseph and Tom were putting cotton baskets on a wagon, Joseph lost his hold on one of the baskets and it fell over, causing half the cotton to fall onto the ground.

"Now, see now, you clumsy little nigger, pick all of it up," Master Kit yelled.

"I'm no nigger!" Joseph yelled, glaring back at Master Kit.

The other slaves quietly watched the commotion as they picked cotton.

Master Kit looked at Joseph with his mouth agape, then marched over to the boy. "See now, what did you say to me, half-breed?"

Joseph glanced at Tom, who shook his head. Then the boy said, "I didn't say nothing, Master Kit."

Master Kit slapped Joseph. "You think you so smart? Turn around, Joseph."

Joseph slowly turned around while he kept his eyes on the man.

Master Kit took the switch from his side and gave Joseph five lashes on his back, making the boy scream in pain with each one. "Now, see now, if I call you a nigger, you a nigger." He grabbed Joseph's collar. "I don't care what them Indians told you! You Master Plecker's now, and if you drop another cotton basket again, the next beating will be with a whip! You understand me, boy?"

"Yes, Master Kit," Joseph said, his voice crackling.

Master Rice approached down the dirt row on a black horse, then dismounted. "What's going on over here?" he said, slowly marching toward Joseph, Tom, and Master Kit.

"Nothing, I got it handled. Still some Indian in this one," Master Kit said as he pointed at Joseph. "Now get on."

Joseph immediately walked to the wagon, wiping the tears off his face.

Master Rice replied, "I'd give it a year, and he'll be like the rest of the niggers."

The wagon rode off with the boys, and some of the slaves began to sing a hymn. Joseph's brow lowered while the hymn echoed across the cotton fields. Joseph and Tom arrived at the cotton gin barn and began off-loading the cotton baskets.

"You gonna watch what you say next time," a grumpy, middle-aged slave named Louis said. The dark brown man drove the wagon around the cotton fields, praised Master Plecker, and showed his dislike of the slaves with lighter complexions.

Joseph scowled back in reply while he struggled to carry a cotton basket inside the barn. Then he murmured, "Louis is nothing but a coyote."

As the day wore on, the pain on Joseph's back increased. He later asked Bo to look at it, and Bo told him there were three large welts. He let Joseph remain behind and wait for another wagon to come by with cotton in it, to give him a little time to heal. Stella later checked Joseph's back to make sure it wasn't bleeding. Five days passed before Joseph fully healed from his beating.

On July 10, 1860, while the summer heat reigned in Tahlequah, Annabelle, Lisa, and Lizzie entered the supply store with Sunni, Lisa, and Brock's daughter. Working was Annabelle's way of distracting her mind from thinking about where Joseph was, and she often carried Sunni around in the store, doting on her. Lisa continued to keep Sunni close because she feared Brock might try to take her. Her refusal to allow Brock to meet their daughter and her allowing Jacob to raise Sunni as his own had already angered Brock enough that he'd had Joseph sold into slavery to punish her family.

"Annabelle, I'm going home to bring back a sack of cornmeal I forgot about," Lizzie said in Cherokee.

"All right. It's been slow all day, so don't feel rushed to come back."

Lizzie replied, "I prefer to be here today. I won't be long." She left the supply store, and while she traveled through the dirt streets of Tahlequah, she saw Paul, Nancy's former mulatto slave who had saved her daughter Eve.

Paul smiled and waved, and she reluctantly waved back. "Miss Lizzie, it good to see you today. How are you?" he said as their paths drew them closer.

Lizzie replied, "I'm fine. I need to go home to get some cornmeal. I'll talk to you later."

"I can carry it for you."

Lizzie turned around and gave Paul a fake smile. "I can carry it myself. I've been doing this for years."

"Well, I was saying I would do it for you if you let me. I also wanted to give you this blue flower in case you wasn't having a good day. I think you should have good days."

Lizzie took the flower and exhaled. "Paul...I appreciate your kindness, but stop it. I don't want your kindness. I really don't want it."

"Miss Lizzie, everyone should be treated with kindness, even beautiful women who don't want it."

Lizzie tilted her head. "I see your English has improved. When did that happen?"

"Mrs. Nancy decided to help me a little because I work for her now."

Lizzie scoffed. "She is a piece of work. No more flowers, Paul. I don't want to owe you anything."

"You never have owed me anything. I wanted to show you I'm happy and to call you my friend. I'd also like to spend more time with you if you will allow it."

Lizzie gulped as she looked at him. "No, Paul...stop chasing me like a child. I don't want you. I don't want *anyone* right now." Her voice began to rise. "And you giving me these flowers to make me happy is making me mad!"

"But you said not long ago that you liked the flowers. What did I do wrong?"

Lizzie threw her hands up. "Be a friend, Paul. Be a friend. I really don't want to become closer to you at all. You can find someone else, because I'm not going to allow this to go past you being a friend." She grunted, dropping her gaze. After a moment, she looked back up at him and sighed. "I'm sorry. You're good man. I just can't tolerate you right now."

Paul pouted. "I will always care about you, so don't tell me how to feel. I'm not a slave any more, and all I ask is to not be treated like one. If I is a good man, why don't you want to give me a chance?"

Lizzie began to walk away. "I don't have to answer that. I suggest you live with that answer."

"I see how you work, Lizzie Lightning. Any time you care, you push people away...even people who love you. If it because Joseph gone, you can always talk to me. I know how it feel."

Lizzie's eyes narrowed as she turned around and stepped toward Paul. "I will never have to explain myself to you or any other man! You think you're so smart!" Lizzie's high-pitched southern voice deepened with each word. "I'll tell you something, mulatto! I buried my momma as a child. I found my papa dead and buried him as a child. I'm strong enough to deal with this. I don't need to talk to anyone about it!"

"I want you to know I care."

With her eyes locked on Paul's sympathetic face, Lizzie sighed. "You're a good man, but right now that's not enough because my nephew is what's on my mind." She placed the blue flower on Paul's chest. "Don't give me another flower unless I ask for one."

Lizzie strolled away as Paul watched, his lips curving up to form a little smirk. "A strong woman needs a strong man," he said.

Lizzie glanced back at Paul as she moved through the towns-people. She felt the corners of her mouth curve upward but smacked her lips to stop it. "Bye, Paul."

"You something else, Lizzie Lightning. I'll certainly pray for Joseph's return," he mumbled with a smile.

———◆———

On July 20, Joseph ate stew for supper with the other slaves, but he remained mostly silent. Tom and Mary attempted to keep his spirits up, but Joseph remained focused on his family. Stella noticed heartbrokenness etched into Joseph's frown and decided to tell a lighthearted story of two squirrels to help cheer him up. His frown didn't budge, and later, as the others slept, he stared up at the ceiling.

"Still awake, I see," Stella said. "What's wrong, Joseph?"

"I miss my family," Joseph said. "I miss hearing the coyotes and wolves at night. I miss seeing the great herds, the cougars, and the birds flying over our farm. I thought they would have found me by now."

"I know how it feels to not be with family. I was born on this plantation, but both of my brothers were sold away. That was years ago, but I never forget who they was and that what matters, Joseph. It's bad when you forget."

Joseph frowned. "Why do people forget?"

"Because it's more painful when you know who you missing. It's hard living years with a hurt heart, so people forget. It's how we survived all this time."

"I will never forget my family."

Stella smiled. "Good, you already do the first step to have hope. God good, and even if White man ruling, they ain't nothing compared to him. Now try to sleep so it easier for you to work."

"Okay, thank you."

"You welcome."

Stella's encouragement helped Joseph finish out the week

and pushed him to pray whenever he got the chance. Tom even started to pray with Joseph, hoping they would be rescued soon from the plantation. The boys' friendship continued to grow as they tried their best to be cheerful while they worked.

On July 25, while the other slaves ate their lunch, Joseph ducked behind the cookhouse to pray. He kept a wary eye out to not get caught praying and end up getting more lashes.

"Ah, there you are again," Riza said, startling Joseph so that he jumped and looked up at her wide-eyed. "Calm down. You should work on your hearing."

"Hi, Riza," Joseph said. "I was praying."

Riza knelt down next to Joseph. "I know what you were doing. You think the Creator is listening to you today?"

Joseph smiled at Riza. "I think he is. You can pray with me if you want to."

"It has been a while so…all right. I'll pray with you. After that, I'll have to get back to the mansion quickly. I'm supposed to be getting Mrs. Wilma's crackers. Our plan to escape is almost ready."

Joseph's eyes bulged. "Really, Riza?!! I think it's good you're here. Let's pray."

Riza chuckled at Joseph's abrupt cheerfulness but gladly took their prayer seriously. The two finished praying, and she stood up and brushed a few leaves off her blue cotton dress.

"Will you come by tonight?" he asked her.

"Sure, and maybe I'll have some extra food for you. Bye, Joseph."

"Bye, Riza."

***

On her way back to the mansion, Riza saw Clint approaching her and smiled at him. Clint gave her two yellow flowers.

"Thank you, Clint. These are pretty."

Clint shyly replied, "I thought you would think they was pretty. I hope they make your day better."

Riza smelled the flowers. "They smell great, and maybe I'll be able to bring you some extra food tonight. You're always so nice to me."

"Well, you always be nice to me. I have to go before Master Rice come looking for me."

"Yeah, I need to get back to work too." Riza resumed walking toward the mansion, then turned and smiled at Clint.

He blushed as he walked toward the cotton fields whistling.

As night fell, Riza managed to steal some of the leftover food from the Pleckers' supper and took it to Joseph and the others. It was satisfying for her to be able to make the younger children happy, though she kept a straight face. As the full moon shone down on the plantation, Riza left the slave house and decided to go through the weeping willows' garden that made a direct path to the house-slave house and the mansion. When she started to go past the trees, she could hear moaning.

Riza slowed her footsteps and listened, soon hearing a woman say, "Master Rice, please, I'm tired."

"You better watch your mouth, Pearl. I don't have patience for this tonight," Master Rice said.

The moaning continued as Riza slowly moved closer. Then she saw Master Rice holding Pearl against a tree with her arms around his shoulders as he raped her. Riza's mouth dropped, and her eyes widened. "I don't believe it," she whispered. A chill ran down her spine as her heartbeat increased. Pearl lifted up her head and looked right at Riza, a tear running down Pearl's face. Riza put her hand over her mouth.

"Are you crying again?" Master Rice asked.

"No, Master Rice. My arm's getting tired."

Master Rice stopped and set Pearl down. "Turn around then."

Pearl turned around and placed her hands on the tree. Master Rice then resumed raping her.

Riza slowly backed up and moved along the other trees so Master Rice didn't see her. She entered the house-slave house and remained silent as the others greeted her. She sat down and quietly watched Susie play with Doris and Daisy.

"Riza, what is wrong?" Dorothy asked.

Riza looked at Dorothy. "Nothing. I'm tired. It has been a long day." A moment later, she mumbled, "I'm tired of this place."

Dorothy's mouth curved downward, forming a small frown. "I know I said I don't want to know about certain things, but never be afraid to speak to me. I know your childhood ended the moment you came here, but I'm always here to help you."

"Thank you. I think I'm going to go to sleep now." Riza lay down and went to sleep, her only escape to suppress what she'd seen. Fearing she would one day experience being raped, she awakened in the early morning hours while everyone else still slept so she could pray for protection in secret.

The next day, Riza kept to herself and spoke little, focused on her assigned tasks and maintaining a fake smile so she could be left alone. During the lunch break Wilma gave the house slaves, Riza decided to go to the apple tree on the side of the mansion and take three apples quickly so she wouldn't get caught. When she was eating the last apple, still hiding on the side of the mansion, she saw Pearl in her brown cotton dress approaching her. Pearl stood before Riza with her hands on her hips.

Riza took another bite of her apple, and her gaze shifted away from Pearl to the distant cattle.

"You know them apples ain't for you," Pearl bickered.

"I'm not bound by the same rules as field slaves," Riza countered. "Think I'll have a piece of chicken while I'm cooking it for Master Plecker, so I don't get tempted to throw up while picking through leftovers."

Pearl sneered. "You think you so special. Don't tell no one what you saw last night, or life gonna get hard for you."

Riza shook her head. "I feel sorry for you. I'm guessing that's been happening for a long time. I saw you cry." She dropped her gaze. "That's all of it I want to talk about."

"Then this be the only time we talk about it." Pearl curled her lower lip. "You ain't got no idea, Riza…what I go through on different nights. So you give me your word, little girl."

Riza pouted. "I don't have to give you nothing. What did you do that causes Master Rice to do that to you?"

Pearl shrugged and shook her head. "I ain't did nothing wrong. He just pick me one day when I was fifteen years old. I used to pray that it would stop, but nothing happened. I still wonder if God even hears the voice of a Negro woman."

"Maybe God has a plan to stop him so he can't do it to nobody else. Maybe he'll send someone to stop Master Rice."

Pearl scoffed as she glared down at Riza. "What plan that be? Who gonna stand for a Negro woman? It can't be you. You nothing but an Indian girl, and I know time not on your side. I see the way he look at you. He waiting for you to turn into a woman."

"I'll never be what you are," Riza defiantly said. "I'm who I am, and that White man will never get pleasure from me."

"I ain't never enjoyed it. Being told where to go and when to go, but that my life."

"If that's all you have to say, you can leave before the overseers start looking for you. I have no reason to speak about what I saw. I'm sorry."

Pearl dismissively waved. "Like your sorry mean anything."

"Well, I'm sure not gonna replace you."

Pearl's face scrunched. "Don't talk to me like that. You ain't nothing but a redskin girl with long, pretty hair."

"Like you said earlier, look at where I work and look at where you work. The masters would actually miss me if I left them." Riza stood up and headed back toward the mansion.

"Riza, you don't speak to me like that!"

Riza smacked her lips and kept walking.

"That rude grass nigger. I can't wait for the day Master Rice touches her!" Pearl spat.

Two weeks passed as the tension between Riza and Pearl festered. Stella thought nothing of the obvious dislike the two had for each other because of Pearl's past treatment of Riza.

Riza later decided to meet with Joseph every other day to pray after lunch, to gain favor with him but also to try to rebuild her own faith. She later decided it was good for the Indian children to get together and pray in Stella's slave house.

***

On August 8, Lizzie heard a carriage arrive in front of the Lightning-Strongman farm. She slowly approached from around the family home with her bow drawn until she saw Eli and Samuel on the front seat.

"They're home," Lizzie shouted in Cherokee as she ran to the wagon, hoping they had found Joseph.

"Lizzie, we need help. John isn't doing well," Samuel shouted in Cherokee.

Lizzie opened the carriage door and saw John lying down on the seat. She placed her hand on his forehead, finding he had a fever. She looked back and saw Maria standing by the family house. "Maria, we need your help!" she yelled in Cherokee.

Maria rushed over to the carriage as Eli, Lizzie, and Samuel got John out of the carriage to carry him into the house and place him in his bed.

As Lizzie and Maria worked to get John comfortable, the front door opened and David walked inside. "Pa, Samuel, did you bring Joseph back?" he yelled in Cherokee.

Lizzie walked out of the bedroom and shook her head. "David, go tell your momma your father is sick right now," she said in Cherokee.

David ran to the supply store and told Annabelle, Grace, and Lisa. The women rushed home with David and immediately went to work caring for John.

John regained consciousness later in the evening as Annabelle sat in front of their bed in a chair. "When did we get back?" he asked in his native tongue.

Annabelle replied, "Earlier today. Samuel said you passed out yesterday, and you have been asleep for most of the day."

John frowned when he looked at Annabelle. "I'm sorry. I failed us again."

"Don't blame yourself. I know you, Eli, and Samuel tried so hard. Samuel told me while y'all were out there in the swamps you refused to sleep for a whole day. So don't apologize to me. Focus on healing. You're no good to your family dead, and I don't know what I'd do if I lost you."

John softly grabbed Annabelle's hand. "I will try to do this differently, so the next time I don't return to you sick. Where are the children?"

"They're eating supper with the rest of the family. The twins stayed with you for hours holding your hands. The flowers next to the lamp are from them."

John smiled while he looked at the yellow flowers. "Well, when they finish eating, send them over. I think my sun and moon have worried long enough."

Annabelle kissed John on the forehead and smiled at him as she left the bedroom. To her surprise, she saw David sitting in one of the rocking chairs, holding onto Joseph's bow. "David, did you eat already?" she asked in Cherokee.

David replied, "No, Momma. I couldn't eat. How is Pa?"

Annabelle walked up to David and placed her hand on his shoulder. "He's doing much better, and he's awake now. You can go speak to him before your sisters do. The moment they learn he is awake, I doubt they'll leave his side."

David wiped a tear from his face. "Are we really going to be able to find Joseph?"

Annabelle hugged David, and he began to cry. She said, "I believe in my soul we will find your brother and bring him home. I miss him too, and I know he misses his big brother. Go speak to your father." She gave David a kiss on his cheek, and he dried his face.

David entered the bedroom and greeted John. As Annabelle listened to them talk, her brow lowered and she deeply exhaled, her eyes fixed on Joseph's bow now leaning against the wall where David had left it.

The next afternoon, Molly Hills, the wife of Reverend Hills, visited the Lightning-Strongman farm. She and her husband had been heartbroken when they learned of Joseph's kidnapping. To Annabelle's surprise, Reverend Hills had gone up to the courthouse a few days after Joseph's kidnapping and condemned Mr. Sawyer's actions. The green-eyed White woman wanted to pray for the family and encourage them through their hard times. Molly's empathy was appreciated by Annabelle, and she was welcomed to have lunch with the family. After lunch, Molly said her goodbyes and promised to keep Joseph in her prayers.

CHAPTER 8
Fire, Rebellion, and Ashes

O N THE EVENING OF AUGUST 12, 1860, Joseph, Susie, and Tom sat behind Stella's house in front of a small fire. "When will Riza arrive?" Tom calmly asked.

"She should be arriving soon," Susie said. "Mrs. Wilma's guest left today, so she had extra bedsheets to clean up."

"Oh, okay. I have to go to the outhouse. I'll be right back."

"Okay," Joseph and Susie said.

"Are you nervous about Riza's plan for us to escape?" Susie asked in Cherokee.

Joseph replied, "I am, but I trust her. She reminds me of my aunties."

"I wish I was as brave as her."

Joseph's head tilted. "I think you are."

Susie grinned. "Thank you, Joseph."

"I know what it was like for Tom to be taken, but you never told me everything."

"Oh." Susie's gaze shifted to the fire and then back to Joseph. "Two years ago, I was enjoying time with my family, visiting my daddy's old friends outside of Tahlequah. They are like cousins to me, and we always had a good time. My momma called for me and my little sister, Lacia. I told her to run to Momma and that I was coming. We were catching lightning bugs and having fun.

I only wanted to catch a few more and let them go. I watched Lacia go to the house."

Her eyes welled up, and she took a deep breath. "I turned around and chased a few of them, then turned back around to the house as my momma called me, but a White man grabbed my arm. I tried to pull away, but he picked me up. I screamed for my parents."

Susie wiped away her tears as they streamed down her cheeks. "I bit that man on his shoulder. He screamed and pulled me off, cursed at me, and threw me onto a wagon. I heard my momma scream for me, and then those White men shot at my parents. I screamed for my momma as the wagon started driving off. The White man that was driving the wagon got shot in his shoulder, but he kept the wagon going. I tried to jump off the wagon, but the other White man that had first grabbed me caught my arm and threw me to the back of the wagon. I kicked him as I heard my papa yelling for me, but then that White man punched me. The next day I woke up with a black eye and chains on my wrists. The last thing I remember is my parents screaming for me."

Joseph felt his heart race as he listened to Susie.

"I was sold to the Plecker family twelve days later. I've been here for two years, and I trust Riza to lead us home."

"The last thing I remember is screaming for my momma," Joseph said with teary eyes.

"I'll be very happy for you to meet my family."

"I want you to meet my family too."

"The last time I saw my momma, she was having another baby. She was on her fifth month. I want to see my baby brother or sister."

"My baby brother has probably forgotten me. His name is Jonathan."

Susie rubbed her thighs and exhaled. "I know Mr. Plecker is evil, but he's not the most evil man here."

"Oh, Wade?"

"No, it's Master Rice. He smiles when he punishes anyone, and before you got here, he came up to me while I was throwing away old food to the pigs. He told me to hurry up, and so I did. When I went past him, he put his hand on my shoulder and made me stop walking. He said I'm going to turn into a pretty young thing like Riza, then rubbed his hand on my back and grabbed my butt." Susie continued wiping away her tears while Joseph's eyes widened. "He ran his hand through my hair and said I'm going to be a fun little thing in a few years. He said I'm going to be something to look at like Dorothy. It's like he's waiting for us to become older and make us his toys for pleasure. I can't stay here and become that. I'd rather die than be a slave used for pleasing a man."

"I promise that won't happen to you."

Susie shook her head. "You can't keep that promise, Joseph. You're a mixed-blood boy, and he wouldn't think twice about killing you. I feel nothing but evil from him. The best thing we can do is run."

Joseph held Susie's hand. "I'm with you."

Susie half-smiled. "And I'm with you, my friend."

The fire reflected off their tears before they cleaned off their faces and resumed waiting quietly for the other native children to join them.

<hr>

On the evening of August 19, Riza and Susie left the mansion and met at the willow trees while the sunlight barely pierced through the drooping leaves.

"Riza, why did we have to come here? We'll get in trouble if Mrs. Wilma knows we are here," Susie said.

"Our time to escape is tomorrow," Riza said.

Susie's eyebrows shot up. "Tomorrow is Master Plecker's party, when some of the other plantation people come over! Riza, are you crazy? There's no way we would get away!"

"There is a way, and I know how to make sure they won't be looking for us. All you have to do is trust me. Please, trust me."

"All right, I'll trust you. When do you want to tell the boys?"

"I will tell them tonight. Now let's go back inside before Mrs. Wilma starts whining for us."

As the girls walked away, Pearl stepped from behind a tree and took a bite of bread. The corner of her mouth slowly curved upward, forming a leer. As she later worked in the fields, she gave Master Rice a slight smirk.

After sunset, Riza and Susie went to the slave houses looking for Joseph and Tom. Riza gathered the boys outside while Stella made them stew from leftover food. Riza's demeanor was different. She was nervous and secretive. The news that tomorrow would be the day of their escape made Joseph excited, but Tom seemed skeptical about the plan.

<hr>

As Riza explained her plan to the children, Pearl walked out to the giant willow trees.

"What do you want, Pearl?" Master Rice asked.

Pearl submissively replied, "Master Rice, I know Riza planning to run away tomorrow during Master Plecker's party. She gonna do something bad so no one gonna know she gone, and she taking the Indian children with her."

Master Rice crossed his arms. "How sure of this plan are you? I don't want to waste no time on Riza if this is hopeful wishing."

"I swear I heard it from her mouth today. She done cursed the whole plantation and planning to do something bad."

"All right, I'll have to let Mr. Plecker know. We'll have to prepare for that little redskin's plan."

"Go get her now! Punish her for her rebellion against you!"

Master Rice slapped her. "Pearl! You don't tell me how to do my job, ever! Is that understood?"

Pearl's eyes bulged as she held her pulsating cheek. "Yes, Master. I don't want her to do nothing bad. She only a child."

"Well, she's not only a child, but I can't expect your Negro mind to understand how dangerous these Indian children are. They not like you. They think, and watching Riza all these years, I know that smart-mouthed girl will try her hardest to win. Go back to your house and don't tell nobody I know, because I promise you, if nothing happens and I feel like you lied to me,

I'm not the only one that'll be requesting your services when I feel the need." Master Rice grabbed Pearl's chin. "You understand me?"

Pearl's body began to shake, seeing the seriousness in Master Rice's brown eyes. "Yes, Master Rice, I do, but I promise you, I tell the truth."

"We'll see. Go back to the slave houses like I told you."

She turned and rushed back to the slave houses as Master Rice marched to the mansion.

Master Rice entered the mansion and told Dorothy to immediately get Mr. Plecker. Soon, Mr. Plecker, Kenneth, and Dorothy came down the elegant staircase with skewed frowns.

"Brian Rice, what encourages you to come here so late? It's 9:00 p.m.," Mr. Plecker said.

"I apologize to you and your household, but there is an emergency that must be addressed now," Rice said. "There must be no other ears but yours to hear this."

Kenneth squinted while he looked at Dorothy. "You can leave now, Dorothy," he said. "You're working longer hours than normal, so go get rested for the party."

Submissively nodding her head at the menfolk, Dorothy left the mansion.

"What is so urgent?" Mr. Plecker asked.

"It's Riza, sir, that little redskin is planning to cause some trouble tomorrow at the party so she can escape with the other Indian children," Rice said.

Mr. Plecker's eyebrows shot upward. "What?! She wouldn't dare do such a thing!"

"Pa, I have no hard time believing such a thing. She always has good timing," Kenneth said. "She used to always time when we needed to get supplies and then wait for Momma at the front door. It made Momma uncomfortable that Riza knew when she wanted to get supplies, so that's why we always go at different times. Little Indian girl is always thinking too much. She's not like the niggers in the fields."

"Who did you hear this from?" Mr. Plecker asked.

Rice answered, "I heard it from Pearl. I have little doubt she ain't telling the truth, but I did tell her if she lying, she gonna get a punishment like she never got before."

Mr. Plecker folded his arms. "Why didn't you bring Riza here?"

Rice replied, "Mr. Plecker, what good will that do us? If it's not true, it would only give that little savage some ideas. Call me a man of morals, but I believe she not guilty until she get caught."

"Well, I won't have that little Mohawk bringing me grief. We'll double-check all the gun cases tonight and lock them up. We take no chances. Inform Wade and Kit of Riza's plans, and I'll have two of Sally's overseers notified as well."

"So Sally is coming to the party this year?" Kenneth asked.

Mr. Plecker replied, "Yes, your sister decided at the last minute she was coming along with Darius. I do wish you'd spend more time with Darius. He is your brother-in-law and a brilliant economist."

Kenneth's head tilted a little. "Pa, I'd rather not talk about this right now when Riza is planning to embarrass us and ruin your party."

"All right, let's check the gun cases now and inform the others of this rebellion."

The men quickly went through the mansion and the gun cases. Mr. Plecker locked all the cases and put the key in his trousers. The others were informed of Riza's plans and waited patiently for the morning.

⟡

During the night, Riza went to sleep next to Susie, anxious for the morning. While asleep, she found herself going through a field of green grass and saw a brown wooden bridge over a stream. She approached the bridge and felt tempted to cross it.

"Hello, Riza," said a man in her native tongue.

Riza turned around and saw a man with a gold aura around his body and felt nothing but peace. "Who are you?" she asked in Mohawk.

"My name is Ojistah, and I have an important message for you."

"What message would that be?"

"You're still her Shining Star no matter how old you become, and every prayer you've made has been heard."

Riza's eyes welled up and before she could stop it, she began sobbing uncontrollably. "What are you? How do you know that?"

Ojistah approached her and placed his hand on her shoulder. "I'm an angel. You have done such a good job being strong, not only for yourself, but for others too. The other message I have for you is to be patient."

Riza wiped away her tears. "Patient for what...to be freed from those White people? No, I can't. If you can be sent to me to tell me about my momma's words, you can help me and the others get out of here!"

"The Father has a special plan, Riza, and you must trust him."

Riza scowled. "No! I'm done waiting! Why does he want me to wait around for? To know what it's like to be raped by a White man, or get beaten by one? I already know how it feels to eat trash after Mr. Plecker is done eating. How much lower do I have to live?"

"I don't know the whole plan, but I do know you need to be patient and trust him. There is more going on than you can see."

Riza shook her head. "I'm tired, Ojistah. I can't deal with these White people anymore. Do you see the way Master Rice looks at me?" Her arms began to quiver. "Do you know what it feels like to know the older I get, the more that man looks at me? I won't wait...not this time!"

"Riza, please listen and know you're not alone. You're a natural leader, but you have to stop thinking about yourself and think about the others too."

Riza's voice rose, "I'm thinking about the others! They want to leave too!"

"You're letting your fear control your actions. The Father does not give you a spirt of fear, but of power, and of love, and of a sound mind. I'm not allowed to stop you. I can only give you advice and the messages I was meant to give you."

"Have you ever seen a woman being raped?"

"Yes, I have, and I know you have too. It's bothering you a lot more than you're willing to admit."

Riza gulped and slowly backed away from Ojistah. Lips quivering, she said, "No…I can't do this anymore. Look at how many years I've lost to these White people. Cleaning their floors, cooking their meals, feeding their babies, cleaning their dishes! I'm not a slave!" She ran across the bridge.

"Riza, no! The bridge isn't complete!"

With each step, Riza could hear the wood breaking. She clenched her teeth and tried to run faster, but her foot went through the bridge and she gasped. The bridge collapsed, causing Riza to fall through. She screamed in terror and jerked awake. She looked around and saw everyone was still asleep.

Riza laid back, placed her hand on her racing heart, and began to cry. "Jesus, I can't do this anymore. Please don't ask me to wait."

As the sunrise on August 20 warmed the land, the slaves began work earlier in preparation for Mr. Plecker's summer party. Riza was shaken by the dream but anxious for the day, and as she walked inside the mansion, she noticed Wade was in the kitchen. Wade's presence caught her off guard, but she kept a straight face. While she and the others worked, Wade followed her throughout the mansion, testing her patience. She glared at him as she moved past him to the cookhouse.

"You give me another look like that, and I'll have your hide beat, Riza," Wade barked.

Riza said nothing as she entered the double doors leading to the kitchen.

As the day went on, Susie noticed Wade and Rice were not out in the fields watching the field slaves like normal. "Riza, I'm scared. When are you going to do it?" she asked.

"When all the guests arrive and sit down, I'll give them something to remember," Riza said. She fixed her brown eyes on the two oil lamps in the kitchen. "Make sure Doris and Daisy are outside when I give you the signal."

Susie whispered, "Okay."

The guests arrived one by one or in family groups while Mr. and Mrs. Plecker welcomed them into their home. When Dorothy left the kitchen, Riza took the oil for both lamps and spread it out on the silver platter. She took the spoons and forks and soaked them in oil too, then walked out to the dining room as Wade watched her. She moved to the opposite side of the table of Dorothy, thinking she couldn't see the oil on the silverware if she was over there.

Riza purposely tripped over a chair, flinging the oiled silverware onto the beige dining room drapes.

"Riza! Are you all right!" Dorothy yelled. She ran over to Riza and helped her stand up.

"I'm so sorry, Dorothy. It was an accident. I'll go wash the silverware immediately," she said.

"You clumsy grass nigger! It's almost time for lunch," Wade snarled.

"Master Wade, please give her time. She can get everything clean in time for everyone to be seated," Dorothy said.

Wade growled, "Hurry up, and, Riza, don't you make another mistake."

Riza immediately gathered the platter and silverware, went into the cookhouse, and quickly began to wash them. The guests began entering the dining room, laughing and conversing in their fancy clothing. Riza and the other house slaves started bringing out the food as Wade watched from the kitchen.

Master Plecker went to Wade and whispered, "Have you made sure Riza didn't make any of the food?"

"I've watched her this entire time, Mr. Plecker. Her and Susie haven't touched the food until now," Wade said.

Master Plecker replied, "Good. Very good."

As Riza was returning to the kitchen, she saw Susie bring out another platter of food and winked at her. Susie winked back and placed the platter on the dining table while the guests continued cheerfully talking among themselves. As Riza returned to the kitchen, she noticed Master Rice was still watching her closely too, but a woman called for him. As she helped prepare other dishes, she saw Susie through the kitchen window, outside with Doris and Daisy. Then she watched Dorothy put another platter of silverware on the kitchen counter, and when she picked up some baked rolls, Riza purposely hit her elbow on the edge of the platter, forcing the silverware to go everywhere.

"Riza!" Dorothy yelled. "For God's sake, be more careful, child. Give me the rolls." She walked out of the kitchen, down the short pathway to the mansion with the hot rolls, as Emma and two other house slaves quickly began to pick up the silverware.

"Quickly clean this mess up!" Wade shouted.

"We do this as quick as we can, Master Wade," Emma said.

Wade looked down at Emma, his nose crinkling. "Move faster!" Looking back up, he realized Riza was gone. "Riza... where is Riza? She didn't go out the door. I would have heard it. She went to the house!" He rushed down the pathway, through the door, past a doorway that led to the living room, and stormed through the double doors into the foyer. "Where did you go, Riza?"

Riza raced up the other staircase in the living room and into one of the bedrooms. She reached into the lower cabinet and pulled out a candle and a lamp chimney, then lit the candle and put it under the lamp chimney. *Now I'll watch them burn,* she thought. She ran at full speed through the second floor and down the living room staircase while Wade was running up the other staircase by the front door. She slowed down and slowly approached the dining room through the living room as the guests ate and laughed. Riza quickly grabbed another candle sitting on a red oak desk and lit it, then she grabbed two pieces of paper off the desk and wrapped them around the candle.

As the two pieces of paper began to burn, Riza tossed both candles at the oil-soaked beige drapes. One candle landed on the floor and lit the oil-soaked red carpet on fire. The other candle hit its target, and fire rushed up the beige drapes. Everyone screamed in terror as Riza ran from the living room to its back door and sprinted down the cookhouse pathway.

Riza saw Doris and Daisy playing by the willow trees and smiled. She ran to Stella's slave house and threw the door. She saw Tom huddled against the wall with Joseph and Susie standing before him. "It worked! It's time to go!" she yelled.

"Riza, I'm scared," Tom said.

Riza angrily replied, "Tom, we don't have time for this! We have to leave *now*! The mansion is on fire! Tom, get up, let's go!"

"Please, Tom, we have to leave now!" Joseph yelled.

Tom replied, "They'll catch us. I know they'll catch us."

Riza growled, "You coward! Stay here with the slaves if you don't want to be an Indian anymore. Joseph, Susie, we are leaving."

Joseph and Susie frowned as they looked at Tom. Susie waved bye to Tom, and the three Indian children ran behind the slave houses and then toward the forest.

Kenneth charged out on his horse and fired a shot in the air with his rifle.

Riza's eyes widened, and she grabbed Joseph and Susie by the arm and tried to run into the forest at a different angle.

Master Kit quickly stepped out from behind a large elm tree with his rifle and two other men and three dogs.

"Riza, what did you do?" Kenneth angrily asked. He looked away from Riza and saw smoke coming from the mansion. "You clever girl. You started a fire. Let this be the first day that you'll never rebel again." He turned to the other men. "Let one of the dogs on them."

"Go get 'em, Toby," one of the men said as he released the brown dog and it charged, barking, toward the children.

Joseph and Susie screamed and ran, but Riza quickly picked up a sharp stone she saw on the ground. The moment the dog lunged for Susie, Riza tackled the dog. The dog bit into Riza's sleeve but missed her arm. She could smell the dog while her heart raced, and the tearing of her sleeve echoed as she rolled with the dog. She quickly hit the dog in its eye with the stone, causing it to cry out in pain. Jumping to her feet, Riza kicked the dog as hard as she could, causing it to yelp and limp away.

During the commotion, Susie had tripped while trying to run, and Joseph had stopped to help her get up. As the men approached them, the three children heard a rifle cock. Joseph and Susie froze in place, and Riza looked to her left.

"You're in so much trouble, Riza Plecker. I don't even know how to describe it," Kenneth said.

Riza squinted, her nose flared, and she shouted, "My name is Riza Moon! I will never accept that slave name!"

Leering, Kenneth strutted up to her with his rifle still drawn on her. "Riza Moon…I haven't heard that in years." His leer dropped from his face. "You're a piece of work, girl. Drop the rock."

Riza reluctantly dropped the rock, and Kenneth hit her in the face with the rifle's stock, knocking her down.

"See now, we should just hang this little savage," Master Kit said.

Kenneth boldly replied, "No! That'd be a waste, Mr. Kit. Her skills would be greatly missed, and I think my father would like to determine her punishment." Kenneth glanced at the other two overseers. "You two go see if they need help putting out the fire while Mr. Kit and I take these three troublemakers back to the mansion."

The two men ran to the mansion with the dogs as Master Kit and Kenneth stood before the children. Kenneth said, "Get up, Riza. I know you can take a harder hit than that."

Joseph and Susie went to help Riza, but Master Kit stepped forward. "See now, did we say for the two of you to help her?" he asked.

Susie nervously replied, "No, Master Kit."

Riza stood up and held her nose as it began to bleed.

"Now, the three of you walk to the mansion, and if any of you try to make a run for it, we'll shoot you dead," Kenneth said.

The children marched to the mansion with Kenneth walking on one side of them and Master Kit on the other side. They forced the children to stand before the damaged mansion and watch the small amount of smoke still seeping through the windows.

"Now look at this...who would have ever thought a child could do this?" Master Kit said, as Kenneth went inside.

The children avoided eye contact with the White people standing around outside, coughing and crying about the terrible fire. Riza could feel her throat tighten, and the Mississippi heat seemed to increase. Her eyes shifted onto Joseph and Susie, whose breathing had become heavier too. Sweat trickled down her sideburns as she bit her lip.

Kenneth left the mansion with Master Plecker right behind him in his dirty blue vest and brown trousers. They marched toward the children.

The closer he got to the children, the wider Master Plecker's eyes opened. He slapped Riza, knocking her to the ground. "You ungrateful animal," he yelled as he rolled up his white sleeves. He then slapped Joseph and Susie, knocking them to the ground too.

"See now, Mr. Plecker, do you want this unholy savage hanged?" Master Kit asked.

Master Plecker replied with a hysterical tone, "Hanged? Hanged? No, this child would welcome death! She is that crazy. No, she and the other two will be made an example of like no other slave ever has."

Riza stood up side-eyeing Master Plecker, her nose still bleeding.

"Take all three of them to the stump and strip Riza naked. I will waste no time breaking your spirit, Riza Plecker," Master Plecker said.

"My name is Riza Moon," Riza yelled as tears of rage trickled down her face.

Master Plecker grabbed her jaw. "You'll think twice before speaking to me like that again, little girl! Riza Moon is *dead*! Do you hear me?!" He then shoved her face away. "Take them inside so they can see my ruined dining room."

Master Kit and Kenneth forced the three children to walk inside the mansion. The air was thick with the smell of burned wood and smoke. The entire dining room wall had been burned black, the drapes were completely gone, the red carpet was scorched, and part of the dining table was burned. Glasses and plates of burned food still sat on the burned table. Riza gulped while she looked at the damage.

"Well, that's enough. Take them to the stump," Master Plecker commanded.

As the children were taken to the stump, tears of anger and fear streamed down Susie's cheeks. Joseph's shoulders tightened as his hands shook and he rubbed them together, and Riza's hands were balled into fists.

"Try your best not to give them tears," Riza murmured.

Joseph's and Susie's mouths dropped, and they looked at each other. Wade commanded the children to stop in front of the stump. Half of the stump was lit by sunrays piercing past the oak tree leaves. They stood before the stump while Master Kit and Master Rice gathered all of the slaves. The overseers had the slaves stand silently to the left of the children.

Master Plecker began to slowly pace. "Now, I'm a fair master. All I want is for all of you to know your place." He pointed at the three children. "These rebellious animals here want to keep breaking those rules. Matter of fact, Riza is the reason my beautiful home caught fire. My beautiful home…with my beautiful wife inside, with two of my beautiful daughters inside, and even my son-in-law." He pointed at the other slaves. "If any of you test me in such a way, you will be shot dead! There will be no mercy. As the Bible says, you're to treat your masters with the upmost respect, but today that commandment was violated. So first up are her followers, a full-blood Cherokee rebel and a half-breed nigger!"

"Bring little Susie," Rice said.

Susie screamed in terror as Wade dragged her to the stump.

"Hold her down. She strong for her age," Rice said.

"Please have mercy, Master Plecker," Susie screamed. "I won't do it again."

"Be brave, Susie," Riza said.

Master Plecker fixed a steely glare on Riza. His lips tightened, and he marched over to where Kenneth held her and then back-handed her already bloody face. "You disrespectful little grass nigger! I'll show you I can play a more dangerous game than you. Rice, forget about the whipping for Susie. Give her the hot stick."

"Yes, sir," Rice said.

Rice and Wade tied Susie's hands down to the old tree stump, and Rice walked away to an open fire pit. "I already had it ready just in case, sir. Where do you want it?"

"On the back of her neck," Master Plecker replied with a sneer.

Rice lifted up a smoking stick from the fire pit, the tip of it glowing orange. Leering, he approached Susie.

Tears ran down Susie's face as she watched Rice casually walk over with the smoking stick. She pulled at her restraints. "I'm sorry," she cried.

Her restraints moved slightly, so Wade grabbed Susie's arms. Rice then poked Susie on the back of her neck with the hot stick. As it sizzled on her neck, she wailed in pain. Tears of anger ran down Joseph's face as he was held by Kit and forced to watch helplessly.

"Again!" Master Plecker yelled.

Rice pressed the hot stick on her neck again, and Susie cried louder, her head trembling against the tree stump. Wade let go of her, and she breathed heavily. Rice poked her again, causing her to urinate on herself while she tried to break the restraints.

"She is a piece of work. She's trying to break out of the rope again," Rice joked. "Take another, sweetie." He pressed the hot stick onto Susie's back, burning a hole into her blue dress and scorching her skin.

Joseph's jaw dropped and his eyes bulged at the sound of Susie's cries. He had never witnessed such cruelty. He looked over at Riza, seeing nothing but fury on her twisted face. He looked at the slaves and saw that some seemed unfazed by Susie's torture while others wept.

"All right, that's enough, Mr. Rice," Master Plecker said.

Rice untied Susie's hands and forced her to stand.

Susie breathed heavily as she struggled to her feet. After glaring up at Rice with her eyes narrowed and her nose crinkled, Susie turned slowly and began to walk to Joseph and Riza. Rice whistled, and she turned around. "I saw that look, little girl," he irritably said. He punched Susie in the face, and she fell to the ground motionless.

"Susie!" Joseph shouted as the other slaves gasped.

Susie lay motionless on the ground.

Joseph broke free of Master Kit's grip and ran to Susie. "Susie, wake up! Susie, please wake up! Susie!" he cried in Cherokee. He looked at her bruised face, blood leaking from her mouth, and lowered his head to listen. Hearing her breathe, he looked up and pleaded, "She's alive. Please help her."

"Dorothy, take that rebellious little redskin to the house to get rested," Master Plecker said.

Dorothy rushed over to Susie and caressed her face, then struggled to pick her up and carry her. Another slave stepped up to help her carry the little girl.

"No, Ethan. If she can't carry that animal, she can drag her."

Ethan calmly let go of Susie and stepped back in line with the other slaves as Dorothy made her way toward the house-slave house with the child's bloody body over her shoulder.

Master Rice pushed Joseph toward the stump. "You're next, you little half-breed nigger," he said.

Joseph turned his head and scowled up at Rice, who then grabbed Joseph by the arm and forced him to kneel. He and Kit held Joseph down as they tied him to the old tree stump.

"Now, to reinforce how I do things. First, he's getting the switch, then give him the whip, Rice," Master Plecker casually said. "Joseph, you can thank Riza for this. You see, I know she was the brains of all of this chaos. Since she wants to talk about bravery, let's see how brave you are, taking on the lashes also meant for Susie. The two of you are from the same tribe, after all."

"I think it's best Kit give the lashes with the switch first, and I do the whippings," Rice casually said, licking his lips. "I'll need my strength when it comes time for that pretty face over there."

Kit picked up the switch, which was made of five weeping willow branches tied together. "See now, this ain't gonna be nothing like the last time, boy," he said with a hint of playfulness in his voice. Leering down at his prey, he struck Joseph on his back with the switch.

The pain surged through Joseph's body with each of the ten strikes across his back, buttocks, and legs. He tried his best not to cry, but the pain was too intense.

Finished giving Joseph his lashes, Kit began to chuckle.

"You ain't felt nothing yet, boy," Rice said. "I promise you not gone ever forget this day." He cracked the whip, making Joseph flinch.

As the first strike hit Joseph's back, he let out a wail.

"Woo, that was a new sound! You hear that, Kit?" Rice struck Joseph again.

Joseph growled and clawed at the stump, attempting not to cry.

Rice leered and cackled each time he drew the whip across the boy's flesh again, until he finally stopped.

As blood ran down Joseph's arms, back, and legs, he kept his head on the stump, still trying to register all the pain he felt.

"Take this boy out of here," Rice said.

Stella stepped forward to take Joseph.

"No, he's gonna watch this," Master Plecker said. "Move him out of the way."

Stella quickly moved Joseph out of the way and stood to the left of Riza in front of the other slaves.

Joseph looked at Riza. In her clear and fearless brown eyes, he saw sadness.

Then Master Plecker took two steps closer to Riza, wiping sweat off his forehead. "The most dangerous creatures in the world tend to be beautiful," he said, addressing his audience of family, guests, and slaves. "You are growing into a rare beauty, much like Dorothy, but you still got Indian thoughts. Today the savage will be broken, and you will bow before your master."

"Bring that pretty face over here," Rice said.

Kenneth forced Riza to step forward to the bloody stump as he held her arms back.

Rice grabbed Riza's face. "I must say, I will enjoy this. After all, my hand got burned helping put out that fire you started!"

Riza bit Rice on his hand, making him howl in pain. She spit his blood on the ground as he held his bleeding hand, roaring, "You little she demon! Strip her down!"

"Don't you touch me!" Riza yelled.

Kenneth and Kit held Riza while she struggled to break their grip and kick Rice as he ripped off her blue dress.

Dropping her dress to the ground, Rice looked her up and down and whistled. "Look at that. She been wearing cloth around the girls to hide them," he said, his tone lustful. "You can't hide you becoming a young woman now. Mm-mmm, looking nice and firm. You a high-price slave that'll be nursing soon."

"Mm-hmm, look at her," Kit said, leering. "Hips starting to spread, and she's even got more rump on her already than my wife."

Master Plecker's face scrunched. "That's enough. Tie her down. I don't have all day. I have guests to attend to," he said with a deepening authoritative tone.

Riza was tied down to the bloody stump, and the hot stick was brought out. Rice burned the back of her neck with it, but she held in her scream. Out of frustration, he poked her four more times on the neck, making her groan in pain.

"Would you look at that, she won't scream," Rice said. He took the hot stick and leered as he placed it near her left cheek. "I must admit. I like that pretty face of yours," he whispered before pressing the hot stick on the side of her head, right above her ear, scorching her hair.

Tears ran down Joseph's face while he watched Riza suffer.

Kit strolled up with the switch and gave Riza a hard strike on her legs. "See now, I bet you'll think twice about running away, won't you!" he yelled. He took another swing, making Riza groan in pain.

As Kit beat Riza, Kenneth quietly stepped away with his hands on his head. He bit his lip and paced as he heard the switch striking Riza in the distance. After twelve lashes, Kit was breathing heavily and coughing while Riza kept her head down, tears running down her face.

As Kit backed up, Rice cracked the whip and took a step forward.

"I'll handle this," Wade said, his tone deep.

"But it was my turn," Rice said.

Wade gave Rice a blank stare and held his hand out for the whip, until Rice reluctantly handed it to him. Turning his attention to Riza, Wade said, "Mohawk, you're going to learn your place as I rip the skin off your back." He cracked the whip, giving her a large wound across her back.

As he continued whipping Riza, blood ran down her body and onto the stump. He took his time, inflicting each wound mercilessly. She trembled in pain as she whispered something urgently.

Wade stopped and walked up to get in her face. "You think praying is going to change things? You stop praying! I want to hear you scream, you understand me?!"

Riza kept her head down and kept praying.

Wade grabbed her by her hair, punched her in her cheek, and slammed her head on the bloody stump. "Let's see you keep praying now!" He cracked the whip on Riza's back again and again until she began to cry. He took off his vest, brushed back his sandy hair, and wiped the sweat off his forehead. "I can't tell what's making me sweat more. The heat or the anger you bring out of me!" Then he gave her another strike, making it twenty lashes across her back, shoulders, arms, and legs.

"All right, I think that will suffice, Wade," Master Plecker said. "Have her taken away so she can think about her actions and recover."

"As you wish."

Riza remained motionless on the old blood-stained tree stump as Wade and Rice untied her.

Wade kneeled down and stared at Riza as she stopped crying. "I see it in those eyes of yours, you ain't got nothing left. Even a prairie nigger can be domesticated."

Riza stood up and abruptly spit blood into Wade's eye.

"Ah! You little she demon! I'll kill you!" Wade swiped at his eye to get the blood out as Riza took a step back.

"No, that isn't necessary." Plecker calmly approached Riza as she covered her breasts and genital region with her hands and arms. He said, "You want to know why I enjoy little Indian slaves? Because your kind is a rarity, and I like fighters. They will do what it takes to survive. So imagine how disappointed I am in you, girl." He stopped in front of Riza and sighed. "Look at you now, Riza Plecker...dirty, covered in blood, and barely strong enough to stand on your own two feet the good Lord gave you."

He cupped Riza's chin with his hand, and she crinkled her nose. "My pa was a good man...treated his slaves well like a good master should. He would walk me out to the cotton and tobacco fields and tell me everything about the Negro. How they thought, how they lacked the intelligence of their mulatto counterparts. And he would talk about the Indian. Then one day, he took me out to a wrestling fight between an Indian and a Negro. At first, the Negro pinned down the Indian, but then there was an uprising of strength from the Indian. He got free and beat the Negro. Can you guess how the Indian won?"

Riza gulped, asking, "No, how did he win?"

"My sweet Mohawk, he used his strength and that savage Indian mind. Right then and there my pa showed me your kind's place in our world. The Negro is the lowest, strength without the mind of a savage, but even though the Indian is superior, the Indian is still meant to serve. Joseph and Tom are not rarities... there are thousands of them. Soon, the mixed-blood breed will replace the full-blood Negro, and even the full-blood Indian. It is God's order, the order of this world."

Riza couldn't stop tears that escaped her eyes, but she inhaled to prevent herself from crying. "It's not Jesus's order. I can't believe that."

"It's the truth, no different from the truth that you belong here. This is where you will survive. This is your home, Riza

Plecker, and you are my property. You have no family left. There's nothing left of them but ashes."

Joseph's eyes widened, and he let out a weak gasp. *The White men killed her whole family!*

Riza's lips quivered as she replied, "You're lying."

Master Plecker clicked his tongue while slowly shaking his head. "I tried to spare you the pain of the truth, but your rebellion forces my hand. It's true. You are the last of your tribe. There's no one left for you to return to. This is your home. It's been your home ever since you were brought here. And your redskin daddy—"

Riza's voice cracked as she yelled, "You're lying!"

"My sweet Mohawk, the truth is the truth. Your body is almost ripe, and then your womb will be ready. Your womb will bring forth strength...it is your role." He looked down at Riza and brushed back a wisp of her hair from her dirty face. "And I'll have my way, little girl. In the name of Jesus Christ, you'll serve this estate as you have these past few years, and your children will serve, and the ones after them. That's the Lord's order, and you will follow it."

Riza's weakened, bloody body quivered as she hesitantly said, "You call yourself a Christian man, but nothing you do is Christian. My family isn't gone. I can read, and I know every lie you've spoken." She glared at Master Plecker with her ferocious yet tired brown eyes. While tears glided down her cheeks, she murmured, "I can't serve you anymore."

Master Plecker's mouth unhinged. "What did you say, girl?"

Riza gulped, her right hand tightened into a fist, and she answered with her voice cracking, "I can't serve you anymore." Speaking the Mohawk language, she said, "My name is Riza Moon...I can't serve you." She slowly shook her head as more tears escaped her eyes, bellowing in English, "I won't serve!"

Master Plecker's tightened lips curved downward. He huffed. "That's your answer after almost burning my home to the ground. Well, I'll have to break your soul. Too bad your redskin daddy wasn't around to teach you how to submit like a woman should." He drew his revolver and shot the tip of Riza's left pinky finger off.

Riza screamed in agony and held her hand, her crying etched with anger.

Joseph's eyes bulged as he watched blood ooze down her arm.

"To the end…a fighter," Master Plecker said. Abruptly, he aimed the revolver at her head.

Master Plecker's and Riza's eyes locked onto each other for a second.

"For order," he said, his voice etched with evil.

Riza gasped, and Joseph's heart dropped when he heard the thunderous gunshot. Then she fell back lifeless as the slaves watched wide-eyed, some covering their mouths.

"Riza!" Joseph cried.

Riza lay motionless, her eyes barely open and her blood pooling out on the ground around her.

Joseph tried to hobble to her, but Stella quickly went after him and pulled him back. He fell to his knees as she held his arms and cried with him. He sobbed uncontrollably, "Riza!"

Smoke off the revolver signaled a silenced flame.

A few seconds later, Riza's eyes widened and she coughed. Pressing her hand onto her right shoulder, she groaned in pain.

Plecker's eyes shifted to Joseph. "Pick him up before he's next," he roared.

Stella immediately helped Joseph stand up, as Riza continued to moan in pain.

Master Plecker looked at Riza with furrowed brow as he told his men, "Cut most of her hair off so she looks more like the other niggers, and then carefully take her to the house slaves. Let her rethink about her current living condition." His voice rose and he raised his pointer finger. "And I said *carefully*. I want her alive."

"Yes, sir," Rice said. Turning his attention to the other slaves, he yelled out, "All right, get back to work, or one of you will be next."

"Make it quick, boys. I don't need her bleeding to death."

Master Plecker looked down at Riza as her moans of pain turned into crying. "You are the last Mohawk. Be grateful the Mohawk bloodline will continue through you." He walked away, heading toward the mansion.

Stella then quickly carried a crying Joseph away as he watched over her shoulder. Rice and Wade started cutting Riza's long, wavy hair as she screamed. Stella rushed into her slave house with Mary behind her to tend to Joseph's wounds. Clint and Tom followed them.

Joseph looked over at Tom. "You told on us, didn't you?" he cried.

"I didn't tell anyone. I swear I didn't," Tom said with a saddened tone.

Joseph angrily replied, "Either way, you betrayed us! You slowed us down when we could've gotten away! I don't want to speak to you!"

"Enough of that mess, Joseph," Stella said. "Save your strength."

Tom sat down in a corner, heaving sobs racking his body, and he wiped snot from his face while he watched Stella and Mary clean Joseph's wounds.

<hr>

Rice carried Riza to the house-slave house and set her down at the doorstep. He knocked on the door, and Dorothy opened it.

"Oh, God! Riza!" Dorothy yelled, scooping Riza up to carry her inside the house. "What did you evil men do to her!" She laid Riza on the table, and she and Emma went to work as fast as they could to stop the bleeding in her upper right shoulder.

Riza's eyes were wide open, and she mumbled while the two women worked on her.

"Once y'all finish cleaning Riza up, y'all get to tending the rest of the guests," Rice said from the still open door. "Mrs. Wilma wants the guests comforted after Riza's rampage."

"Do you not see how hurt she is?" Dorothy furiously yelled.

"You watch your mouth, Dorothy! Or you'll get another beating, but this time it'll be like this little redskin got." He threw down the two pieces of cloth Riza had used to hide her developing breasts. "She was hiding herself well. Looks like she's going to be a real nice shape like you. Mm-mmm, looking like you haven't pushed out nothing." Dorothy grimaced as she tried to clean Riza's bullet wound. "Now be quick about cleaning her up." Rice walked off.

Dorothy glanced back at his departure, her eyes burning with fury.

"We do our best for her," Emma said. "All Susie need now is rest, but we could lose Riza, so we work fast. Then go to Master." The two women worked tirelessly to stop the bleeding, clean Riza's wounds, and bandage her.

Riza soon came out of shock and cried in pain while they worked on her.

Emma gave her water, saying, "Well, this here a blessing. The lead ball went right through her, so we ain't got to dig it out. You stay here now and finish Riza up. We don't need no more trouble. I see you in the cookhouse once she okay." She rushed out of the house, bustling off toward the cookhouse.

Riza continued to moan while Dorothy wiped away the last spots of dried blood. "I'm so sorry, Riza," Dorothy said as her tears hit the wooden floor. Riza began to cry again as Dorothy held her left hand and kissed it. "You're gonna get over this. I know you will. You a strong spirit."

"I...I hate them all," Riza coughed. "I hate everything they are, and...I hope one day they get what's coming to them."

"Don't hate. Don't do what they do to us, sweetie. Please don't let what they did to you turn you into what they are. I wish I could've saved you."

"Master Wade would've had you whipped if you tried to save me. All of this is my fault. I should have waited."

"It was brave of you, but a dangerous thing you did. You took my girls outside to the willow trees, didn't you?"

"I had Susie do it before I set the fire."

"Thank you for thinking of them."

Riza half-smiled at Dorothy.

Susie awakened as the afternoon sunshine of the next day illuminated the house. Her eyes widened when she saw Riza's damaged body. She crawled toward Riza, wailing, "What did they do to you, Riza?"

"I'm glad you're awake, Susie," Riza said with weakened voice. "I'll heal. Like you will."

Susie held Riza's uninjured hand. "How did they know?"

"I don't know, but I guess Tom betrayed us. He was the only one who knew about our plan."

Susie's eyes grew wide. "He isn't one of us anymore."

"After we heal, I want to hear what he has to say. This was my fault. I had a dream that we were supposed to wait. I ignored the dream the Creator gave me. I'm sorry, Susie," Riza cried. "We should've waited, but I hate this place so much. I hate that we're slaves."

"You tried to save us, that's all you tried to do. There isn't anything to apologize for. We all want to get back to our families. I remember you talking about your momma and how she would brush your hair while you ate apple slices and—"

Riza suddenly began to cry harder, and Susie gaped at her. "Did I say something wrong?" Susie asked.

Riza rubbed away her tears, answering, "No, it's…I have a lot to think about. Thinking about my family hurts. All I feel is pain."

"I'm here with you."

Riza looked up at the ceiling and deeply exhaled. "And I'm here with you too. I can't lose anyone else."

The two girls remained in the house, spending the hours comforting each other between drifting in and out of fitful sleep.

A few hours later, the old wooden door creaked open. Susie's eyes widened as Mrs. Wilma slowly stepped into the house. The sunlight outlined the middle-aged woman's body as she moved toward the two girls.

Her green eyes narrowed, and her thin lips tightened once she stood before the girls. "I'm disgusted. No, I'm more than disgusted. I'm…just absolutely appalled! The outright rebellion the two of you displayed," Wilma bellowed. "I made sure the both of you were fed. I made sure the two of you knew proper manners, and this is how the two of you behave!"

Susie's body began to tremble in fear.

"You have destroyed my beautiful dining quarters and endangered the lives of so many people!"

"We're sorry, Mrs. Wilma," Susie replied, her eyes welling up.

Wilma took off her beige straw hat and rubbed her forehead. "I didn't ask for your response, little Susie. The two of you have no idea what it means to be a mother," she scoffed. "Dorothy almost had Daisy taken from her. I guess that will be both of y'all's punishment. Your firstborn will be sold."

Susie's tears hit the wooden floor as she begged, "Mrs. Wilma, we're sorry. We won't do nothing like it again!"

Riza coughed and struggled to lift her head. She breathed heavily, replying, "It was me. Susie didn't plan it. I did. Please don't take away her child because of my actions."

"You have spit in my face, Riza Plecker," Wilma sternly said. "I never wanted this for either of you."

Tears streamed down Riza's face, and she shook her head. "Please have mercy. You always told us it is the sign of a true Christian. I will give up my firstborn for what I did, but please don't punish Susie."

Wilma's gaze shifted off the girls and then back to them, now fixed on Riza's damaged body. "Look at you, Riza…beaten within an inch of your life. And with most of your hair cut off. Now you truly look like one of them. You have disappointed me. You were meant for greatness…to replace Dorothy when she became too old, Riza. You break my heart, little girl. Out of mercy and, yes, even out of love for the two of you, I won't push for such a punishment. However, if there is another rise out of you, Riza, there will be no mercy. You will behave and be proper as a young Christian woman should. You better remember, I'm your mistress. I almost sold Daisy, so don't let that savage mind fool you into thinking that I'll excuse you again." She turned her head toward Susie and pointed at her, saying, "The same goes for you. You're not field niggers, and it's best y'all remember it."

"Yes, Mrs. Wilma," Susie replied.

"You best wipe those tears from your face, little girl. You will receive further punishment for this upheaval. Y'all won't get fed tonight, and both of you will work tomorrow. The two of you will no longer have the honor of wearing a house-slave's clothes. You will have to earn that privilege back. You'll wear field nigger dresses until I say. That's all for today." Mrs. Wilma turned around and left the house, the door closing behind her.

Wilma then instructed Dorothy not to feed the girls.

Furious with Mrs. Wilma's decree, after the Pleckers' supper, she grabbed a basket and filled it with bread and cooked beef. Dorothy had Doris take the basket to Susie and Riza.

During the night, Riza's body twitched in pain while she tried to sleep, and she wept in the darkness as she prayed to the Creator for freedom.

CHAPTER 9
Pressing Forward in Faith

ANNABELLE TWISTED AND TURNED IN bed. She awakened gasping for air and yelled, "Joseph!" She began to cry while she pulled her knees up to her chest and the bedsheets to her face. She could feel her body trembling.

Grace entered the lonely bedroom and immediately placed her hand on Annabelle's back. "What's wrong?" she asked in Cherokee.

Annabelle replied, "It's Joseph. I had a dream about him." With the moonlight gleaming off her tears, she turned to Grace. "Something is wrong. I can feel it."

"Calm down and tell me about the dream."

"He screamed for me, and I heard the cracking of a whip." Annabelle's grip tightened on the bedsheets. "I know my baby is in trouble."

Grace sat down on the bed and continued to rub Annabelle's back. "We have to have faith. I know with John out searching for Joseph, it's been harder, but we must hold on."

"It was so real. His scream still haunts my soul. He's never screamed like that."

Tears shimmered in Grace's eyes. "We'll speak with Elder Joyce in the morning. We have to remember every dream doesn't have a meaning."

"I can't shake the feeling this one did have meaning."

"Either way, we must play our role. I know you want to go after Joseph, and if things were safer, I'd go with you."

"Even being born a slave, I never understood how they could hate so much. It's like a curse on their people."

"It probably is, but what we can do right now is pray for Joseph. Even if the dream was a reflection of what he's experiencing, we can pray for Jesus to strengthen him. Pray for someone to be there to help guide him and be his friend."

"John just left yesterday with Eli and Samuel to search for him again, but I feel like a terrible mother for not going after him."

"What good would it bring us if you were captured? You know the answer. The Brown family is still after you."

"I'm powerless."

"Not through prayer, you're not. Come on, let's pray, and first thing in the morning, we'll go to Elder Joyce. Tsula and Lizzie can feed the kids."

Annabelle's mouth curved downward into a slight frown. "Okay, I'll walk in faith."

"Do you want me to sleep with you? Jannie is in a deep sleep."

Annabelle half-smiled. "Yeah, I could use your company. You're a good auntie to agree to sleep in that small bed with her."

Grace sighed. "She's still a wild sleeper. I'll put Rain in the bed with her so neither of them wakes up and comes in here. Hopefully they grow out of wanting someone in the same bed soon."

"That's my other prayer."

The two women smiled at each other, and Grace left the room to put Rain in the same bed as her sister. Grace returned to Annabelle, and the two women prayed together, then went to sleep.

✦

The morning sunshine beamed into Joyce's home. She set her wooden cup down on the supper table and cleared her throat,

147

then said to Lizzie, "I can feel the pain coming off your spirit. What concerns me more is the anger growing within you. It'll cause you to move off your feelings. Remember, forgiving doesn't mean you are excusing the actions of another."

"I know Brock Jackson is responsible for Joseph's kidnapping," Lizzie said.

"No matter how deeply this evil man is involved in Joseph's kidnapping, he won't escape the Father's wrath. Lizzie, be patient in how he's dealt with."

"I'll try my best not to react. He makes it hard. I can feel the hate coming off him."

"It's because your spirit has grown stronger, but you can't fight evil with evil. It'll only set—" Joyce began to cough and covered her mouth.

Lizzie's eyebrows lifted as she stood, saying, "Elder Joyce!"

Joyce put out her wrinkled hand, and Lizzie slowly sat back down. "I'm okay, baby," she said, finally taking a deep breath. "As I was saying, don't feed your evil wolf. It'll set you back, Wildcat. It won't make you stronger."

Lizzie's nails slowly scratched Joyce's supper table. "I can still remember his scream. I should've been faster."

"And what if you had been killed and they still managed to take him? Don't get lost in the past. Don't fall into the sea of regret and self-blame. Continue to push away the old you and love the change occurring in you. You must trust in Jesus to guide you to the next step. One step, a day at a time, in every area of your life...use the past as lessons."

A tear shimmered in Lizzie's eye, and she looked down to her hands. "I don't want to bury someone else before their time."

"Stay away from such negativity when you're not in control of the future. Even if you had the gift of premonition, you wouldn't have control. Accept the pain you feel, but destroy the thoughts that go against the Father's promise."

Lizzie exhaled. "Yes, ma'am."

Joyce folded her hands. "And what did I say about there being no shame in letting tears fall in here?"

Lizzie's eyes widened, and her gaze fixed back onto Elder Joyce. "I'm...I'm trying to trust and let go."

"By pushing forward and having faith is how you please Jesus. Not by going to the church every Sunday or fighting to control your situation. I know you're in pain, and it's not all about Joseph." Joyce smiled. "I know you are trying, Wildcat. Now we can talk about the other reason you came here."

Lizzie gulped and drew her brow together. "The other reason?"

"Yes, the other reason. Even with all the anger in you, I can see it in your beautiful eyes, and when you actually smile...it's still for him."

Lizzie shifted in her seat with eyes now fixed on Joyce's wrinkled hands. "I'm not proud of myself."

"You're not wrong for loving him. People often move under the delusion you can only be in love with one person. It does take strength to move forward, and for some people, Jesus will bring that person right back to you after they've felt the consequences of feeding their evil wolf. When this happens, the other person needs time to heal and grow...then they can move forward. Other times, we have to move forward in acceptance that the Father has someone even better for us. Hard seasons are meant to mature us. Your thorn is your mentor, and what's for you is for you."

"I still feel a little heartbroken, but I shouldn't feel this way. Joseph being gone makes it even harder for me."

"Your feelings matter, baby...they do. If feelings weren't important, we wouldn't have been gifted with them. However, we have to move by the spirit because often our feelings can betray us. I've prayed hard for you in the spirit. I've seen your path moving differently."

Lizzie rubbed her eyes to hide the tears that escaped, and Joyce shook her head with a smile. Lizzie's eyes shifted back to Joyce. "How so?"

"It's a challenging path not meant to harm you. You're built for the challenge. You'll have to learn how to love again even though you love Ja—"

Suddenly there was a knock on the door.

Lizzie quickly stood up. "I'll get it." She wiped her eyes again and opened the front door. Her eyes locked onto Annabelle and Grace. "What are you doing here?" she asked as she smacked her lips.

"Well, this answers the question of where you left to in such a hurry," Grace said.

Lizzie's nose crinkled. "Whatever."

"Annabelle had another nightmare about Joseph."

"Come on in," Joyce said.

The two women walked into the pine-scented home.

Joyce invited, "Come to the table. I believe me and Wildcat were almost done. Whether she chooses to stay is up to her."

Lizzie grabbed the bottom of her braid and began to undo it. "Elder Joyce, can we continue later?" she asked. "I'll listen to them at home." She forced herself to smile, but Joyce squinted with her eyes fixed on the fake smile.

"You return to me in an hour, Wildcat," Joyce said. "We need to finish."

"I promise, ma'am." Lizzie left the house and hastily closed the door.

Joyce said, "Lord Jesus, I go from one refusing to let anyone see her vulnerable…to you two."

"Is she okay?" Annabelle asked.

Joyce replied, "Her anger is rising again. The best thing for her is to stay away from Brock Jackson. The other things I'll work with her on. She loves hard, and people who struggle with their feelings can act on impulse. Now tell me about your dreams, child."

Annabelle told Joyce about her dreams, sobbing as Grace embraced her.

Joyce put her wrinkled hand on top of Annabelle's hand. "You must be careful in the interpretation of dreams. Your dream could be the fear of what he's going through taking form, or it could be your spirit reaching out to him. Because of this, your spirit is interpreting his feelings, whether he's being tortured or not."

Annabelle wiped away her tears. "I can't lose another child. I don't have the strength to go through it again."

"We must hold onto faith. You don't know what's to come, or why the Father allowed Joseph to be taken. Hard as it is, there's more going on than what you can see. Don't allow what has happened to poison you with hate."

"I was hoping the information we were able to get on the plantations would bring me ease."

"What do you feel is pulling you deeper into fear?"

Annabelle frowned. "If he's in Mississippi…"

"I see. If he's in Mississippi, it's certainly more troubling, but we'll press forward in faith. And we'll pray for Joseph to remain strong in his faith. Annabelle, your feelings are important. It is necessary to feel in order to heal in life. However, we must be careful not to move on our feelings."

"Yes, ma'am, I remember."

"In life, the Father challenges us to move in uncertainty because we're being taught to move by faith, not by sight. It doesn't matter the situation. I'll give this example. Sometimes people are allowed to fall in love with the person the Father knows will fit with us best, but there's a delay in the relationship progressing. The Father is interested in molding. You see, we as people are quick to say we're ready when the truth is, we're not. In most cases, the poison needs to be driven out before the person is ready to grow into their purpose. They can't imagine causing the other person pain, but the truth is none are perfect. We can cause pain to people we love. It's another reason we're meant to move by faith, not by sight. Why we're to move by the Creator's words.

"Look at the mess White men have created with their hate and greed. Their motives have attacked all of the people…including themselves, and they've even managed to poison the word of the spirit because they wanted to control what was said. That's why we have to move by faith. You have to be mature enough to ask yourself the right questions. You can't change the past, but you have freedom in how you act in the future. How are you going to act now? Give me your hands."

The two women held onto Joyce's hands.

"There's nothing like the prayer of a mother. We'll pray for not only Joseph's return, but for his protection and guidance on what should be done."

The wise woman led the prayer with Annabelle and Grace following her lead. She then had the young women smudge with the smoke of burning sage. With the smell of burned sage coating the house, Joyce prayed for both Annabelle and Grace individually.

"Thank you, Elder Joyce."

"Continue to be careful of Brock Jackson," Joyce instructed. "Nothing but evil releases from him."

"We will, Elder Joyce," Grace said.

The two young women gave the elder a hug, and wiped tears from their eyes. Grace opened the front door.

"And tell your sister to come right back here," Joyce commanded. "That little girl better not make me come over there."

Grace's eyes widened. "I'm sure she'll keep her word."

"Mm-hmm, your sister is hiding. As of now, it's half and half she'll return, but if you say something she'll come. I'm expecting Lea to arrive soon, but it's okay if Lizzie returns while my grandbaby is here."

"I promise I'll tell her."

"Good. Now, Annabelle, remember the prayers. The current facts are not final."

"Yes, ma'am. I will," Annabelle said.

"We will see each other again, Elder Joyce," the two young women said.

Elder Joyce replied, "We will see each other again."

As the two women left, Joyce leaned in the doorway, coughing again. She took a deep breath and exhaled before returning inside her home. Lizzie kept her word and returned to Joyce's home to finish her counseling.

———◆———

That same morning, Susie and Riza were forced to put on brown cloth dresses as a symbol of demotion under Mrs. Wilma's reign.

Susie and Riza were to prepare breakfast, clean the banisters, change the bed linen in all of the rooms, polish the silverware, dust the foyer and living room, and help prepare supper.

Riza struggled as pain surged through her body. She attempted to walk down the elegant staircase leading to the front door. *I can't keep this up. Every step hurts my back, my legs, and my shoulder*, she thought. Her body shook uncontrollably with each step.

Mrs. Wilma sighed and scowled as Riza slowly moved down the stairs. "No more savagery left in you, Riza? Hurry up now."

"I'm trying," Riza said.

Wilma looked away with a sigh, her mouth curved downward. She turned back, her brow now lowered. "You disappoint me, Riza. Using your rare intelligence to cause an uproar."

Riza pouted. "I'm sorry, Mrs. Wilma."

Wilma scoffed and grinned. "I bet you are. Hobbling down the stairs like an old woman." She began tapping her fingers on her wrist. "I guess there's no point in making you work when the old slaves are moving faster." She bellowed, "Dorothy, come here."

Dorothy came out of the living room.

"Yes, Mrs. Wilma?" Dorothy asked.

"Help this child down these stairs," Wilma said.

Dorothy helped Riza walk down the rest of the stairs.

"Riza Plecker, I'm dismissing you. However, if you ever lead another rebellion. I will shoot you, and I will sell your firstborn. I'm too old for this, and you manipulating others won't be tolerated. Do we have an understanding?"

"Yes, ma'am," Riza said, grimacing.

"You certainly are a gifted Indian girl, but what you did was evil. Never force the hand that feeds you. Take her out to heal, Dorothy."

"Yes, Mrs. Wilma," Dorothy said.

Dorothy helped an injured Riza exit the mansion.

Wilma sighed. "Lord, I hope that girl has no more fight in her. She certainly tried it this time. It would be a tragedy to lose her."

Dorothy and Riza entered the house-slave house.

"Can't stand that ugly White woman," Riza snarled.

"Enough. Take this time to heal," Dorothy said. "I'll talk to Master Kenneth and see if you can get off tomorrow too."

"Thank you, Dorothy."

"You're welcome, and maybe the truth will come out. I don't think Tom told."

Riza frowned. "I hope he didn't." She lay down, and Dorothy returned to the mansion.

———————◆———————

At the cotton gin, Joseph struggled through his pain to manage the baskets of cotton. He tried to focus on his anger at Tom to push the pain from his mind. He ignored Tom while they worked, and his responses to Tom were short when they did have to communicate.

Seeing Joseph struggling with the workload, Bo had him only take the cotton out of the baskets.

"They not telling us nothing," Bo said. "I sorry, but we can't go to the mansion. No one know if Riza alive. All the house slaves been kept from us. Never seen a child get beat like her."

"I want to go there so badly," Joseph said, frowning.

"If you go, they will kill you. We have to wait and pray for the best."

Joseph sighed. "Why won't they tell us if she's alive?"

"'Cause not a lot of us live when we get shot. She got hurt bad, and then they dragged her like a dead animal."

Mary entered the barn with a smile. "Riza is alive," she cheerfully said. "She hurt real bad, but she alive."

Joseph smiled hearing the news, but then he lightly cried.

"Good, the Lord heard our prayers," Bo said. "Well, only thing we can do now is work and give her time to heal." He patted Joseph on the shoulder. "See, the Lord does hear our prayers." Bo continued to comfort the boy as they worked, and he tried to keep peace between Joseph and Tom.

A week passed while Joseph, Susie, and Riza struggled to heal. Joseph continued giving Tom a cold shoulder, believing he had betrayed them. One day as they returned to the slave house, Tom stepped in front of Joseph.

"Get out of my way, traitor," Joseph snarled.

"I didn't tell on anyone," Tom said.

"How did they know what we were doing?"

"I don't know. Did someone else hear us talking to Riza? Did Clint hear us talking?" Tom said a little too loudly.

The boys suddenly saw Clint wave and head toward them. "Hey, y'all," he said. "I glad you looking better, Joseph. I sure did think Master Rice was gonna kill you."

"Clint, please tell us the truth. Did you hear us talking to Riza about leaving?" Joseph asked.

"Well, no, I didn't. I walked inside when y'all was here, but I heard no talk of y'all leaving."

"Was there anyone else that could've heard us, like Louis?"

"Naw, Louis wasn't around. I think only thing not normal I seen was… Well, I don't know 'cause it not the first time I seen her do it. But I seen Pearl walk to the big willow trees, and she stay there awhile, then come back to the fields later. Wait, I know she was, 'cause I was walking Jerry the donkey to them fields, 'cause I finish my food early. I saw Riza and Susie together. They go to Master's house, and later Pearl come back. She had to be by them."

"Why would Pearl tell on us?" Tom asked.

"I don't know. She always seemed so nice to us," Joseph said.

"She don't like Riza, and she told on somebody before," Clint said. "She told on Donald a few years ago when he stole some corn and ate it."

Joseph frowned. "I want to go speak with Riza, but I'm not allowed to anymore."

Clint replied, "I go do it. I went to talk with her four days ago, but she was 'sleep when I opened the door. She look peaceful so I don't wake her up."

"Yeah, go and ask her what she thinks," Joseph said.

Clint nodded and went back to work.

"Thank you for believing me," Tom said.

"We're friends. I couldn't understand why you would tell on us. I'm sorry," Joseph said.

"Do you think Pearl really did it?"

Joseph huffed. "I don't know. But if she did hear Riza and Susie talk about it, she could've told on us. I think Riza can figure it out."

Once Clint finished feeding the animals, he snuck to the house-slave quarters and met with a resting Riza. "How you healing?" he asked.

"I'm healing," Riza calmly said. "How is Joseph?"

"He moving better. He very sad though. Everyone thought you was gone die."

"They're not the only ones." Riza sighed. "Why am I even alive?" she mumbled.

"What you say?"

"Nothing, Clint. I don't think Tom told on us. Someone had to overhear us."

"I did see you and Susie talking not long ago. Not long after Pearl come rushing from the willows."

Riza's brow began to crease. "She better not have told on us. I can't stand that jealous woman. Ugh, even the thought of her tellin' on us makes me feel sick."

"I sorry, Riza."

"No, it's not you, Clint. She makes me so angry, and now I have to get used to using my hand again. It feels weird missing a part of my finger. Thank you for visiting me."

"Next time I bring you a flower."

Riza grinned. "That would be sweet of you."

"Well, if Pearl really did it, she wrong. Hit her with one of them apples. She got a big head, you ain't gonna miss."

Riza cackled but it quickly turned into a pained moan.

Clint put his hands out. "You okay?"

"I'm fine. It just still hurts to laugh. That was funny, though. I didn't think you had it in you."

"Well, I trying to make your day better."

"Yeah, you are, and you're doing a good job at it." The two friends talked for a little bit before Clint had to get back to work.

If it really was Pearl, she'll have more than words thrown at her, Riza thought.

CHAPTER 10

Unexpected

ON AUGUST 30, 1860, RIZA was tasked with picking apples off the five apples trees behind the mansion. While carrying a full basket back to the kitchen door, she was overtaken with pain and dropped the basket, sending apples rolling about. She stared at her left pinky finger, feeling the pain surge through it. She sat on top of the basket and rested.

Pearl walked up from behind Riza, holding another woven basket. "Master Rice said to use this older basket and get some of those walnuts while you out here," she said.

"Hate that man," Riza snarled.

Pearl smiled and mockingly replied, "Is your feelings hurt with that pretty hair gone, or 'cause now you not allowed to hide that you turning into a woman?"

Riza sharply replied, "You talk a lot for someone that can't read."

Pearl's smile dropped from her face. "I know I can't read, but I can understand signals."

Riza squinted her keen eyes. "What would you know about signals?"

No "I just sayin' I know I can't read, but I ain't no dumb nigger, unlike a redskin."

Riza stood up and clutched her right hand into a fist. "What did you say? Did you hear us making our plans?"

"I don't know what you talkin' about. And what if I did? You ain't gonna do nothing."

"I'll tell everyone Master Rice is raping you."

Pearl bickered. "You think you so smart. You ain't nothing but an evil little girl using them signals. Just 'cause we ain't never had no homes, don't make you better."

Riza squinted again. "It was you...you told them. Somehow you heard us talking, and you told on us. How could you?"

Pearl shrugged. "Master Rice promised me a favor if I told him secrets, and you no kin of mine. You wasn't taking me with y'all."

Riza's voice raised, "You think someday that man will treat you nice? I'm thirteen, and I know that White man will never give you nothing. You dumb puppet. I promise I'll make you pay for what you did."

Pearl sneered. "I'd like to see you try, little girl. You ain't that pretty no more." She walked away.

Riza's anger began to boil over. "And you were never pretty," she barked. She picked up an apple and threw it at Pearl, smacking her on the back.

Pearl turned and glared at Riza, her mouth agape. Riza threw another apple, but Pearl ducked it. Riza grunted and quickly threw two more apples. Pearl dodged one, but the second apple slammed into her forehead.

"You crazy girl!" Pearl screamed. Then she dodged another apple and took off running to the fields.

"You better run, you nappy-headed slave!" Riza bellowed. She then kicked the basket Pearl had brought her and screamed.

She later told Susie that Pearl had ruined their plan to escape. When evening arrived, Susie snuck to Stella's slave house to tell her and the boys. Furious that Pearl had told the masters, Stella told her to sleep in one of the other slave houses. She blamed Pearl for all of the drama and said she no longer wanted to share any meals with her. The other slaves soon became split as news of what Pearl had done spread. Some slaves believed Riza only cared about the other Indians. Bo sided with Stella, believing Pearl had betrayed the children to target Riza.

By late September of 1860, the children had recovered from their injuries. Joseph was now scarred with two marks on each of his legs and four scars on his back. Susie healed well, but the back of her neck was now darker than the rest of her body. Riza called the scars on her back the spider's web and had discoloration on the side of her head from the burn. Her gunshot wound healed well with a scar, and she felt no more pain in her functional half pinky finger. She was now assigned to always be by Mrs. Wilma's side and no longer allowed to go to the other slave houses. The other children were given the same tasks they had before but were threatened to be shot dead if they attempted another escape.

Joseph and the others remained under high watch and were often taunted by the overseers. Kit took pleasure in making Joseph flinch anytime he reached for his switch.

⁕

Eli, John, and Samuel returned from Louisiana in September of 1860, having had no luck in finding Joseph. They'd been forced to return with low supplies, and because the harvest season had arrived and the weather was starting to change. After supper, John remained at the table, resting his chin on his hand as the rest of the family sat by the fireplace.

George sat down next to John and adjusted his black vest. "I understand your pain, but we must remain hopeful," he said in his native tongue. "Joseph has a strong spirit and a good heart."

John replied, "I feel like I acted too slow when those men took him. I thought I was doing the right thing, making Annabelle take the girls and go hide inside the room. Now she is having nightmares about our son. I failed her."

"You did the right thing, John. You protected the family. You didn't fail. What would've happened if the girls got hurt by gunfire, or Annabelle? Your momma walked on, and your Aunt Shay has walked on before their time. I didn't handle their passing like a man. I failed to teach you boys how to be a man."

"Uncle George, you taught us how to farm and work the best we could with this land. You didn't do a bad job with us."

"No, Grace didn't do a bad job with you and the others. I was too busy getting drunk. You never knew this, but the year your Aunt Shay walked on, I drank almost every day and would pass out in the fields. Grace was forced one day to steal from a White family in one of the outskirt towns. I found out when I walked into the barn one day and saw all the extra bags of flour and cornmeal. We got into an ugly fight…it felt like I was talking to Lizzie, but the tears in your sister's eyes showed me I was hurting the family. I thank the Father for giving me a chance to change."

John frowned. "Those were hard times. I don't remember all of it."

"I know what you do remember is William passing on when we were forced to come here. I never thought I would bury a child, but you did good healing after a few years."

"Losing William was hard. I thought that was the end of our pain."

"So did I, but life isn't fair. You know that. I don't like being patient, and I know you don't either, but be patient so we find Joseph at the right time."

"We won't be able to make another trip to Louisiana. It'll take too many days to check the last plantations, and you need help harvesting. We've already lost too many crops because I haven't been here or in good health to keep them healthy."

"This will be the time our faith will truly be tested. Maybe Joseph will find a way to escape, and by a miracle, will make it back home. The path that will be chosen for Joseph to come home to us is unknown, but the Father is forever faithful, and his will is good. We must hold to that and not bow to these White men."

"You're right, Uncle George."

George placed his hand on top of John's shoulder and smiled. "It took me a long time to be right. Let us hope it won't take you as long."

The two men chuckled and continued to talk to about the family.

Tsula looked over at George and John as they talked, then let her gaze shift to Samuel while she nestled Katelyn. "How many plantations did y'all need to check in Louisiana?" she asked in Cherokee.

Samuel replied, "Thirty-four. We needed to check out eleven more. All the ones we checked did have at least five Indians there and a few mixed bloods, but we didn't recognize any of them. I feel bad we didn't take some of them with us."

"Don't feel bad. Y'all did a good job going through all that land to find Joseph, and there's no way you could've taken slaves without a fight. The next time I think you will find him."

"Yeah, I think we will too."

"I'm grateful Eli went with you again."

Samuel smacked his lips. "I can take care of myself."

"Don't be that way. I only said that because we needed some-one there with you to tell the difference between the masters and the slaves. You're cute, but you're lacking in the mind, unlike me. I got both." Tsula giggled at Samuel as he struggled to keep a straight face.

As days passed, everyone agreed that another trip to Louisiana would take too long, and they wouldn't be able to return safely with the change of season ahead. George became ill, forcing the men to work harder on the remaining crops and Lizzie to help them with the carrying and gathering of crops.

Annabelle read her old Bible constantly to remind herself God could make a way for her son to be returned to her. Joyce remained a powerful voice of encouragement for the family, but her recent lack of activity and constant coughing concerned Annabelle. It was unusual for the old woman to not do her morning walks. An unexpected cold front arrived in September, confirming it would be difficult to travel to Louisiana again before spring.

On the morning of October 9, 1860, Annabelle walked to the supply store with Grace. "I hope Maria and Lizzie aren't having a hard time cleaning up Sky's mess," Annabelle said in Cherokee.

Grace replied, "Yes, she spit up all over her clothes. If Maria didn't push us so hard to leave, I would've stayed."

"At least Lizzie stayed while Lisa and Tsula walked the children to school. I hope we—" Annabelle's eyes widened and her lips tightened at the sight of Brock Jackson slowly riding his horse in their direction.

Grace's eyes fixed on the man, her brow furrowed and her left hand tightened into a fist. "Let's keep going, Annabelle." She intertwined her arm with Annabelle's, and they began to walk faster.

Annabelle's gaze remained anchored on Brock. She took deep breaths and finally took her eyes off him.

Brock greeted a Cherokee man in his path, but his eyes quickly locked onto the two young women again as he drew closer. "Well, look what this morning brings me," he said, pulling his gold pocket watch out of his brown vest.

"We have no words for you, Mr. Jackson," Grace said with a deepening tone.

"My dear Grace, we have plenty to talk about after what your sister did. She tortured a US official after you plunged two arrows into him."

The two women stopped walking, and Grace yelled, "After he helped kidnap my nephew! He is lucky to be alive!"

"Are you threatening a White man, Grace Lightning?"

"It's Five Killer."

A leer slowly grew on Brock's face as he placed his pocket watch in his vest. "My, my, so you think a change of name is going to save you? I understand your family is upset, and I excuse John's reaction. I'd imagine I would tie someone down to get information on my son if I had one…but what your sister did—"

"My sister did nothing! Mr. Sawyer is a kidnapper and a liar! How dare you stand before us and make light of Joseph's kidnapping?"

"Careful, beautiful, your cousin had a smart mouth on her, and it didn't stop me." His malicious blue eyes focused on Annabelle, and he cackled. "Woo-wee, momma bear, the way you're looking at me…" Brock put his hand on his chest. "As if I were there when the boy was taken."

"You have no soul," Annabelle said with a scowl.

Brock rubbed his chin and shrugged. "I had nothing to do with it. Though I warned Lisa…but she couldn't get it into her savage, prairie nigger mind. I understand though, I'll never see my daughter while she's being raised by a half-breed nigger. At least with poor little Joseph, I'm sure he's just as comfortable with the chains he most likely has on his wrists as he was living here…playing Indian."

Face crinkled in an angry glare, Annabelle let go of Grace's arm, gritted her teeth, and reached for Brock's leg. Grace immediately pulled her back as she grunted.

Brock laughed, saying, "My goodness, Miss Annabelle. You are truly becoming more and more like them. I forgive you though. I know it must be hard. But don't be so angry now."

"You'll go to hell!" Annabelle yelled.

Some of the townspeople stopped and watched them, talking among themselves.

"Calm down, Annabelle," Grace said. "Remember what Elder Joyce said."

Continuing to leer, Brock replied, "My dear, let me give you some real wisdom. You are still young…with a firm-looking body. All you have to do is lay on your back or climb on top. Afterward, I'm sure you can squeeze out two or three more pups to make up for your loss. And while you're at it, you can teach your redskin sister-in-law how to watch her mouth. Miss Lizzie Lightning will be dealt with for her unnecessary aggressions."

"Don't threaten my family, Brock!" Grace growled.

Brock scoffed. "It's not a threat, but a simple pure warning. I can't truly touch her since Hunter's actions led to that half-breed boy being taken. However, she may find out the hard way that her constant disrespect and beauty will get her into more trouble than she knows. A man would pay a heavy wage for her."

Grace's eyes narrowed. "Goodbye, Brock."

"That's Mr. Jackson."

"Not anymore, it isn't."

"Well, then...I guess the name Five Killer truly isn't your last name. Lightning is more dangerous than a man that's killed five. I suggest you watch your mouth too. I'll send a prayer up for little Joseph since today is his special day."

Annabelle's widened eyes began to well up, and a vein in her forehead began to appear.

Brock lightened his voice as he said, "Oh, yes, I've looked at the records. Ten years old is something to be proud of for a half-breed in chains." He snapped his horse's reins and rode off.

"Your blood will soak the ground!" Annabelle screamed.

Grace's eyes widened, and she quickly pulled Annabelle back and coaxed her to walk away.

Brock slowly turned his head around, murmuring, "I'm sure you would try it, but you're not the dangerous one." He smirked. "Watch that mouth, momma bear."

As he rode away, other Cherokee turned their backs to him to display their disgust.

The women arrived at the store, and Grace spoke with Annabelle to calm her down. Maria and Lizzie soon arrived and were angered at the news of the confrontation with Brock. In the early afternoon, Annabelle returned home on her break from working at the supply store. She sat in her silent house with Joseph's bow on her lap. Her hands held onto the body of the bow as she slowly breathed in and out to stop her tears. A sudden knock on the front door caused Annabelle's gaze to turn to the door.

"Yes," she said in Cherokee.

The door slowly opened, and Grace calmly walked into the sunlit house.

Annabelle took Joseph's bow off her lap and set it aside.

"There's no need to hide your pain from me," Grace said in Cherokee.

"It's his birthday. It's my baby's tenth birthday, and there's nothing I can do for him."

Grace closed the front door and sat down in a rocking chair next to Annabelle. "We can't control what's happening to him, but we can think of the good times and continue to pray for his return."

A tear slid down Annabelle's face, and she exhaled. "I'm tired of praying."

Grace's brow lowered as she frowned. "I understand you're struggling, but prayer is our weapon. They're not going unheard."

Annabelle wiped away her tears. "It feels li—"

A soft knock was suddenly heard at the door, and the two young women turned their heads. "Who is it?" Grace asked.

"It's Victoria. I wanted to check in on Annabelle, if she's there," she answered in Cherokee.

"Come in, Victoria," Annabelle replied.

Victoria entered the house, saying, "I couldn't help but come see you, Annabelle. I saw the look on your face this morning when I went to the store. To ask how you're doing would be foolish of me."

"Thank you for checking on me."

"You are my friend. And the pain in your heart is showing in your eyes. I wanted you to know I feel your pain, and I'm her—"

Tears broke from Annabelle's eyes, and she heaved and wailed, "I only want my baby boy back alive. I want to hug him and kiss him. I want to see the smile I gave him!"

Grace rubbed Annabelle's back as her own tears now fell to the wooden floor.

Victoria quickly stepped up to Annabelle and knelt down before her friend. "I'm sorry, I didn't come here to make you feel worse," she said, tears now falling down her cheeks.

Annabelle hugged Victoria and cried harder. "It wasn't you. Thank you for caring about my baby. I want to leave. I want to bring him back."

"Oh, Annabelle, you know why we can't." Victoria hugged Annabelle and swayed with her sobs.

"I don't care. I can't stand the thought of him having chains on him or saying 'Yes, Master.' He shouldn't be experiencing the pain I had."

Victoria shook her head with her watery eyes fixed on Annabelle's eyes. "I know you want to bring him back, but it's too dangerous."

Annabelle turned to Grace, saying, "Please, Grace, can we please try? I only want to try one time. We traveled to Mercy, why can't we check a few plantations?"

Grace's voice crackled as she replied, "No."

Annabelle let go of Victoria and grabbed onto Grace's arms, sobbing, "Please! I only want to try one time, and if we fail, I promise to come home. We can take Eli and Lizzie."

Grace put her hand on Annabelle's wet cheek. "We can't risk it. With all of my heart, you know I want him back, but we can't move on fear or anger. We might bring more problems to our family if we do this wrong or if you get captured. As punishment those White men might even kill you. What would we tell the children if this happened?"

"I won't get captured. I will kill them all before they put me in chains or kill me."

"Annabelle," Victoria said with a frown.

"Sister, I love you and because I love you, I won't help you turn into them. I won't let you."

Annabelle laid her head onto Grace's chest and continued to wail.

Grace kissed the top of Annabelle's head as she embraced her sister.

"I will stay here as long as you need me to," Victoria said as she rubbed Annabelle's back.

"I only want to say happy birthday to my baby boy," Annabelle cried.

The sunlight glistened off Grace's tears as she replied, "I know."

An hour passed before the young women were able to calm Annabelle down as they sang hymns and challenged her to focus on the good memories of her son. Afterward, they returned to the supply store, and Annabelle worked alongside her family.

After closing the store early, all of the women went to Elder Joyce's home to support Annabelle as she struggled with her grief. Elder Joyce had Annabelle smudge and prayed over her. The old woman promised to continue to go into deep prayer in search of answers.

The women returned home, and Annabelle was surrounded by her family. She forced herself to smile to support her other children, who were processing Joseph's absence too. After the children went to sleep, Annabelle cuddled with John, and they talked about Joseph to cope with their son's absence.

<hr>

A frown remained fixed on Joseph's face the entire day despite Tom's effort to cheer him up. All he could think about was his family, and after he ate supper with Stella and the others, Stella began to have them all sing slave hymns, a common activity after supper.

I wish this singing made me happy, he thought. *The singing is always happier in here than when they start singing in the fields. Right now, I can't even smile when I think about Jesus.* After the hymns were sung, he went outside to look at the full moon. As he sat behind the slave house, he heard someone step on a branch and turned to his right.

"So that's what it's going to take for you to notice me here," Riza whispered.

"Riza, you're not supposed to be here," Joseph whispered.

"Master Plecker can only watch me for so long. Susie said you weren't doing well, and today was your birthday, so happy birthday."

"Thank you, Riza, but I don't think it will make me feel better."

Riza frowned. "You miss your momma, don't you?"

"Yeah, and my brothers, my sisters, my pa, and everyone. I thought they would've found me by now."

Riza squatted. "I miss my momma too. What is your momma's name?"

Joseph gave a half-smile. "Annabelle. What's yours?"

"My momma's name is Violet, but family calls her Vi. I understand. I haven't seen my momma in years. You never get used to missing them."

Joseph bit lip as he exhaled. "I'm sorry they killed your family and your tribe. My pa said when he was a child and was forced to walk to Indian Territory, they lost a lot of people. All of his grandparents died and his cousin William. But the White people killed all of your people."

Riza looked away from Joseph and glared up at the full moon. "I don't believe him." She deeply inhaled and exhaled. "I can't believe a liar…a false Christian."

Joseph reached forward and calmly held Riza's hand. He said, "I hope he's lying, but what will you do if they did kill your whole family?"

Riza turned to Joseph and shrugged. "I can't think of an answer. I trust the Creator. I trust Jesus. Even if those evil people killed them, I'll survive knowing their spirits are free."

"You can come live with my family if your family is gone."

Riza smiled with the moonlight reflecting off her watery right eye. "Thank you."

"Will we escape from here?"

"I think at the right time we will. I had a dream we were supposed to wait, but I ignored it because I wanted to leave now." Riza's brow lowered while she slowly tapped her fingers on the ground. "It was my fault, and I'm sorry."

Joseph pouted. "It was Pearl's fault. She told on us."

Riza sighed. "Yeah, but if we had waited, Pearl would've been the one to get beaten." Her mouth curved downward. "I planned the escape months ago when I learned of the party. I look in the mirrors now, and I only see a piece of who I was. We'll try again at the right time."

"You're really smart, Riza. I think you scare Master Plecker."

"I think so too, but he also scares me. The next time, if we do this and fail, I think they'll kill me. I've created the one thing we didn't need and that's fear." Riza hugged Joseph. "I have to go back before Mrs. Wilma comes to the slave house to make sure I'm there. Try to enjoy the night." She stood up and stretched.

Joseph half-smiled. "It felt good to hit Pearl with that apple, didn't it?"

Rizza grinned and then quickly ran to the house-slave house while Joseph watched.

Joseph looked up at the full moon and sighed. "I miss you, Momma." He entered the slave house and spent time with the other slaves as they celebrated his birthday.

On October 11, 1860, Riza was instructed to give the leftover food to the pigs. It was nearly unbearable to pour good food into the pigs' slop bucket. When nobody was looking, she ate a fresh muffin Wilma hadn't wanted. As she finished giving the pigs the food, a wagon filled with cotton baskets rolled by with Pearl and a few other slaves in it.

"After you done with that, how about you roll around in that mud with them," Pearl taunted.

"I think you need to spend time with your family instead of me," Riza stated.

The other three slaves cackled as Pearl angrily looked around. "Stop the wagon," she commanded. The driver stopped the wagon, and Pearl stood up. "How does it feel to be a real nigger, Riza? I see that hair takes a long time to grow back, and you wearing the dress of a field nigger. Now you ain't nothing but a nigger!"

Riza squinted and her nose crinkled, but then she scoffed with a leer slowing etching across her face. "Tell Master Rice I said hi, nigger."

Pearl screeched and was about to jump out of the wagon when the two men sitting with her held her back. "Come on, Pearl. Riza a child," one man said.

"Let's go before they say more mean stuff to each other," the other man said.

The wagon rode off while the men held Pearl down and she yelled, "You ain't nothing, redskin! They should've shot you dead! Grass nigger!"

Riza scrunched her face and threw the slop bucket down.

She clutched her brown cotton dress and marched over to the white mansion grunting. Her mind raced as she took deep breaths. Later in the afternoon, while standing at attention next to Wilma, she was instructed to get more tea and so took the silver tea set to the kitchen.

"Emma, Mrs. Wilma would like an apple, some pinto beans, and muffins with the melted cheese on top of them," Riza said.

"It is too soon for her snack time," Emma said.

"Are you telling her when she wants to eat?"

"Why, no, I wouldn't dare." Emma immediately started to prepare the food, fearing Wilma's wrath.

Riza cleverly put some milk in Wilma's tea while she prepared it, then walked out to the white patio where Wilma was relaxing as she watched the slaves work. "Mrs. Wilma, I have your tea hot and ready for you," she softly said.

"Why, thank you, Riza. You did that quite promptly," Wilma said. "You keep this up, and I'll have to consider allowing you to wear a nice blue dress again instead of that ugly attire the field slaves wear. Look at them go, and in good spirits. I guess because winter will be coming soon."

Riza politely replied, "They do seem happier today, Mrs. Wilma."

"Believe it or not, child, but watching them out there in those fields makes me think of your Master Cornelius. I miss my oldest boy. He spends too much time at his own plantation and forgets to come see his momma every week. It's frustrating. The boy is only ten miles away east but only comes here every two or three weeks."

"I imagine that must be disappointing."

"Disappointing? Why, when the time comes for you to produce your own, you will understand it is more than disappointing. My oldest won't spend enough time with me, and my youngest spends too much time here. It feels like my three girls were the only ones to understand balance."

As Wilma prattled on, Riza saw Emma coming with the food. She abruptly excused herself so she could grab the food and prevent Emma from speaking to Wilma.

Wilma quickly stood up and watched Riza march toward Emma. "Riza, where are you going?"

"To get your food, ma'am." Riza took the platters from Emma, returned to the patio with the food, and proudly presented it. "Mrs. Wilma, here is a meal prepared for you."

Wilma's eyebrows rose. "What is this? I never asked for such a meal at this time!"

Riza joyfully replied, "I believe we are grateful to be of service to you, ma'am, especially on such a beautiful day."

"You're quite right, my dear. It is a beautiful day." Wilma's brow lowered while she looked at the food. "And you have a reputation. Please, dear, have a muffin."

Riza put her hand on her chest. "What? Mrs. Wilma, I could never take what is meant for you."

"I insist. Now take a muffin to satisfy me."

Riza half-smiled at Wilma's demand and took a muffin to keep herself on good terms with the woman. She ate the muffin while Wilma watched. "It is good. Thank you, Mrs. Wilma."

Wilma cheerfully scoffed. "It was nothing, child. I merely feel some rewards are meant to be given when appropriate behavior is displayed." She then sat down and ate the meal as she casually watched the slaves work.

A few hours later, Wilma jumped to her feet holding her stomach. "Well, I must excuse myself to the outhouse. Make sure all of this is cleaned up by the time I return. I'm expecting a few guests in about half an hour." Her stomach then growled, and she quickly marched to the outhouse.

Riza gave a notorious smirk as she picked up the silverware and ran to the kitchen. "We are expecting guests in a while, Emma," she said. "I have to go attend to Mrs. Wilma now." She handed Emma the dirty silverware and quickly ran outside.

"What was that about?" Dorothy asked as she entered the kitchen's back door.

"She seemed happy to me," Emma said.

Dorothy's brow lowered, and her cheek pinched. "I know, but why?"

As the slaves continued to work in the cotton fields, a wagon with empty baskets went past the fields. "Louis, you come this way in a little bit. I almost done with this," Pearl called out to the wagon.

"Okay, I come back through," Louis said.

"Pearl," Riza said.

Pearl lifted her head up as Riza jumped off the wagon with a slop bucket.

"Here's a gift from your family!" Riza flung pig feces and mud onto Pearl.

Pearl screamed in disgust as the feces and mud dripped down her skin and brown dress. Riza ran away laughing while Pearl continued screaming and attempting to clean herself off.

Riza threw the slop bucket by the pig pen and then calmly walked into the mansion with a big smile.

"Riza, where were you?" Dorothy asked.

Riza answered, "I was at the patio, making sure I didn't forget anything."

Dorothy put her hand on her hip. "Stay out of trouble. You've been doing good these past few weeks."

Suddenly there was a knock at the door.

"It must be Mrs. Wilma's guest today," Riza griped.

"It's most likely Mrs. Daphne since you scared the others away," Dorothy joked. She and Riza opened the mansion doors, and a cheerful, blue-eyed Daphne came in with another young blonde.

"Ah, Dorothy, it's always a pleasure to be welcomed by you," Daphne said. "Riza...I see your hair has started to grow back," she added, her tone hinting disgust.

Riza gave Daphne a forced smile as Dorothy closed the door. "Mrs. Daphne and Mrs. Judy Mays, please let me escort you to the living room," Dorothy said. "Riza, please bring out some tea for them."

Riza went into the cookhouse while Dorothy walked Daphne and Judy Mays into the living room. When Riza left the double doors with the silver tea set, Mrs. Wilma was climbing down the staircase.

"Riza, are they here?" Wilma asked.

"Yes, ma'am, they are. Dorothy took them to the living room," Riza said.

"Good, I spent more time in the outhouse than I felt like I was going too. Please take the tea out to the patio. I'd like to enjoy my company out in this gorgeous weather."

Riza smiled. "Yes, ma'am."

Wilma entered the living room. A brown grandfather clock ticked in the background as the young women spoke to each other. "Ah, girls, I'm so happy you came. The last few times, I couldn't enjoy the company of both of you at the same time."

Daphne cheerfully replied, "Well, today things worked out quite well."

Wilma excitedly replied, "Yes, let's go to the patio in this beautiful weather. The heat has finally decided to weaken. I had Riza take the tea out to the patio."

Daphne snobbishly replied, "How can you allow that grass nigger to even serve you after what she did. Her whole hand should have been shot off. I wouldn't trust her to comb my hair."

"It was a challenge, but I do believe at last Riza and I have a stronger understanding. Though I doubt she and the overseers have such similar feelings, which is understandable."

"Well, of course not. That little savage spit blood into Wade's eyes. What kind of sick child does that?"

"She was rebellious. But now that little flame has been snuffed out. No more talk of Riza." The three women walked outside to the patio and conversed as they drank tea. "What's on your mind, Judy Mays? You've spoken so little."

"Not much is on my mind," Judy Mays said with her calm southern accent. "To be honest, I'm impressed a thirteen-year-old child could come up with such a scheme. These Indian children certainly have potential."

Wilma replied, "Now don't you start showing sympathy. You were there while she set ablaze my beautiful dining hall. It has only been this past week that it looks as beautiful as it once did. How have things been in Columbus?"

"Things have been quiet. The children are doing very well,

and Edgar has established some nice strongholds in the industry businesses."

"Which ones?" Daphne asked.

Judy Mays put down her tea and smiled. "The railroads. He has been quite adamant about getting involved with the trains. I support his decision. It's the best way to send goods, and hopefully, it'll encourage more people to travel by train."

"How is he balancing that and the tobacco fields y'all have?" Wilma asked.

"Well, we have seven employees that we can afford to pay, and it has proven quite beneficial."

Wilma replied with a flabbergasted tone, "Employees…what about your slaves, Judy Mays?"

Judy Mays curled her lower lip and exhaled. "Edgar and I have decided not to buy any more slaves. We have our ten, and they're faithful. We're satisfied with that and want the children to learn more than the economics of slavery."

"Sweetheart, you're not turning abolitionist on us, are you?"

"Why, no, I feel the railroad profits are more beneficial to my family's needs, and we still have our tobacco fields. We want to have more reach in providing for the family."

"I understand, Judy Mays. I have always had interest in the railroads," Daphne said.

"Well, ain't nothing wrong with supporting Edgar's interest," Wilma said. "Those railroads will always be around, like these slaves ain't going nowhere. It's only a matter of time before we go further west and get more land for our cause."

"Riza, more tea, sweetie," Judy Mays said.

Riza walked over and poured tea into Judy Mays's cup.

Judy Mays half-smirked. "I must admit, I feel bothered that after all these years I keep forgetting which tribe you're from."

"I'm Mohawk, Mrs. Judy Mays," Riza calmly said.

"No wonder. I hear your tribe has always been violent animals," Daphne snobbishly said. "They have almost no form of self-control. It's quite sad."

"On the contrary, it took patience to do what she did," Judy

Mays said. "I'd say your comment of no control is lacking in evidence, Daphne. You underestimate the Indians."

Riza fought back a grin when she looked at Judy Mays.

Mrs. Wilma said, "Don't encourage such disgusting, disrespectful behavior. She's lucky to be alive, and to have both of her hands."

"In no way am I asserting what she did was proper, but merely it took intelligence to do such a terrible thing. I was there as you were when the fire took place. All I'm saying is that proper treatment yields better results."

A smug leer etched on Daphne's face. "Well, when was the last time you had a slave run away? Besides your precious Annabelle?"

Judy Mays narrowed her eyes and sharply replied, "The last runaway was twelve years ago." Her face went blank. "Please don't be rude. I'm not near my children, and in this position, I will say what I want. Don't mention Annabelle again."

Daphne's eyes widened, and her jaw dropped while she held her tea. "I meant no offense by it, Judy Mays."

"I must admit it's impressive to not have lost any property in twelve years," Wilma said. She drank some more tea and then placed her cup down. "However, I have such a hard time believing that most will respond as needed with a kinder form of authority. Riza and Dorothy are exceptions in my opinion. The rest are too lazy and dumb to respond as I need them to without some form of harshness."

Judy Mays replied, "I understand your viewpoint."

"I am bored by this. Please allow me to show you my apple and walnut trees. They have produced a lot this year." The women set down their cups and stretched. "Riza, have some crackers prepared for us. I'm enjoying seeing my old younger friends."

Riza replied, "Yes, Mrs. Wilma."

The women spent the rest of the day together while Wilma showed off her apple and walnut trees. Judy Mays separated from Wilma and Daphne and walked up to the patio. Riza was putting out the crackers, but turned around once Judy Mays came within a few feet of her.

"You can give as many fake smiles as you want, Riza," Judy Mays said. "I see nothing but sadness in you now. No more fire."

Riza gulped. "I am sorry for the fire, Mrs. Judy Mays."

Judy Mays scoffed and confidently took two steps closer to Riza. "Who are you trying to fool, little girl? You tried your best to run away. I don't accept fake apologies."

"I on—"

"I only care about the truth, and you showed your true colors." Judy Mays picked up a cracker and took a bite out of it. "Unlike the others, I don't like the idea of you losing your spirit."

"Thank you, Mrs. Judy Mays."

"Hmph. For your sake, continue to act right. You're a clever girl. You'd be surprised how quickly things can change for the better or worse." Judy Mays began to walk away but stopped. She slowly turned around, and her blue eyes anchored on Riza. "I've watched you grow, Riza, and I believe in being honest with you. You're not the last one." A half-smile formed on her face, then she turned around and marched back to the other women.

Riza put her hand over her heart and half-smiled.

After a few hours, the women returned to their carriage. "I truly enjoyed our gathering today, ladies. I look forward to another one," Wilma said.

"Of course! Today was a glorious day," Daphne said.

"If all works well, I'll be able to spend more time with you ladies next week," Judy Mays said. "I'd certainly enjoy it."

Riza looked at Judy Mays standing by the carriage.

"Riza, behave yourself, dear. Be the lady I know you can."

Riza smiled and nodded, saying, "I will, Mrs. Judy Mays."

Wilma chuckled as Daphne and Judy Mays got into the carriage. "My word, Judy Mays, you've always had some way with her over the years," Wilma said. "Please do come back soon."

"I wish you hadn't moved out here to Caledonia when Columbus is flourishing," Judy Mays said. "I do look forward to another visit, maybe in a few days."

The carriage began to ride off when Riza shouted, "I know a slave that spoke of a Negro named Annabelle."

Judy Mays suddenly stuck her head out of the carriage door window as it rode away. "What did you say, Riza?"

Riza remained silent while the carriage continued to drive off.

"She couldn't have said what I heard."

"What did she say? Do we need to stop?" Daphne asked.

Judy Mays sat back in the carriage and exhaled as she looked at Daphne. "Nothing, I mean it can wait. I'll speak with Riza when I return."

Daphne's brows drew together. "Why would you ask that deceitful savage anything?"

"She raises my interests. Especially if she…I mean she's just a nice form of entertainment when she's controlled. She's different."

As the two women rode away, Wilma approached Riza with her arms crossed. "Why would you say such a thing?" she asked.

"I was letting her know something that I've heard," Riza said with her head lowered. "Mrs. Judy Mays seemed interested in the name."

"Speak when you've been spoken to, Riza."

Riza nodded. "Yes, ma'am."

"Come along. I'd like to see my silverware polished."

Riza pouted as she reluctantly followed Wilma into the large mansion.

———◆———

As the autumn breeze carried in the change of weather, it seemed almost unnatural how fast the days were cooling by October 15, 1860. After Lea left, Joyce sat in her favorite rocking chair with her tea. The house suddenly became filled with a beautiful light.

A woman with a face that flickered blue and white light like lightning appeared and stood before Joyce. "Hello, Joyce. My name is Hope," she said in Cherokee.

Joyce coughed as she propped herself up. "I feel peace and calmness from you," she said. "You're a powerful spirit…an angel."

The angel smiled at Joyce. "Yes, I am. Most humans are too scared to think that I am."

Joyce cheerfully replied in Cherokee, "You are so beautiful. Please, sit down. I've never had an angel in my home. I'm honored and curious as to why you appear to me."

"Joyce…I've been told to take you home today. The Father has decided for you not to suffer anymore in this world."

"This isn't anything but a cough I've been struggling with. I can tough this one out like the others."

"I'm sorry to say, this time the sickness will win. All of your hard work here won't be unfruitful, and change is coming to this land."

Joyce's smile faded, and her mouth formed a slight frown. "Please, tell me if you know…will slavery of the Negroes and my people end?"

"Yes, slavery by the chains will end, but another form of slavery will take its place. It will take time for all forms of slavery to be destroyed in this land because so much blood has been spilled to keep it alive. A great war will also begin, and it will be like nothing this land has seen before."

"All I ask is for my loved ones to make it through the war."

"Your family will survive the war, but there will still be some losses."

"Joseph Lightning, is the boy alive?"

"He is alive, and there is a plan for him to return at the right time. Before you ask, I don't know his location."

"I was worried the Father would call for me at a bad time, but I have faith that things will become stable once again. How old are you with such a young, beautiful face?"

Hope giggled. "You know it's rude to ask a female her age."

Joyce began to cackle as she reached for her tea.

"I'm more than 800 million years old, to make it simple. I was born after the evil one rebelled against the Father."

"Well, now I'm jealous for you to have so many years and look so young. I thought I looked good for my many years."

Hope giggled. "You've aged well for a human. You can stand

up correctly and walk very well. That's more than some of these humans who are only eighty and have to use a walking stick."

"I guess I do need to be more grateful. I would ask to wait for Lea, but she was here earlier today, and we had a good talk. I'm very proud of her. She has learned everything I asked her to learn. She is a strong child."

"You will see her again."

"Yes, I know. It's just...I know it will break her heart when she realizes I have walked on."

"I can arrange that your spirit leave your body and stay behind to comfort her for a moment before I take you home."

"I would like that for her, and there is a letter for her that I wrote a year ago, to help her cope when my time came. I do want to write a letter for the Lightning family. Their family has tried so hard to support our people, and now they have their greatest trial. Even that wildcat," Joyce joked.

"Her love for you will cause her to grieve, but she'll heal."

Joyce walked to her old wood table, grabbed several pieces of paper, and started writing. Afterward, she added the letter meant for Lea and sat back down in her rocking chair to take another sip of tea.

"I think the letters read beautifully."

"You read them already?! I was a bit worried it sounded preachy, but I have high hopes for that family, like many others. However, I feel they're the ones that need the support I can give right now. Especially Annabelle...that child has endured so much."

"You've done more than you know, Joyce, and now is the time."

Joyce suddenly felt sleepy as her heart and her breathing slowed to a stop. The letters fell from her hand and landed on the wooden floor. Hope picked up the letters and put them on Joyce's lap with a smile.

As the evening arrived, there was a knock at Joyce's door. Soon the door slowly opened, and Lea entered. The teenager quietly walked over to Joyce in her rocking chair.

"Grandma Joyce, wake up. I forgot my bonnet," Lea said in Cherokee.

With no response forthcoming, Lea frowned. "Grandma Joyce?" She shook her. "Grandma? No, please, I was just here. I don't understand. Grandma, please wake up!" she cried.

Clutching her long braid while she wept, she knelt down and held Joyce's hand. She noticed the two letters on Joyce's lap and picked them up. "Why did you leave me now? Grandma, please come back for a moment. I love you so much."

Lea felt the warm touch of a hand on her right cheek and looked over to her right but saw nothing.

"I was hoping she wouldn't take it this bad," Joyce said. "How she reminds me of my daughter Amber."

"Your daughter is waiting. Are you ready?" Hope asked.

Joyce leaned over and caressed Lea's right cheek again while the girl continued trying to see what she couldn't. "I think one more hug would be too much for my baby. I'm ready now, Hope, as long as she knows I have walked on to the gates of heaven." With that her spirit walked away into the lights of heaven with Hope.

Still holding her right cheek, Lea quivered beneath the rush of intense and all-encompassing love she felt filling the house. "Thank you, Grandma," she said as tears ran down her face. "I'm not angry at you for joining our ancestors."

CHAPTER 11
Paying Respects

I N THE EARLY MORNING, LEA went to the Lightning-Strongman family farm and told them the devastating news. Annabelle and the others were shocked and gave their blessings to Lea. Lea gave Grace the letter she found.

"She knew she was going to walk on," Lea said, speaking Cherokee, her voice breaking. "I still can't decide if I would've wanted her to tell me or not."

"Things will be all right, Lea," Grace said. "Your grandma always spoke about you the most. I know you'll make her proud no matter how many years pass."

"Thank you, Grace. We will see each other again."

As Lea left, Grace sat down at the supper table and stared at the letter.

Tsula came up to Grace while holding Katelyn and wiping tears from her face. "Grace, what are we going to do? Elder Joyce had the strongest spiritual connection," she said, her voice breaking. "She had the gift of seeing. We have no one left like her."

Grace looked up at Tsula as she wiped away her own tears. "We do what she has been trying to teach us all these years. We grow closer to the Father and ask for help and wisdom. We stay together as a family as she told us to and trust in Jesus. She did what she was meant to do. It was her time."

Tsula deeply exhaled and was about to walk away when she saw the letter in Grace's hand. "What does it say?"

Grace looked at the letter bundle for a long moment and then opened it, pulling out several pages. "She wrote more than one letter. Tsula, this is for you and Luke. Lizzie, come here. This is for you. Annabelle and John, this is for you. Lisa and Jacob, this is for you and Samuel and Maria. Uncle George, she wrote something for you and Michael."

"You read it to us, Grace," George said.

Grace handed the others their letters and read the letter meant for George and Michael. "George, over the years I have watched you grow from a boy to a troubled young man with a family," she read. "I prayed for your freedom from alcohol since I learned about your struggle. I'm glad to see you've been freed from it and happy to see you become the man your family needs. Remember to ask Jesus for help in all you do and lead your family with love. I wish Shay could see her prayers were answered, but I do believe she looks down and sees the man she married so many years ago. Keep growing in spirit and lead like you were meant to.

"Michael, you were always the quiet one in your family, and that's a good thing. You remained as yourself and never changed to be like the rest. To follow your path is harder than to follow the paths of others. I pray that you continue to heal and don't blame yourself for Joseph's kidnapping. Evil waits patiently for any opportunity to cause the most pain. Don't forget to move forward. I saw the young lady who likes you. Don't keep her waiting. There's nothing wrong with falling in love while searching for Joseph. I know that through the Father you will grow to be a great leader in your family."

"That meant a lot to hear those words from her," George said in Cherokee. "May she rest with our ancestors and the Father in heaven." He slowly got up and marched outside to the fields.

Annabelle unfolded the letter and held it so John could read it as well. The letter read, "Annabelle and John, it has brought me great joy over the years to see such a beautiful young couple grow and have children of their own. John, I'm always amazed by the Creator's work in a person's heart. You've grown into a strong leader. Your parents would be proud. Annabelle, you're a Cherokee woman in my heart and eyes. Strong, loving, and focused on growing the Father's kingdom to the best of your ability. I've been told by a heavenly spirit that slavery will end. I can also tell you Joseph is alive and you will find him, so don't lose faith, Lovely Child. No matter how dark things look, hold onto your faith, not only for your sake but for your children. I know David has not handled Joseph's absence well. Keep an eye on that boy. He has a bit of Lizzie in him. I love you both and am so pleased our paths were meant to cross. We will see each other again."

Annabelle let out a weak gasp as she became overwhelmed with joy and sadness. She hugged John while she tried not to cry.

Lisa and Jacob read their letter. "Lisa and Jacob, the hidden lovers, I've decided to call y'all. I'm happy the two of you have held strong to the love you have for each other. I'm also saddened and embarrassed the two of you had to hide your love for each other, a man and a woman. The love I see between you two is symbolic of how Jesus loves the people. It's an unbreakable bond. Lisa, no matter how you feel, you're a strong Cherokee woman to endure so much. You moved forward as you should've. You know better than most, life isn't fair, but the Father has a way of healing past pain. Jacob, continue to be the head of your family and never forget to ask the Father for guidance. You're not perfect. Don't be too critical of yourself. Continue to love each other, Sunni, and your children to come."

Lisa mumbled, "It'll never be the same without you, Elder Joyce. I hope the stars shine brighter now that you have walked on."

Samuel gave the letter meant for them to Maria, not wanting to show any sadness. Maria sat down and read the letter. "Samuel and Maria, I have enjoyed watching two shy people become as one. Maria, I was impressed with your effort to learn the Cherokee tongue and to pass that knowledge onto Rosita. I love your daughter's spirit. She'll grow into a loving, strong woman, and I know she'll walk a great path. Sky will also grow into a special woman when the time comes. I'm sure Tsula will do her best to keep her nieces on her side. Be prepared to lose that fight, Samuel. You and Tsula have been one of the most entertaining set of twins I've known in all my years on this earth. Make sure to keep that bond between the two of you and your children."

Maria lightly laughed as she wiped tears from her face. "You should read this, Samuel," she said.

Samuel hesitantly walked over to Maria and began to read the letter.

Tsula and Luke were reading theirs. "Tsula and Luke, I pray more blessings will come your way. Clever Fox, you have always been entertaining to say the least, and I'll miss you, not your instigative ways. You and Lizzie will fight until the end of time, and that's all right. The two of you love each other and must remain strong in that. I'm blessed to have witnessed you become a great mother. I know your mother smiles down at you. Remain close to Samuel—the two of you are stronger together, as twins should be. Luke, remain strong and close to the Father. You're a patient man, and that will help guide you in making the right choices for your family. Remember to also listen to Tsula. The two of you are one, and she has a strong mind, so listen to her as a husband should."

Grace began to unfold her page as Lizzie went to her room and closed the door. She stared at Lizzie's door, sighed, and un-folded the letter. She read, "Eli, I'm proud of how you have come to help lead your family. Remain a faithful man and remember who Grace is. She's a natural leader and looks for your respect because it will be impossible to love her without respect. Trust in the ways of the Father. There's no shame in not having an answer for everything.

"Grace, I'm so proud of how you have been a rock for your family. My time has come but yours remains. I know you'll be a great mother. I'm sorry I won't be there when that time comes, but my spirit will be watching. Continue to grow with the spirit your mother left you and hold strong to your faith. I've written to

Annabelle that I know Joseph is alive and he'll be found. I know this as a certainty and that the age of chain slavery will die. I sit here with a heavenly host, having enjoyed her presence greatly. Be mindful of Lizzie. She has come a long way, but still struggles with her emotions. Be mindful of David too.

"I've also told Lea a hidden truth about my own family. My own two children that died coming here were from my first husband, and the rest of my children were from my second husband. My two children were the last of that branch. They didn't have any children of their own, which broke my heart. My second husband, Christopher, was actually a half-breed. His father was a runaway slave, and his mother was from our Bird Clan. He was born with most of her looks and passed as such. So all of my children and their children and so forth have a little Negro blood, and I felt it was time for the whole truth to be learned. Lea's letter contains the truth, and I hope she continues to pass on that truth. I hope she gains some pride in having a little Negro blood. Remember not to sacrifice so much of yourself. Keep your prayer life strong and help your sister the best you can. We will see each other again."

Tears dripped from Grace's eyes, and she smiled as she handed Eli the letter to read next and leaned on him for comfort.

As the day continued, Lizzie stayed in her room staring at Elder Joyce's letter while she sat on her bed. After unbraiding her wavy hair, she picked up the letter, unfolded the paper, and read.

"Lizzie Lightning, you're a special and loving woman. You've solved many of your problems with fighting over the years. Some of those times were justified and other times you acted on your feelings, letting your temper rule you. I'm happy for you, Wildcat, for the progress you have made over the years. I have strong hope that you'll continue having the courage to change. Your family hopes the best for you. I know you still love Jacob, and that's okay, baby. The love you have for him is real. It's a hard path the Father has destined you for, but there's a reason for it. To truly love someone when they're not ready or can't give the same amount of love back to you is difficult. Some day you will fall in love again even if your love for Jacob doesn't die. You know I'm not saying you need a man to fulfill you. We've had many talks, and you know a husband does not complete you…a husband is meant to be your partner.

"Accept your current role in the family, but be careful. That anger of yours is building again because of Joseph's kidnapping. Let it go, Wildcat. I've learned that Joseph is alive. Have faith in the plans the Father has for you and the family. You have the spirit of a warrior, but the love in your heart must be stronger than your instinct to fight. Those twin girls and Rosita look up to you, and they must learn to trust the path the Father wants them to follow.

"I'm sorry I didn't get time to have one more talk with you, but I had a wonderful vision of you in my dreams. I wanted to wait and see what was on your mind the next time we talked, but I saw a blue flower bring you joy. Give the man who gave you that flower a chance and ask the Creator to help you heal where I couldn't help you. You love hard and because of it, you guard yourself strongly. I don't know if the man is your husband, but I do know you should try to give him a chance and pray about it. Remember to walk by faith, not by sight."

A tear fell onto the letter as Lizzie mourned in private. She tugged on her wavy hair as she tried to control the pain she felt. She had now lost her mentor. *I'm afraid I'm not able to open my heart again to someone who isn't family,* she thought. She began to pray, asking for guidance and help against her unbelief.

A soft knock suddenly echoed on Lizzie's door. "Auntie Lizzie, are you still going to teach us how to cut the chicken today?" Rain asked in Cherokee.

"I will come out soon, Rain," Lizzie said. "Auntie needs to rest a little."

Rain's voice became cheerful. "She's going to show us!"

Lizzie could hear Jannie and Rosita give a quiet cheer. She waited for the strength to compose herself and opened her door to go teach the girls. She smiled when she saw her nieces and Rosita, because it reminded her of Joyce's words. She was practicing to be a mother with the girls. She thought, *I'm not hiding that I want my own family from the others anymore.*

The next day, the morning sunrays covered the land of Tahlequah. David stood by the old redbud tree with his gaze fixed on the rising sun.

"Son, you haven't eaten breakfast," Annabelle calmly said in Cherokee. "Come eat with the rest of the family."

"I'm not hungry, Momma," David replied in a somber tone, his gaze fixed on the sunrise.

Annabelle slowly stepped around to stand in front of him and saw the tears welling in her son's eyes. "David, no matter how much pain you feel in your heart, I'm here for you."

David turned to his mother. "Why did she leave us now, when we need her guidance the most?"

Annabelle felt her own tears building up and hugged her son. "She didn't walk on to leave us or to hurt us. She was called home…it was her time."

David hugged his mother, crying, "How will we find Joseph now?"

"Oh, sweetie, your brother is alive, and Elder Joyce saw in a vision that he would be returned to us. We have to hold onto hope."

"What if she was wrong, and it was just a dream?"

"She has never lied about what she's seen and has always tried to remind us to walk by faith and not by sight. She'd always tell me and your aunties we'd have to continue to grow spiritually because she didn't know when she would be called to the gates of heaven. She was gifted, but she never took Jesus's place, David. It's true she was the strongest of us, but in her humble ways, she also made sure we sought the Father."

"She was always good to us. She helped raise my momma when she lost almost everyone."

"And with the knowledge you have of her love and kindness, you're to spread the love she showed Camille and she also showed me. Do you hear me?"

David nodded. "Yes, Momma."

"She is right," Lisa said in Cherokee.

Annabelle and David turned their heads to see Lisa standing a few feet away.

Lisa continued, "We honor Elder Joyce by spreading the Father's love. Even when it's hard and to those who don't deserve it."

"It was Mr. Jackson, wasn't it? He had Joseph taken away," David said with a pout.

Lisa's brow lowered and her mouth curved downward. "We're sure he was involved, but you promise me to do as you're told. We've already lost your brother. We can't lose you too because of revenge. Do you understand?"

"Yes, ma'am."

Lisa put out her arms. "Come here."

David walked into the embrace, resting his head on her shoulder.

Lisa continued, "Let revenge come from the throne of the Creator. I promise those who took your brother will be dealt with. We already have to keep an eye on your Auntie Lizzie. We don't need you getting into trouble too."

"I want to help."

"David, your being here and protecting your siblings and younger cousins *is* help."

"But—"

Lisa shook David, saying with a stern tone, "No! You do as you're told to protect the family. You do not follow your feelings. Is it understood?"

David's gaze shifted to the ground. "Yes, ma'am."

Lisa calmly put her hand on David's cheek and forced his gaze to hers. "Is it understood?"

Tears broke from David's eyes, and he nodded, saying, "Yes, Auntie Lisa."

Lisa hugged David and rubbed his back. "We will find your brother."

Annabelle also rubbed David's back. "Be patient, son. We won't stop until he's back home."

Annabelle's gaze went up when she noticed John standing on the steps of the family house, observing the women comforting his son. She could see the small frown on her husband's face. He nodded at her, and she nodded back as she continued to rub David's back. John slowly turned around and went back into the house. The two women walked David to the family house as he cleaned his face. Grace fixed David a plate, and he ate his breakfast with the rest of the family.

Annabelle sat down next to John and glanced at a sleeping Jonathan in his cradle.

"He is a good sleeper," Maria said as she held Sky.

Annabelle replied, "Yes, far better than the twins. The Lord at least heard that request."

Maria giggled, saying, "I heard that. I went the opposite way with Rosita being a good sleeper, but Sky will wake up to anything."

The twins and Rosita suddenly began laughing, and Maria turned her head toward them.

John calmly put his hand on top of Annabelle's, and she looked at him. He leaned to her ear and whispered, "Is David accepting her death?"

Annabelle whispered, "He is trying to accept it, but he is also worried about Joseph."

John leaned back and sighed. He turned and watched the twins and Rosita teasing David and him playfully responding. He leaned back to Annabelle's ear and whispered, "Thank you for being a strong, good wife. I love you."

Annabelle closed her fingers in between John's fingers, saying, "I love you too."

John kissed Annabelle on her forehead and smiled.

"Ew," Rain said.

"Ew," John said.

Rain cocked her head. "Yes, ew."

John stood up. "I'll teach you not to say ew when Momma gets a kiss." He playfully ran around the table after Rain, growling.

Rain ran around the table laughing and grabbed onto Lizzie's waist. "Auntie Lizzie, don't let him get me!"

"Go to the other houses if you're going to make all that noise," Annabelle said. "I don't want you waking up your brother."

Rain let go of Lizzie's waist with a grin slowly etching across her face as she slowly walked past her father. She then bolted for the front door, and John began to chase her as she laughed and ran to Annabelle's house.

Jannie looked at her mother with a smile, and Annabelle nodded at her with approval. The long-haired girl then ran outside to join the fun. Maria also nodded, allowing Rosita to join the fun, and she ran out of the front door.

Annabelle grinned at Lizzie and Maria as she shook her head and looked at a sleeping Jonathan. She then looked at David, who continued to eat his food. *Jesus, please give us the strength to make it through this storm, I miss my baby boy,* she thought.

On October 18, 1860, the Lightning-Strongman family went to the church grounds for Elder Joyce's funeral service. The partly cloudy day was accompanied by a cool fall breeze.

Annabelle held Jannie's and Rain's hands while they approached the church. Her eyes widened when she saw hundreds of Cherokee gathered on the church grounds. Among those paying their respects were Molly and Reverend Hills and the entire Cherokee council, including Chief John Ross.

As the family started to greet those already present, Annabelle felt both of the twins' grips tighten on her hands. She glanced at both of her daughters and saw tears shimmering in their eyes. She felt her chest tighten but held back her tears.

Uncle George led the family to the front of the gathering where Elder Joyce's body had been placed into a wooden coffin. The Lightning-Strongman family stepped up to the coffin and looked at the lifeless body of Elder Joyce with lowered eyebrows and frowns.

Elder Joyce had been dressed in her orange and red-trimmed dress that had seven stars embroidered on the bodice. Her long, wavy silver hair had been brushed down her shoulders, and her hands had been folded.

George cleared his throat and, with tears glistening in his eyes, gave his thanks to Elder Joyce while the family listened. Annabelle felt her heart break even further when she heard his genuine words. Tsula and Luke then gave their thanks, with Tsula kissing Joyce on the forehead before tears broke free from her eyes. She held onto Luke with Katelyn in her other arm and wailed as he wiped away his own tears. Michael, Maria, and Samuel then gave their thanks to Elder Joyce. Samuel held Rosita in his arms as she cried into his chest. The three wiped their tears as they followed Tsula and Luke.

Grace stepped up to the coffin with Eli holding her hand. Her cheeks glistened with tears as she shook her head. "Saying thank you isn't enough," she cried in Cherokee. "You taught with love and always tried to guide us through the spirit. If it wasn't for you, I wouldn't have learned how to help lead my family when my momma and Auntie Shay walked on." She let go of Eli's hand and put both of her hands to her chest. "If it wasn't for you, I wouldn't be who I am. Thank you, my mentor...my grandmother!"

Every eye surrounding the coffin began to shed tears.

Eli put his hands on Grace's shoulders calmly and kissed her cheek. Grace put her hands on top of Eli's hands as she continued to weep. Eli gave his thanks and then the couple slowly walked away from the coffin.

Jannie broke down in tears, and Annabelle knelt to give her daughter a hug. "It's okay, Moonlight. You know she walks in the kingdom of heaven now," Annabelle said as tears trickled down her cheeks.

Jannie replied in her native tongue, "I'm going to miss her. Why did she leave us now?"

"Oh, sweetie, when the Creator calls us home, it's time for us to go. It doesn't mean that she didn't love you." From the corner of her eye, Annabelle noticed more tears running down Rain's face. "Oh, come here, my sunshine."

Rain tightly hugged Annabelle and cried into her mother's shoulder.

John and David approached the coffin with John carrying Jonathan. John gave his thanks and patted David on his back. David struggled to give his thanks to the elder as he tried to hold in his tears.

"There is no shame in tears being shed here," John said in Cherokee. "Her spirit is listening to your words, son."

Tears fell from David's eyes as he gave his thanks. John and David then walked toward the rest of the family.

Lisa and Jacob then stood before the wooden casket, and Lisa began to wail even harder. She gave praise to the Father for putting Elder Joyce into her life. Jacob also gave thanks to Joyce for the love she showed him. Lisa put her hand onto Elder Joyce's chest as tears hit her hands. She leaned over and kissed Elder Joyce's forehead, and the couple slowly approached the rest of the family.

Lizzie stood firmly at the edge of their group, her gaze anchored on the coffin.

Annabelle approached the coffin, still holding Jannie's and Rain's hands. She sobbed as she looked at the lifeless body of her mentor. "Your wisdom was from the heavens. Without you, I wouldn't be speaking to you as I am now. I am Cherokee because of you. You helped my spirit and soul heal. There will never be another you, and I'm blessed to have witnessed what greatness is. I learned how to truly be a woman from you. I will try my hardest to pass this on to my daughters, and to their daughters when that time comes. We will see each other again, Grandmother. Thank you."

The twins then gave their thanks, and they joined the rest of the family.

Annabelle stopped and glanced back at Lizzie, finding her unmoved. She turned around and kept walking.

"I have often fed my evil wolf, but you still loved me," Lizzie said in Cherokee.

Annabelle's eyes widened, and she looked back at Lizzie who was now standing in front of the coffin. More sunlight had broken through the clouds and reflected off Lizzie's tears as they streamed down her face.

Lizzie continued, "I was filled with so much anger, bitterness, and hate, but you worked with me. Now you are with the ancestors...my momma, Auntie Shay. There will be no other like you!" She then broke down in tears and held Elder Joyce's lifeless hands. "Thank you is not enough, Grandmother! I love you. We will see each other again! I know this." Lizzie gave a kiss to Elder Joyce's forehead, but then left the church grounds as she was overcome with racking sobs.

Annabelle looked at Grace, and Grace turned to her. "She'll be back," Grace said. "We have to let her return on her own."

Annabelle nodded, calmly rubbing her thumb across Jannie's and Rain's hands. Several minutes passed as others in the tribe arrived and paid their respects to Elder Joyce's family. Pastor Bluebird then walked up to the coffin and began giving a brief speech. Lizzie returned with a clean face and stood next to her family. The church's choir then began to sing hymns, and the large crowd sang along. Annabelle could feel the Holy Spirit come among them with peace.

After a few more hymns were sung, Pastor Bluebird gave the eulogy for Elder Joyce. "Harmony, you may come up now," he calmly said.

Annabelle glanced to her left and saw Harmony embracing Lea, who was sobbing over her great-great grandmother. She gave Lea a kiss on her forehead and let go of her. *Oh, Lea... Keep your baby girl close, Harmony*, Annabelle thought.

The brown-skinned woman wore a black cloth dress and had her dark brown hair put into a hair bun. Harmony's bloodshot brown eyes scanned the crowd. Speaking in the Cherokee tongue, her voice rang, "From the depths of my soul, thank you for honoring my great-grandmother. There are many great stories of her we could all share. The presence of her love made everyone feel like you were her favorite. She was the greatest representation of what a Cherokee woman should be. She could be as calm as the winds of the spring, but she wouldn't hesitate to make her presence felt like one of the great storms. May

Jesus's love bring us peace as we do not say goodbye in our tongue, for our ancestors knew of the Creator's kingdom before White men got lost on the ocean and came to our shores.

"During *Nunna Daul Tsuny,* our Trail of Tears, she lost so much like many of us who were old enough to experience the evil of White men. She forgave them, though, and she taught me how to forgive them. As she was teaching me, she made it clear that our forgiveness of them is not forgetting what they did, but having the strength to let the Creator deal with their hate. Unforgiveness is enslavement, and I refuse to be a slave. I will be like my grandmother, free. Loving and free…strong and free in the spirit of our Creator and as our ancestors and the angelic hosts rejoice in her arrival at her new home within the Father's kingdom. There are no words strong enough to show how much I will miss her, but I will continue on her legacy, as will the rest of my family." Harmony began to sing a poem.

Annabelle's heart felt heavy as she heard Harmony's words. She looked down at the twins whose water-filled eyes were mesmerized by Harmony's powerful, saddened voice. She continued to rub her thumbs on the twins' hands to soothe them.

Harmony finished her poem, and the crowd shouted with praise to the Creator for the time they'd had with Elder Joyce. "We will see each other again, Grandmother," Harmony shouted through the tears streaming down her face.

Elder Joyce's body was then lowered into her grave, and Annabelle's family left the church grounds. As they walked away, a hawk flew over the burial site.

"Momma, is it true what Auntie Lisa said, that the eagles and hawks can carry our prayers up to heaven?" Jannie asked.

"Yes, they can, and every thanks and prayer for Elder Joyce has been heard," Annabelle replied. She spent the rest of the day redoing the twins' hair and processing the loss of their spiritual anchor.

Supper was the calmest Annabelle had ever experienced, with little being said but a lot of reassuring hugs and kisses being shared.

CHAPTER 12
Holding onto Hope

I N C ALEDONIA, M ISSISSIPPI, R IZA LEFT the mansion and headed toward the pig pens where she began to dump left-over food into the food trough. When she saw Master Rice approaching her, she quickly headed back to the mansion to avoid him.

"Come here, Riza," Rice said.

She kept going toward the mansion, ignoring Rice's call.

"I said come here, redskin, or do you need to get a beating?" Rice yelled.

Riza stopped and scowled. "What can I do for you, Master Rice?" she asked.

"You sure do like to test me," Rice bickered. "You know that's not a smart thing to do, little girl."

Riza continued to look at Rice with a lowered brow.

"My apologies. You not that much a girl anymore...are you?"

Riza sharply replied, "I'm thirteen years old. I'm sure that still makes me a girl."

"What if I told you I know what you did to Pearl? You dumped all that pig crap on Pearl, and it landed on cotton she was pick-ing."

Riza dismissively waved her hand. "I have no idea what you're talking about, Master Rice."

Rice squinted. "Are you saying Pearl is a liar?"

"Master Rice, all I'm saying is, why are you trusting a nigger? You need to think about believing what you hear from a woman who opens her legs for you."

Rice slapped Riza, causing her to fall. "You little grass nigger! You think I'm gonna tolerate a lie like that? I should beat your hide again."

Riza growled, "I didn't do what she said!"

"Explain all the messed up cotton we can't use no more."

"Mud from the wagons, or maybe one of the other slaves did it." Riza's tone dripped with sarcasm. "Remember, I'm not allowed to go to that part of the plantation, and I haven't been there."

Rice glared at Riza and pulled out his whip. He cracked the whip, barely missing Riza as she lunged out of the way. He said, "You keep talking to me like I'm your equal, I'll do more than whip you. Now did you or did you not ruin that cotton?"

Riza stood up and fixed a glare on Rice. "No, Master Rice, I didn't throw pig crap on a nigger. May I go do what Mrs. Wilma has instructed me to do now?"

Rice marched up to Riza while she stood her ground and grabbed her chin. "I have a hard time believing you, but since nobody else saw you, I'll have to let you go. I will be letting Mr. Plecker know of this." Rice pulled Riza closer, and she could smell his foul breath. "You keep in mind that I've had fun with an Indian girl before." Rice placed his hand on Riza's back, forcing her to stay in place while he placed his other hand on her right breast. "You not far away from being a young lady." His hand moved down from her back to the top of her buttocks, and he released Riza as her nose crinkled up and tears started to run down her face. "Remember, don't test me, or I'll make you into a woman. You understand me?"

"Yes, Master Rice," Riza said with stern tone.

Rice marched to the fields while Riza watched, gritting her teeth and digging her nails into her dress with clenched fists. Then she walked toward the mansion, stopping to kick one of the trees and scream before she walked inside. *He makes me want to take a bath*, she thought. She continued to work the rest of the day, making every effort to suppress her worry.

During this time, Joseph and Tom had been riding on a wagon to collect cotton baskets and give empty ones back to the field hands. The boys were exhausted and barely able to put the baskets on the wagon as Louis sat back and enjoyed his feet being kicked up on the wagon's seat. While Joseph and Tom took a cotton basket from a field slave, Pearl approached them with her cotton basket.

"Here, you boys take this. It full and heavy," Pearl said.

Joseph and Tom picked up the cotton basket and began to walk back to the wagon.

Pearl followed them. "Y'all know what Riza did to me?" she asked.

"No," Joseph said.

Pearl sharply replied, "That demon girl threw pig crap on me and run away. I told Master Rice, and she gonna get it. Her skin gonna bleed again!"

"You deserve much worse to happen to you," Joseph angrily replied.

Pearl raised her voice. "How dare you speak to me like that. You one of us. Riza *not* one of us, and never will be. You a Negro child, or is you blind? You not Riza or Susie."

Joseph folded his arms. "At least I know I can believe them."

"Riza will turn on you the first chance she get. The masters see both of you as Negro children. Is y'all smarter than our masters? I think not."

"I'm Cherokee. I ain't no nigger, even when I carry this cotton. My momma said to never accept it when people call me a nigger."

"My momma told me that too," Tom said.

"Well, yo' mommas ain't nothing," Pearl snarled. She grabbed another cotton basket and walked back into the cotton fields.

The boys later arrived at the cotton gin barn where Bo was busy working on a broken wagon. They began to take off the cotton baskets, both pouting over Pearl's hateful words.

Bo stopped working on the wagon and asked them, "What's wrong with both of y'all?"

"I can't stand Pearl. She's a mean woman," Joseph said. "And she always asks about Riza."

"Boy, that ain't nothing new. She always gonna have it in for Riza. You stay out the way when two women fight."

Tom replied, "Riza isn't a woman."

Bo replied, "She almost there. Y'all don't know better. Give it another year or two, she gonna look even more different than y'all see now. So, like I say, don't get involved."

"I know Riza won't turn into a mean woman like Pearl," Joseph said. "She keeps calling us Negroes, but we not Negroes! I'm Cherokee, not a Negro."

The boys began to carry the cotton baskets into the barn as Bo calmly followed them. "I understand y'all's anger. I wouldn't want to be a Negro if I had a choice either. Only thing for a Negro is to work the land. As Indians, y'all free, but they scared of y'all. I heard how the White men talk 'bout Indians."

"What did they say?" Tom asked.

Bo answered, "Not one good thing. If they could, they would shoot all of you and take the women as slaves, but there too many of y'all. That's what I heard them say. I'd say I didn't have Negro blood and be a Indian if I could. I'd die free instead of having a whip on my back."

"Well, I never said I don't have Negro blood. My momma is Negro," Joseph said. "I just said that I'm not Negro. I'm a half-breed like Tom."

Bo smiled at the two boys as he grabbed a hammer off a shelf. "I've heard both of you talk about yo mommas," he said. "Y'all miss them and wouldn't lie to someone about who they is. I guess y'all can claim what y'all want, but would it shame yo'r families if y'all lie and say you not Negro at all?"

Joseph's and Tom's eyes grew wide.

"I understand y'all don't want to be slaves. Y'all wasn't born slaves. It only make sense y'all don't want to be called what we is. Keep doing good here, and maybe it get easier for y'all. Maybe Riza or Susie give y'all strong babies."

Joseph's and Tom's eyes widened even more as they looked at Bo. Then they left the barn.

Bo began to chuckle as the boys walked back to the wagon. "You give it time and you boys won't see those two like you do now. When you fall in love, you feel different."

Joseph and Tom pulled off some more cotton baskets as Bo watched. "Bo, are you in love with someone?" Joseph asked.

"I did have someone when I was younger, but she was given away to the Miller family. I think of someone special now, but I pray to the Lord on it. I not ready to tell her yet. You got to be careful when you tell women how you feel."

"I think she would like you, Bo. The other slaves always say good things about you," Tom said with a grin.

Bo smiled and helped the boys carry in the cotton baskets. "Thank you for your words. Y'all don't listen to Pearl. She get jealous easy."

Joseph and Tom continued to off-load the cotton baskets and then went back to the fields. In the wagon, Joseph realized that Bo and Michael had similar casual attitudes and half-smiled.

❖

On October 20, 1860, Judy Mays and Daphne returned to the plantation to spend time with Wilma. Riza served the women as they talked, remaining obedient to gain more favor.

Master Plecker entered the dining room. "Ah, Judy Mays, Daphne, what a pleasure it is to see both of you," he said.

"Mr. Plecker, it's good to see you," Judy Mays said. "I was surprised that you weren't here when I came to visit not too long ago."

"Well, I was meeting with the Douglas family out in Tennessee. I think we may have found a good match for Kenneth if he behaves."

The women chuckled and sipped their tea.

"My father wishes me to tell you hello, and if time permits, he would like to go hunting with you," Judy Mays said, playfully pointing at Master Plecker.

"Tell him I said I would look forward to another hunting trip with him. Almost shot ourselves a cougar last time."

"You men and your guns," Daphne said. "I find it amusing how you men can't help but to shoot everything."

Mr. Plecker arrogantly replied, "We're doing what the Indians should've done a long time ago. Stupid prairie niggers never knew how to handle the land like a man should. They did nothing to civilize the land."

"Careful now, Mr. Plecker. That little redskin there might try to burn down your home again."

Riza felt her heart drop when the Pleckers stared at her as she stood at attention in her brown dress.

"Daphne, don't say such terrible things," Wilma said. "That day is best forgotten."

"Riza won't do something so foolish again. We have an understanding," Mr. Plecker said. "Isn't that right, Riza?"

"Yes, Master Plecker," Riza said.

Wilma replied, "It was my fault for thinking she had a Negro brain, but you know the Indian is a bit smarter. The good Lord knew how to make them for us. You got the Indian, they understand commands better, can work the fields, and, in my opinion, do better at cleaning the house than a Negro. Riza just needed to be reminded what her role here is, and we haven't had a problem from her since."

Daphne replied, "I wish Thaddeus had the temperament you do. He would've had her hanged for what she did."

Mr. Plecker folded his hands. "I think the good Lord would see better for me to educate Riza and show her what she did was terribly wrong. I'm glad she has learned quickly how to behave. It would have been a waste to lose her. Especially since I have plans to get more Indian children. Riza, bring in those crackers I like while I enjoy our company."

"As you wish," Riza said. She left the dining room and returned with the crackers.

Dorothy later brought in entrées for the guests. Wilma became more excited and wanted to show Daphne and Judy Mays how she wanted the staircases redone in the mansion.

Judy Mays politely declined to be shown so she could finish her cake. Wilma took Daphne to show her what she wanted while Mr. Plecker followed.

With a slight grin, Judy Mays's blue eyes shifted to Riza. "The last time I was here, Riza, you said you knew someone with a certain name," she said. "What was that name?"

"Annabelle, Mrs. Judy Mays," Riza quietly said.

"Where did you hear that name before?"

"I heard it from an Indian boy. His mother's name is Annabelle."

Judy Mays exhaled when she took a sip of tea. "Never mind, there's no way the boy is connected to who I'm looking for then."

"Well, no, I don't think so, but she's the mother of a half-breed here."

Judy Mays squinted. "Don't play games with me, Riza Moon. I know you're smart enough to know I don't take pleasure in having a slave whipped, but don't test me."

Riza looked at Judy Mays, her brow somewhat furrowed. "I'm speaking the truth. I know he wasn't born a slave, and I know for a fact his mother is a Negro named Annabelle."

Judy Mays continued to look at Riza, her finger lightly tapping her teacup. She looked to seeing if Wilma was still talking to Daphne, then continued, "Why would you tell me?"

"Maybe I have a soft spot for you."

Judy Mays grinned and lightly scoffed. "Since you were a little girl, I've enjoyed your quick wit. I still fail to see why you would say something."

"Honestly, I thought it was the only way I could say thank you for telling me the truth about my tribe. You seemed sad when her name was mentioned, so I said something."

"What proof could you possibly have that this boy is linked to the person I'm looking for?"

"I'm not saying he is. I honestly don't think it's possible because he's from Indian Territory. I'm only saying how many former slaves do you know with a nice name like that? I have no reason to lie about what I know."

Judy Mays continued to lightly tap her teacup and stare at

Riza. "Giving me this information must cost something. You're a clever child."

"You made me feel happy. I wanted to make you feel happy, but if you're talking about cost, we haven't played any mind games lately." Riza withheld her smile. "I know I scared everyone, but I'd like to hear one of your mysteries." Her brow lifted. "You also seemed really interested in seeing this former slave."

Judy Mays's voice deepened. "Let me tell you something, little girl. She isn't a former slave. She is still by law owned by my family."

Riza's face went blank, and her eyes shifted from Judy Mays.

Judy Mays bit her lip and quietly exhaled. "Annabelle is none of your business. She escaped over a decade ago. I know you're different from the others...you and Dorothy. I know there's something else running through that vindictive mind of yours. I'll let it go though."

"Do you miss the slave?"

Judy Mays crossed her legs. "I do miss her. I can admit that much."

Riza's eyes widened. "She was more than a slave to you, wasn't she?"

A leer slowly etched on Judy Mays's face, but it dropped when she noticed Wilma and the others walking back into the dining hall.

"Judy Mays, is everything all right? You look so serious," Wilma said.

"Oh, well, no. I was pleased with how well Riza made the tea," Judy Mays said. "It has the right ingredients in the right amounts."

Wilma smiled. "Good. You must take a look at what I'm talking about doing once you get done with your food."

Judy Mays gave a fake smile. "Of course, I will take a look."

As the afternoon passed, Daphne and Judy Mays prepared to return to Columbus, Mississippi. "It is always so marvelous to come out and visit," Daphne said.

"Yes, I certainly plan on making another trip very soon, especially before this winter takes over the land," Judy Mays said.

Wilma joyfully replied, "Good. I look forward to it!"

Judy Mays smirked. "Wilma, you said you have four Indian slaves now, correct?"

"Why, yes. There's three children you know and our new addition. Why do you ask?"

"I was just making sure I was paying attention. We talk about so much in such a short amount of time."

Wilma giggled. "Yes, that's true."

Daphne and Judy Mays got into the carriage.

"Drive safe now," Wilma called out as the carriage rode off. Then she went inside the mansion with Riza following her.

Later in the night as Mr. Plecker and Wilma lay in the bed and read, Wilma looked over at Mr. Plecker. "Calvin, I was pleased that you joined us today," she said, smiling.

"It was my pleasure, dear. I remember enjoying their company when they were children, and now they're young women. I know it pleases you, having a younger crowd around you," Calvin said.

"I must admit. Daphne does test my patience a bit. Always bringing up Riza...the child has been dealt with."

"She may always bring it up, dear. You'll either have to tell her to stop or tolerate it. I think Riza scares her a bit."

Wilma chuckled. "Poor Daphne, child wouldn't know what to do with Riza. Riza would rule her household. I'm grateful you thought about Riza's punishment. I would've hated to replace her."

"I know, dear. That was part of the reason for my decision. It would grow tiresome teaching another Indian child what their role in this world is. Riza's rebellion was a call for help. She now fully understands her limitations, and I doubt she'll even try something on that scale again."

"When she gets older, she should be placed with a strong slave so she can produce healthy children."

"How about Joseph? I like the boy's flexibility with the animals."

Wilma raised an eyebrow. "What do you mean?"

"The animals like him and are patient with the boy when he

feeds them. Especially the two bulls we have. The other slaves are too stupid to work with the bulls and are scared of them. Since the boy has been feeding them, I've seen less wasted corn feed on the ground."

"No, not him, Calvin. He looks too Negro for my liking. I want Riza to produce nicer looking children like Dorothy has done. Please send her to Tom when they're of age. He doesn't have the nappy hair and has a nice color to him."

"Then what about Susie?"

"Susie is nice looking for an Indian child. She and Joseph are from the same tribe, and I think they'll be more willing to give us offspring we can put over the other slaves. Odds are they'll look more like Susie and be appropriate for serving our guests."

Calvin nodded. "All right, I can agree to such an arrangement in the next few years. Stability is what is most important, and I do believe Susie is the most obedient of the Indian children. Her character will certainly give us more responsive slaves that can think."

"What can you tell me about this young lady you were scouting at the Douglass plantation?"

"She is a nice young thing to look at. She's seventeen and ready for a husband. I think she'll certainly catch Kenneth's attention. She is obedient, speaks when she is spoken to, and dresses respectably. She's what the boy needs in his life."

The corners of Wilma's mouth curved into a smile. "Good. I like her already. He needs someone who will follow him."

"I was thinking about giving him one of Dorothy's daughters as a gift."

Wilma's smile faded. "Calvin, did you know Kenneth had promised Dorothy the girls would never be separated?"

Calvin's voice rose as he said, "That boy did what?! Who gave him authority to make that decision?"

"Calvin, please calm down. I'm sorry I didn't bring it up earlier. So listen to me. Because of Dorothy's faithful services and her disgusting encounters with Geoffrey, which produced those two girls, Kenneth made her the promise. He has always been a sweet boy, and he and Dorothy are only separated by a year. He wants to be a man of his word."

"Still, I won't have any more behavior like this!" Calvin raised his voice higher. "Riza was enough! Enough, I tell you! That little savage is blessed that I'm the man I am, or I would've had her hanged and set on fire. Are there any more surprises I should know?"

"No, dear, I know of nothing else."

Calvin sighed. "I enjoy having those Indian children here, knowing their place. That's the problem with the rest of them out there in the wilderness. They don't know their role in this world. My great-granddaddy had more Indian slaves than Negroes, and his plantation was more productive than my granddaddy's who had almost no Indians. The same with my pa. Riza is the leader, and the more we control her, the more we control the others. No more surprises in this house."

"I understand," Wilma calmly said.

"My boy wants to be responsible and keep his word? Well, then I'll give him both of the girls. Dorothy will stay here."

"What if Kenneth wants all three of them?"

"Bah, I don't want to think about it. I want to give him something if things do work out with him and Reece Douglas."

"That's a pretty name, Reece. When is she planning to visit?"

"I scheduled a trip in January for their first meeting at a gathering. I want to talk to Kenneth first though. I don't want to rush him."

"This is exciting! My youngest is finally going to grow up." Wilma kissed Calvin and snuggled next to him. "All I need now is for Cornelius to show up more often."

Staring into the darkness, Calvin placed his arm around Wilma as she fell asleep.

———◆———

Over the next few days, the rest of the cotton was gathered and brought in from the fields. Joseph and Tom were then assigned to help cook the butchered cattle and gather firewood. The butchering of the cattle was traumatizing for Joseph. It was different from a chicken being butchered. Lizzie killed chickens quickly, but the boys could hear the tied-up cattles' moans while they were beaten to death by three slave men. The smell of the old barn made Joseph nauseous when he saw the entrails, which smelled worse than those of a deer or pronghorn. All of this was done in preparation for the coming winter.

On November 4, 1860, Joseph and Tom were escorted by the overseers to the forest to cut firewood. It was the first time Joseph had experienced such cold. The clothes given to him for the winter were nothing like what he wore in Tahlequah, and even still the cold made his fingers and toes hurt.

Joseph and Tom struggled to bring more wood to the wagon on a sled they pulled behind them. As they worked, Louis gave the boys snobbish looks. As the boys loaded the wood in the wagon, Louis bickered, "You two little niggers need to move faster. I get cold easy, and y'all move too slow."

The man tested Joseph's patience as he clearly had no regard for any of the other slaves.

Joseph blurted, "I'll hit you with this firewood if you talk to me like that again. I'm cold too." His heart suddenly dropped, and he looked behind him to see if Master Wade or Master Kit had heard his outburst, but the men kept watching the other slaves.

"You think you can talk to me like that, nigger?"

"I'll hit you with this firewood too," Tom said.

The two boys stared Louis down while he sat in the seat of the wagon. "Y'all little Negros gone crazy to speak to me like that. I'll beat y'all like our masters."

Joseph angrily replied, "We're half-breeds. The only nigger here is you. I should tell Riza what you said to us so she can light you on fire."

Louis pouted. "She wouldn't do that to me."

"I bet she would if we told her what you said to us," Tom said.

Louis pointed at the boys. "Y'all niggers ain't nothing, and she ain't nothing. Nothing but grass niggers."

"Keep talking to us like that and wood will hit your head," Joseph snarled.

The boys continued putting wood on the wagon while Louis scowled and spit on the ground and some of the other slaves sang hymns. Joseph listened to them, especially to Cecil, who was responsible for starting most of the slave hymns. And he began to think about what Bo had said to him and Tom. Was he really ashamed his mother was Negro, and would he ever lie about being half Negro?" The question terrified Joseph.

Joseph soon found himself humming along with the singing slaves. "We cut good wood for Master's fire," Cecil sang, leading the other slaves in chorus. "We march to cut them trees like angels march to serve the Lord. We hear them trees fall for Master's fire. Yes, we cut good wood for Master's fire. We cut good wood for Master's fire. Trees don't like my axe, but we cut good wood for Master's fire. We pray Lord bless us, 'cause we cut good wood for Master's fire. We cut good wood for Master's fire."

Tom's jaw dropped and he gaped at Joseph. "Why are you humming that song?" he asked.

"I'm not ashamed of my momma, so I hum for her," Joseph said. "Are you ashamed of your pa?"

Tom smiled at Joseph. "No, I miss him." He began humming along with Joseph while they gathered the wood.

To Joseph and Tom, it was a form of rebellion to be proud of being Indian and Negro, and they refused to be seen as only Negro.

During the night of November 10, 1860, a snowstorm arrived in Caledonia. A cold wind eased its way into the slave house and enveloped the group huddled together on the cold wood floor with nothing more than one blanket each. Joseph awoke shivering and looked around, his gaze falling on Mary, also awake and shivering. He rolled over to Mary, and they wrapped their blankets around each other, doubling their shield against the cold.

"Thank you, Joseph," Mary whispered.

"You're welcome," Joseph said.

Soon his and Mary's shaking began to decline as their bodies warmed up.

The next morning as Joseph and the others woke up and prepared their breakfast, there were constant creaking noises from the cabin's structure. Brushed off as a strong wind from the storm, they ate their breakfast and got ready for the day. Finished with her breakfast, Stella went to open the door when the roof collapsed. The children screamed while the snow covered the inside of the slave house.

Bo was about to look for the overseers when he saw Master Plecker on the porch of the mansion. He quickly walked up the dirt trail and then slowly approached Master Plecker, lowered his head, and spoke with him. Bo returned to the slave houses with Plecker calmly walking behind him. Plecker stood before the slave house and crossed his arms. He called for Wade and Rice, spoke with the men, and had them inspect the damage before he returned to the mansion.

"All right, Joseph, Tom, and Clint, y'all going to put a new roof up," Wade said. "Y'all gonna take the lumber over by the cattle barn and use it to put up a new roof. Bo is gonna tell y'all what to do, and if y'all don't finish by night, I suggest you prepare for a cold sleep."

"Yeah, dying in the cold ain't a fun way to go," Rice said.

The two men stepped away to oversee the rest of the day's work.

Bo walked over shortly after with a ladder and tools. "All right, boys, we do this fast," he said. "No choice here. You wouldn't be the first Negroes to sleep in the cold." Then he tasked Joseph and Tom with shoveling the snow out of the house as he and Clint measured the wood.

The two boys struggled to move the snow quickly because the shovels were small and their hands hurt from the cold. They took breaks and placed their hands into their armpits to warm them.

"Bo, are y'all done measuring the wood?" Joseph asked.

Bo replied, "We almost done, but all that snow still gotta be moved."

"We have to hurry, Joseph," Tom said. "If we don't finish this, we might freeze tonight. I don't think Master Wade was joking when he said he would make us sleep in here."

"My hands are so cold, and my clothes are wet from the snow falling on me," Joseph said.

Tom replied, "My clothes are still wet too, but we have to do this. We have to think of Mary and Stella."

As Joseph and Tom shoveled out the snow, Joseph looked at the broken wood lying in the house and smiled. "That's it. I know how we can do this faster." Joseph grabbed the broken pieces of wood and put them into the stove and made a fire.

"That was really smart! It feels a lot warmer already," Tom said.

Joseph smiled at Tom, and the boys worked to remove the rest of the snow and then helped Bo and Clint put on a new roof. The cold made it harder to focus, but out of desperation, they pushed to get it done. To warm themselves, Bo, Clint, Joseph, and Tom took breaks warming themselves by the fire inside the slave house. Stella and two other women brought them food when they were allowed to eat. The slaves finished the roof right before sunset and were about to take the tools back when they saw Rice walking toward them.

"Looks like you boys managed to get this done before the sun goes down," Rice callously said. He stood before Joseph and the others and looked at the roof. "I think you boys need to thank Bo here. I know y'all wouldn't know what to do if he wasn't here." He looked inside the house and saw the light from the fire. "How did y'all make a fire? Y'all can't gather firewood until the sun goes down."

"The boys was smart. It was hard putting the roof up when it was cold, Master Rice," Bo said. "The boys used that bad wood to make the fire. We finished 'cause we was warm and it helped us work faster."

"You little niggers took that wood and it's burning now!" Rice yelled. He slapped Joseph, knocking him down. "The rule is y'all can't use no wood meant for slaves until that sun goes down. So you using that wood because you boys think it no good?"

Rice was about to grab Joseph when Tom stepped in front

of him holding a hammer. "It was me, Master Rice," he said. "I made the fire. Joseph didn't make it. It was my plan."

Rice replied, "So you think you brave now? I always thought you was one of the smarter ones. Riza and the others got off easy for what they did, and now you want to stand in my way. Did I ask you which one of you made the fire?"

"No, Master Rice. You didn't ask us who made the fire."

Rice rubbed his unshaved face while he glared down at Tom. "Be careful, boy. Being too smart comes at a price. Have you seen Riza's back? Those nice tiny scars she has now…well, I guarantee I'll make sure you have some big scars if you overstep your bounds again."

"Yes, Master Rice. I won't do it again."

Rice swept his glare from Tom to Joseph, then Bo and Clint. "I don't like how Indian children keep finding ways to teach these niggers what to do. Give me that hammer in your hand, boy."

Tom gulped and tightened his grip on the hammer.

"I said give me that hammer!" Rice grabbed for the hammer.

Tom held onto the hammer. "I'm sorry, Master Rice."

"Tom, you rebellious half-breed, I'll tear your hide!" Rice pulled the hammer from Tom's grip and swung it at Tom, hitting his arm.

Tom screamed in pain and held his arm. Rice hit him on the back, causing the boy to fall to his knees. Joseph was about to lunge at Rice when Bo grabbed him and pulled him back. Rice hit Tom in the back with the hammer three more times as Bo, Clint, and Joseph watched in terror.

"I'm sorry," Tom cried.

"Boy, you ain't sorry yet. That wasn't nothing, but if you ever do that again, it won't be a hammer I use on you. I'll crack that whip on your nigger back so hard that any Indian blood left in you will stain the ground." Rice kicked Tom. "Now get this half-breed redskin up before I change my mind and whip him too, Bo."

"Yes, Master Rice. I get him now," Bo said. He helped Tom stand, noticing the boy couldn't move his arm. "Master Rice, I don't think he can move his arm."

Rice spit on the ground and glared at Tom. "Take him to Dorothy so he can get done what needs to get done. He's working tomorrow with one arm or two. That boy will work."

"Yes, Master Rice."

Bo escorted a crying Tom to the mansion. Joseph was about to follow them when Rice put the hammer to his chest. "Now, did I say you could go to the mansion?" Rice asked.

Joseph gulped, nervously replying, "No, Master Rice, you didn't."

"Well…now you thinking, ain't you? You and Clint, y'all take these tools back to the barn, and you remember to do as you're told, or I might give Susie some lashes to make up for your disobedience. I think it's only fair since you took her lashes. Don't you, boy?"

Joseph pursed his lips as he calmly took the hammer from Rice. "No, Master Rice. I think I should get the lashes I deserve. Susie isn't Jesus."

Rice laughed. "That must be the funniest thing I ever did hear a slave say. Get out of here before you say something that'll make me mad."

Clint and Joseph quickly left, carrying the tools they could. As they made their way through the snow, to the barn, Joseph noticed some of the other slaves glancing at them.

Later in the day, Joseph and the others ate the food rations they had for supper and waited patiently for Tom's return. Dorothy returned with Tom and explained his arm was probably fractured. She was unsure as to how long it was going to take to fully heal, but said he would be able to use his arm normally again. Guilt fell onto Joseph when he looked at Tom's bandaged arm.

As Tom ate, he noticed Joseph's quiet nature and stopped eating. "It wasn't your fault, Joseph," he said. "I think in some way I deserved this for not leaving with you and the others."

"That's not true," Joseph said. "It was scary and crazy. You would've been whipped like me. I would rather have a bad arm for a little bit than to get hit like that again. You know Wade hit Riza so hard her back tooth fell out."

Tom frowned. "I only want you to know this wasn't your fault. Master Rice is an evil man. I hope one day he gets hurt for what he does to us."

"There be no talk like that here," Stella said. "Master Rice wasn't right for hurting you. But no more of this, y'all children fighting the masters. First Riza, now y'all talking like this. Please speak none of this. Pearl will try her hardest to hurt Riza. That means hurting y'all to hurt Riza, and I can't watch Pearl all the time, so stop this talk."

"Sorry, Stella," Tom said.

"Pray and be good servants. I know the Lord will bless us. Now come sit closer in a circle so we can sing to the Lord. Be happy we got masters we got...it could be badder."

The boys moved closer to Stella, Clint, and Mary and started singing slave hymns. The songs reminded Joseph of the suppers he'd had with his family. There was always a story being told or something funny Tsula had to say. Stella often told Joseph old fables, always cooked for him, would give him hugs, and prayed over him and the other children before they had to work. Slowly Joseph realized the love Stella was showing him and the others.

———◆———

The winter temperatures settled in, continuing to make it hard on the slaves as Christmas arrived. Master Plecker had decided the slaves were to be allowed a free day not to work, Since Riza was still forbidden to go to the slave houses, Clint, Joseph, and Tom walked over to her quarters to visit with her.

As they talked to each other, Clint looked at something that had caught his eye and then said, "Bo go inside Master's house."

"Are you sure Bo went inside?" Riza asked.

"Yeah, I know he did."

"Stay here. I'll be right back." Riza entered the mansion through the kitchen pathway and cracked the double door. She saw Bo kneeling before Master Plecker and Wilma but couldn't fully hear what he was saying.

"Riza, what are you doing?" Dorothy whispered.

Startled, Riza jumped up and then exhaled in relief that it

was Dorothy. "I'm listening to Bo talk to Master Plecker. I think something is wrong," she whispered in reply.

"Bo is inside the mansion? What could he want?"

"That's what I'm trying to learn," Riza replied. Then she and Dorothy cracked the double door and watched intensely while Master Plecker slowly paced and rubbed his blond beard, then nodded his head and looked at Wilma, who was smiling.

"Dorothy, come out here," Master Plecker yelled.

Dorothy quickly opened the double door while Riza backed up against the counter so she wouldn't be seen.

"Dorothy, we'll be having a wedding today. I want you to prepare some dinner rolls to celebrate. I have given permission for Bo to marry Stella."

Dorothy smiled as she looked at Bo and said, "Yes, Master Plecker. I'll start immediately." Then she returned to the kitchen, finding Riza waiting with a big grin. Dorothy said, "I can tell by the look on your face you heard that."

"So, they're getting married today?" Riza asked.

"Yes, they are. Master Plecker has approved, and I'm sure Bo has already run out of the mansion to tell Stella. I'm happy for them."

Riza smiled. "I need to go tell the others."

"I'm surprised you won't stay with me and make the dinner rolls. That's the one thing you like to make."

"I'll come back after I tell Susie and the others."

"All right. Be quick so we can give them all the daytime to celebrate."

Riza was about to leave but looked back at Dorothy, "Will you ever marry someone?"

Dorothy's eyes widened, and she continued to look down at the mixing bowls she'd placed on the counter. "Maybe someday I will. Hopefully on my own terms, out of love, like Bo and Stella. I've seen masters tell slaves who to lay with, and I've seen it happen several times here. All we can do is hope and pray we never see such a day."

Later in the day, Master Plecker allowed the slaves to have a celebration for Bo's marriage proposal. The field slaves gathered in front of the slave houses to celebrate while Kit, Rice, and Wade stood in the background observing. Dorothy, Emma, and two other house slaves brought them dinner rolls. Still on punishment, Riza and Susie remained inside the mansion with Mrs. Wilma. Dorothy and the other house slaves handed out the rolls. The other slaves cheered, clapped, stomped their feet on the ground to make a beat, and danced. Emma quieted the other slaves and put a broom on the ground. It was the weirdest thing Joseph had seen, but it fascinated him.

"Here today we celebrate Master Plecker's blessing to Bo and Stella," Emma said. "Master is good to us, and the Lord blesses us to see this. Bo and Stella, y'all jump the broom now."

Bo and Stella held hands and jumped the broom. The slaves cheered as the couple shared a kiss.

Emma raised her hands and the corners of her mouth curved upward to form a big grin. "Now we'll all see you as husband and wife as Master Plecker has blessed."

Joseph turned to Tom, asking, "Why did they jump a broom?"

"I was told jumping the broom is how we recognize their marriage even though it's not like how White people get married," Tom answered as he took another bite out of his dinner roll. "So, welcoming the new and sweeping away the old to join two families."

Joseph's mouth curved upward, forming a large smile. "I think it's a fun way to show they love each other." He turned his gaze to Bo and Stella, who were now dancing together.

Emma picked up the broom and turned to head back to the mansion with a big grin.

Tom stopped her, asking, "Emma, I forgot to ask Riza, but do you know when she can visit us?"

Emma answered, "I don't know when Master gonna let her come to this part again. The good Lord was with her that day."

"Why do you say that?" Joseph interjected.

"'Cause Master Plecker didn't have her killed." Emma walked away.

Joseph's mouth curved downward, and his eyes lowered. However, as he watched the other slaves celebrate Bo and

Stella's union, he wondered how his parents had celebrated their marriage. All the slaves could do was clap, stomp their feet, and sing to celebrate.

That night Joseph and the others slept in another slave house so Bo and Stella could be alone. Joseph thought it was special to dance the night away, believing that was why they were spending the night alone.

◆

On December 30, 1860, Annabelle was sitting at the supper table, playing with the string on Joseph's bow, when a sudden knock startled her. She opened the door and found Molly in a light blue winter dress and white bonnet.

"Hello, Annabelle. The others said you were here. May I come in?" Molly asked.

Annabelle replied, smiling, "Come in, Molly. We can have a seat at the supper table."

Molly followed Annabelle to the table and sat down next to her.

"We haven't seen you in two weeks. How are you?" Annabelle said.

"I'm doing well. We were out in the Choctaw territory since the snow cleared up. How are you doing?"

"I'm doing all right. Grateful for what we have. We have just enough food to feed ourselves but not enough to give to the others like we could last year."

"I imagine Grace isn't pleased with that."

"No, she isn't, but we try to keep her mind away from it. We make sure she eats good for the baby. She's an unselfish woman."

"That's a true statement." Molly's smile faded. "I do have a hard time believing you're completely well with Joseph still missing."

Annabelle exhaled and looked away from Molly.

"Annabelle, please be honest; it's not a sin to be honest."

Annabelle threw her hands up. "What do you want me to say? That I look at my children now and feel empty? I see the look in David's eyes every time he sees Joseph's bow, and it breaks my heart. That's why I keep it here, so my son doesn't have to be reminded every day in his room that his brother is gone." She sighed. "Elder Joyce was given a prophetic word before she walked on, that Joseph was alive and that one day we would have him back. But I can't help but question why we have to wait so long."

"I understand your pain, but trust what Elder Joyce told you. Trust that the Lord will be faithful."

Annabelle's voice elevated. "No! You don't understand because you have never lost a child!" She gasped as she looked at Molly's frown. "Molly…I'm so sorry, that wasn't right of me."

Molly began to sniffle as she reached for Annabelle's hand. "That was honesty. It was painful honesty, but it was honesty. I've noticed Christians have a terrible time with being honest about our pain. I want to encourage you to hold onto your hope no matter how much time passes. I believe Elder Joyce's words, and I also know God is faithful." Then she smiled, took Annabelle's hand, and placed it on her stomach.

"Molly…oh, Molly, I'm so happy for you!" Annabelle quickly gave Molly a hug.

Molly tightly hugged Annabelle back. "Don't lose hope, Annabelle. Just don't lose it."

"How far along are you?"

"I noticed about two weeks ago the changes started to happen. Reverend Hills is overly excited and already wants me to start knitting baby blankets. Even if I can only give him one child, I'm a blessed woman. Can I pray for you, Annabelle?"

"Yes, I do need some of that."

Molly prayed for Annabelle and spent the rest of the day with the Lightning-Strongman family to share the blessed news of her pregnancy. The family decided to make supper for her to celebrate and welcomed Reverend Hills to join them.

CHAPTER 13
The Winds of Change

IN MISSISSIPPI, JOSEPH AND THE others continued their struggle against the cold winter temperatures while trying to remain on Rice's and Wade's good sides. As the weeks passed, Tom's left arm healed slowly, but he tried his best to finish work quickly to avoid punishment. During some of the breaks, Susie would go to the cookhouse and wait for Joseph, Tom, or Mary to show. When the overseers weren't looking, Joseph and Susie would go to the back of the cookhouse and whisper to each other in Cherokee. Like Riza, Susie was still forbidden from visiting the others at the slave houses. But speaking their first language and socializing with the other slave children was a stress relief and strengthened their friendship. Susie would also relay messages from Riza to Joseph in Cherokee.

In late February of 1861, Kenneth and Master Plecker rode out to Tennessee to attend a gathering at the Douglas plantation. During their trip, they discussed the recent formation of the Confederacy and Mississippi's earlier seceding from the Union. Emma had spread the news Master Kenneth was going on a trip to possibly meet his new wife, which caught the attention of all the slaves. They began questioning what this woman would be like and if it meant Master Kenneth would be leaving the plantation immediately after getting married.

When the men arrived back at the mansion, they were excitedly welcomed home.

"My boys are home! Dorothy, you come out here with some tea," Wilma said. "How did it go? Please tell me!"

"Reece is a nice girl, Momma. I must admit she surprised me," Kenneth said.

Wilma smiled. "Good, good. I want to meet her. We must have her come for a visit."

"Calm down, Wilma. We've already set up an arrangement for another visit to their home, and we can schedule one here for the two to get to know each other better," Mr. Plecker said.

"When are we are leaving?" Wilma asked.

"Next Thursday we'll leave and arrive there on Friday. I'm sure you'll be pleased."

"Good! I look forward to it."

Dorothy came through the double doors with a silver tea set on a platter.

Wilma said, "Ah, Dorothy, you must hear the good news. Kenneth's meeting with the Douglas family was a success. We'll be leaving Thursday to meet them, and next week we will host Miss Reece here. Isn't that exciting?"

Dorothy looked at Kenneth with a blank expression. "Yes, Mrs. Wilma, it is exciting," she said in a dull tone.

"Place the tea in the living room. I'm looking forward to talking more about this Reece," Wilma enthusiastically said.

"As you wish, Mrs. Wilma." Dorothy's gaze shifted back to Kenneth, her lips pursed. "Master Kenneth, do you want dinner rolls?"

Kenneth avoided eye contact with Dorothy as he replied, "No, but thank you, Dorothy."

Dorothy went into the living room and placed the tea on the table, then returned to the kitchen.

⸻ ◆ ⸻

On the afternoon of February 27, 1861, Lizzie walked through the melting snow and entered Grace's home. Annabelle and Grace were sitting in the living room, warming by the lit fireplace adjacent to the front door. Lizzie's long braid swayed as she closed the door behind herself.

"I figured you were going to show up soon," Grace said in her native tongue.

Lizzie replied, "How did you guess that?"

Grace grinned. "The twins were starting to argue."

Lizzie sat down on a wooden chair. "Yeah, I didn't want to hear all that. It's like an urge they can't grow out of. We don't argue like them anymore."

Grace side-eyed Lizzie and joked, "Oh, sister, no, we don't. You stab cutting boards instead."

Lizzie puckered her lips into a pout. "Whatever. I haven't done that in a long time."

Smirking, Annabelle spoke in Cherokee, "You can send a strong message."

Lizzie anchored her brown eyes onto Annabelle while withholding her smile, then her gaze shifted back to Grace. "Don't you have a piece of bread to chew on for that baby?"

Grace sarcastically answered, "I swear I think you're trying to make me fat."

Lizzie chuckled. "Maybe."

Grace smacked her lips and lightly slapped Lizzie on her shoulder. "You and your smart mouth... I'm going to take a nap." She put her hand on her hip. "And then I'll eat something. Talking about don't I have a piece of bread to chew on... I can't wait for you to get pregnant." She stood up and kissed Annabelle on the cheek. "The grits are still warm if you want some, Lizzie."

Lizzie's eyes shifted to the black-colored Castrol stove and then back to Grace. "Okay."

Grace looked out the two windows through which warm sunlight beamed into the house. "With this cold weather, the plants are still sleeping. I'm sure they'll be excited as me when it warms up." She turned around and walked down the house's hallway to her bedroom.

Lizzie's eyes fixed on the burning fire. "How are you doing, Annabelle?"

Annabelle's eyes widened, and she exhaled. "I don't know. I

miss fixing his plate. I miss yelling at him to come inside when it is too cold to be outside. I miss holding him under the redbud tree and looking at the bison. I miss his laugh… I miss my baby so much. Last week was the first time I've been able to sleep through the night. My heart is hurting. I think about what those White men could be doing to my baby. The things he's seeing and hearing while the hate suffocates the land. It's like I'm lying to myself. I feel almost nothing…and this scares me. And I'm terrified of the twins or Rosita going anywhere alone. How are you?"

"I feel the same, but my fear is turning into anger," Lizzie said. "I'm trying my hardest to not be the old me." Her mouth etched into a frown, and her left hand gripped the chair's armrest. "I honestly need Elder Joyce. I hate that she's gone."

"I miss her too. She'd always pray over me for my parents and my brother Todd. I still think about them every day. I wonder if I'll see them again in this life or in heaven. But Joseph is mostly on my mind."

"Brock Jackson will pay for this with his blood one day."

Annabelle grimaced. "We must be careful. My spirit can't take any more losses."

Lizzie turned her head to Annabelle. "I miss my little Joseph. I miss him running into my room every morning. I miss his competitive spirit. I miss the smile you gave him."

Annabelle's eyes began to well up. "Yeah, he does have my smile."

Lizzie's gaze moved back to the fire. "One of the reasons I miss Elder Joyce so much is because she could always read me." A tear fell from her left eye. "She read through every lie I told."

Annabelle frowned. "She was gifted that way."

Tears suddenly streamed down Lizzie's face.

Eyes wide, Annabelle thought, *Oh, Lizzie.*

"Can you believe, she had the nerve to call me out one last time. Love is powerful, and it can hurt so much."

Annabelle's brows drew together. "You mean Jacob?"

"I thought letting him go meant the love would die. I was

wrong. I guess it's a lot easier to fall out of love when a man treats you like dirt or has a baby with another woman."

"You have a strong heart, Lizzie. Even if you still love Jacob, I know the Father has someone else in mind for you to make up for your pain."

"Still being in love with him makes me pathetic."

"No, it doesn't. He's not beating you. He's not killing your soul with his words. You're not pathetic."

Lizzie's voice rose. "Then what do you call it? He's married to Lisa. I'm a fool."

"You loved him before Lisa did. It doesn't make you a fool. It means you had the courage to open your heart. I think it's normal that you still love him. And for what it's worth, you haven't been trying to seduce him away from Lisa. There are women that would try to seduce Jacob...but not you. It shows you have great character."

"Elder Joyce said it's okay if I never stop loving him. She said I'll fall in love again, but that person must come before Jacob. I have to have my life in order."

Annabelle wiped away a tear. "The truth is, I've never stopped loving Benjamin, but I also love John. I believe Elder Joyce's words...no different from what she's said about Joseph."

Lizzie wiped away her tears and looked at Annabelle. "Lisa can never know the truth."

"I won't tell anyone."

Lizzie half-smiled. "I believe you. I hope we can bring Joseph home before the next winter."

Annabelle felt her heart pound harder and half-smiled. "So do I."

✦

On March 10, 1861, Joseph and Tom were instructed to bring the fresh-cut beef to the mansion. The two boys pushed a cart up to the house as a white carriage arrived. They saw Riza and Susie stand behind Wilma as she anxiously approached the carriage.

"Welcome, welcome, Reece," Wilma said. "I'm glad to see you have arrived safely."

A young blonde woman stepped out of the carriage wearing a red Victorian dress and red bonnet. She spoke to Wilma, but the boys couldn't hear what she was saying.

"She's a pretty White woman. Who's she here for?" Tom said.

Joseph replied, "Susie told me Master Kenneth had been visiting some lady to probably marry her. I guess that must be her."

Tom sighed. "So that's who we're bringing the fresh meat for. She is pretty. I think he's going to marry her, and if Master Kenneth leaves us, we might as well be in hell."

Joseph huffed. "Susie said even Dorothy seems a little upset about this White lady."

"Well, let's get this meat to Dorothy so we don't get in trouble. I hate how Master Rice looks at us."

Joseph and Tom walked to the cookhouse door and knocked on it.

Susie opened the door. "Hey, y'all, good timing. Dorothy is short-tempered today," she said. "She yelled at me for setting up the dining room table too slowly. She normally doesn't act like that."

"The new lady is here, and she's pretty," Joseph said.

Susie's mouth dropped a little. "Really? How pretty?"

Tom replied, "She looks nicer than Mrs. Daphne or Mrs. Judy Mays. I think she's younger than them."

"Really? We better hurry up. Dorothy wanted me to tell her immediately when Miss Reece arrived."

"Reece is her name?" Joseph asked.

Susie replied, "Yeah, I think that's a nice name. I never heard it before. Come inside while I tell Dorothy Miss Reece is here."

Joseph and Tom pulled the cart up to the door. As the boys helped Susie put the fresh meat on trays, Dorothy entered the kitchen through the back door. "Continue to move quickly so we can start cooking," she agitatedly said.

"Sorry. We'll move faster," Joseph said.

Dorothy stomped out to the cookhouse pathway with a grunt.

"What's wrong with Dorothy?" Tom asked.

"I don't know. She's been like this since yesterday," Susie said with a concerned tone. "I think she wants Miss Reece to be impressed. We should take a look."

The children went down the pathway, entered the mansion, and quietly stepped up to the double doors. They cracked the doors open and peeked out. There stood Dorothy, eye to eye with Miss Reece who had a marginally smaller frame.

"Right on time, Dorothy. This is Miss Reece. She'll be joining us for supper," Wilma cheerfully said.

"Good afternoon, Miss Reece," Dorothy said.

"So this is Dorothy," Reece said. "I was surprised Kenneth would even mention a slave in some of our conversations. I see why. She is a pretty little mulatto. Even her hair is somewhat decent, Mrs. Plecker. Almost as nice as Riza's."

Wilma chuckled while Dorothy quietly took a deep breath and Riza forced a smile.

Wilma replied, "She is something. She has even produced two very lovely children. Doris and Daisy, y'all come down here right now. We have them polish, dust, and fold the bedsheets because of their young age, but they're efficient."

Doris and Daisy carefully walked down the stairs as Dorothy and the others watched.

Wilma said, "Ah, good. Children, this is Miss Reece. She'll be our guest for a few days."

"Good afternoon, Miss Reece," the girls said.

"It's rare to say this, but these are beautiful girls for mulattos," Reece said. "I'd imagine if you wanted to sell one, you would have extremely high bidders."

Dorothy's eye twitched as she clutched her right hand into a half fist.

Reece continued, "Especially the youngest. My word, Mrs. Plecker, I must admit I'm jealous."

"Don't say such things, Reece, and besides, we have decided to keep the girls together. Dorothy has been exceptionally loyal since she was a child here, and as a reward, we decided no such sale would take place."

"Mrs. Plecker, I've never heard of bargaining with a slave."

"Oh, no, this is no bargain. This was an act of kindness from a Christian household. We find that to be very important. Our slaves know their place. Isn't that right, Riza?"

Riza moved her damaged pinky behind her back and calmly replied, "Yes, Mrs. Wilma."

"I must admit, I'm pleased with the humbleness of your home even though a slave should know their place in any case," Reece said. "Dorothy, I'll have a glass of water."

Dorothy struggled to smile while she stared at Reece's ringlet-styled blonde hair and nodded to her. She then turned to go to the kitchen.

"Dorothy, what was that?" Wilma asked.

Dorothy took a deep breath and turned around with a smile. "My apologies, Mrs. Wilma. I'm so excited to have Miss Reece here," she said. "I'll get her water immediately." She turned around and walked toward the kitchen pathway.

"Hold it. Tell those Indian children to come out here. I saw their little eyes looking through that door. I guess even they're excited about your arrival, Reece."

"Yes, Mrs. Wilma." Dorothy went through the double doors just in time to see Joseph and Tom rush out the doorway and run toward the cookhouse. Dorothy angrily pushed the back door open and bellowed, "Get in here, both of you! Mrs. Wilma wants both of you in there right now!"

Startled by Dorothy's authoritative tone, the two boys stopped immediately, spun on their heels, and ran inside the mansion. On the other side of the double doors, they stood before Wilma with their hearts racing.

"Ah, here are our half-breed Indian slaves, Joseph and Tom," Wilma said. "Look at them, healthy, strong boys. I'm fully confident in their ability to serve you for many years to come."

"My, Mrs. Plecker, they do look strong for boys," Reece said. She pointed at Tom. "That one there is clearly a half-breed. I imagine he might be difficult to control. I heard they hold onto some savage ways."

Wilma chuckled. "No, dear, actually Tom is the *most* obedient, though all are obedient. If there were any we really had to train, it would be Riza, and you see how she is."

Carrying a glass of water, Dorothy returned through the double doors with Susie walking in front of her.

"And here is Susie, full blood and efficient in many household chores."

"Mrs. Plecker, I feel like this will be a supper like no other. Are all of them house slaves?"

"Why no, Joseph and Tom are meant for the fields. That Negro blood calls to the fields, and as they get older, they'll be given higher rank as drivers. The boys are more intelligent than the full-blood Negroes and work faster. It all works well."

Dorothy's eyes widened.

Reece replied, "Really? I'll have to talk to my father so he can consider having some half-breeds on our plantations."

"Indeed. Well, children, go where you're supposed to be so Reece can see the rest of the house," Wilma said.

The children rushed off in their separate directions.

"I have your water ready, Miss Reece," Dorothy said, offering the glass.

Reece gave Dorothy a leer. "I changed my mind. Give it to the trees."

"Well, let me show you the rest of my splendid home before the men come down and ruin my tour," Wilma said. "Come, Riza, in case Reece would like some water later."

Dorothy watched the two women walk toward the living room with Riza following them. With her blue eyes locked on Dorothy, Reece snobbishly lifted an eyebrow and leered again. Dorothy narrowed her hazel eyes.

Back at the cotton gin barn, Joseph and Tom began to tell the others about Reece. Bo, Cecil, Pearl, Stella, Stephen, and other slaves stood in a semicircle, listening attentively. The boys told how she appeared with her blonde hair and how pretty she was. A few of the slaves smiled at the boys' description while others listened with blank stares. The boys continued by answering the questions they could, but they couldn't answer the question most of the slaves wanted to know. Was she going to marry Master Kenneth?

At supper time, Dorothy and the other house slaves set up the dining table. Kenneth sat next to Reece and Mr. Plecker while Wilma and her daughter Sydney and her husband Theodore sat across from them.

"This will be a glorious time. I only wish Sally and Darius could've joined us," Wilma said.

Dorothy and the other house slaves served black-eyed peas, clam chowder, dinner rolls, fried chicken, gravy, and baked sweet potatoes. Then Dorothy and Emma brought out tea and water at Wilma's request.

Dorothy stood next to Riza at attention while the dinner party conversed. Dorothy had to work hard not to speak out against Reece as the young woman spoke and laughed. She thought, *What does Kenneth like about her? She's not prettier than me, and she sounds stupid.*

Noticing Dorothy's twisted mouth and downward gaze, Reece let her fork fall on the floor. "Oh, dear, I'm clumsy at times. Dorothy, come get this fork," she said.

Dorothy forced a smile and walked over to pick up the fork while the others continued to talk. She picked up the fork as Reece smirked at her, then she quickly took the fork to the cookhouse and brought back a clean one. She properly placed the fork on the table and walked back to her place.

Reece suddenly laughed at one of Theodore's bad jokes and purposely hit her spoon out of the clam chowder, sending it to the floor and soup splattering across the tablecloth.

"Looks like you did it again, Theodore," Sydney laughed.

"I feel so terrible about the mess. Dorothy, come clean this up and bring me more clam chowder. It's quite good."

Dorothy forced herself to smile, stepped over to the mess, and began to wipe it up. As she wiped soup off the carpet, she caught Kenneth looking at her and narrowed her eyes for a split second, but Kenneth quickly looked away. When Dorothy was about to stand, Reece purposely elbowed her head and acted surprised at the pain to her elbow.

Dorothy moaned as she stood up with the cleaning rags. "Careful, Dorothy. You have to remember she can't see you," Sydney said.

Everyone but Kenneth chuckled as Dorothy headed toward the kitchen.

"I guess I'm not the only one that's slightly clumsy," Reece lightheartedly said.

The others at the dining table chuckled and then continued conversing as Dorothy entered the kitchen.

Dorothy handed Susie the cleaning rags, hurled the spoon into the sink, and shrieked, "I can't stand that blonde devil!"

Susie, Emma, and three other house slaves had never seen Dorothy so angry and were terrified. "Dorothy, calm down. You don't want Master to hear you say such a thing," Emma said.

"I don't care what gets heard," Dorothy growled. She took a deep breath and hugged Susie. "I'm sorry. I didn't mean to scare you. Emma, give me a bowl of that clam chowder."

Emma gave Dorothy a bowl of clam chowder, and Dorothy stared at the bowl, scowling. Abruptly, she snorted and spit into the clam chowder, then marched out of the kitchen, grabbing a spoon on the way.

Dorothy leered as she moved toward Reece and calmly placed the bowl in front of her.

"That was good timing, Dorothy," Reece said. "I see now why Mrs. Plecker speaks so highly of you."

"Thank you, Miss Reece," Dorothy said.

Dorothy went to stand next to Riza, eagerly watching for her special dish to be eaten.

Reece enjoyed three spoonfuls of the clam chowder as she continued a conversation and then paused to say, "I must admit, I love this clam chowder. It has such a special flavor to it. Can I receive the recipe for it?"

"I'm sure we could arrange such a thing for you," Wilma said.

As Reece continued to eat the clam chowder, a smirk drew across Dorothy's face.

Riza leaned over to Dorothy. "What did you do to it?" she whispered.

"Nothing you need to know," Dorothy whispered.

Riza leaned back over and looked at Dorothy. She tightened her lips and prayed Reece wouldn't fall over dead.

After supper, the Pleckers and Reece continued to talk in the dining room. Dorothy, Emma, Riza, and Susie picked up the dirty dishes and platters off the dining room table. After placing the dishes and platters in the cookhouse, Dorothy and Riza returned to the dining hall. Sydney and Theodore then left the dining hall to walk around the estate before leaving. At this time, Mr. Plecker excused himself and went out to the front porch. After several minutes, he returned inside and stopped in the doorway of the dining hall.

"Miss Reece is ready to go to Sydney's estate," Kenneth said.

"All right, well, your sister won't be hard to find," Mr. Plecker replied as he turned out of the dining hall. Kenneth escorted Reece to the foyer while they talked, with Wilma following.

"Mr. and Mrs. Plecker, this supper is truly one I won't forget," Reece said. "My daddy will be pleased with what I have to say to him."

"We're pleased to hear such a thing," Mr. Plecker said. "I'm assuming the two of you will meet at more gatherings. We'll walk you out to the carriage so you can be on your way to stay with Sydney this evening."

"There is one thing I do want to do first, Mr. Plecker. I do want to thank Dorothy for her service."

"Dorothy, come out here quickly," Wilma shouted.

Dorothy walked out of the dining room and stood at attention.

"Come closer. Reece would like to speak to you."

"Yes, Mrs. Wilma," Dorothy said, stepping closer to Reece.

Reece proudly stepped up to Dorothy, standing eye to eye. "I was impressed with your service. I look forward to putting more of it to use."

Dorothy humbly replied, "Thank you, Miss Reece."

Reece leaned in and murmured into Dorothy's ear, "I'm sure we'll have more interesting conversations." She leaned back and glared into Dorothy's hazel eyes. "You have such beauty. I know you'll look forward to it as much as me." Then she turned around with a peppy smile and said, "All right, I'm ready, Mr. Plecker, Kenneth." She let Kenneth put his hand on her upper back and lead her out the door with Mr. Plecker walking beside them.

Scowling, Dorothy watched Reece leave.

Later in the evening, Dorothy and the other slaves cleaned the dishes and utensils with little conversation as they were afraid of Dorothy's unusual mood.

"Dorothy, you was wrong now, doing what you did," Emma said.

"You didn't see what she purposely did," Dorothy sharply said. "She deserved a lot worse."

"You shouldn't speak like that around these children. You teaching them evil. Letting that pretty lady make you angry. She say you pretty too. I ain't never had a White woman say I pretty."

Dorothy angrily replied, "She gave me a hard time because of how I look."

"What did you do?" Riza asked.

"She spit in Miss Reece's clam chowder," Susie casually said.

Riza began to cackle while she washed a plate.

"Riza, that not funny," Emma said as she shook her head. "You, of all of us, should know 'bout punishment. Or you forget about yo' scars?"

Riza humorously replied, "I think I look good with the spider web on my back. My leg is looking good too."

Susie laughed as the two girls continued cleaning the kitchen.

"You see what you did," Emma snarled. "You spreading evil, Dorothy. You gotta keep peace when Miss Reece come back."

Dorothy angrily replied, "I've kept my peace with that woman by not saying anything. Let's finish up, I'm tired."

The others remained silent, not wanting to further test Dorothy's patience.

Doris walked into the kitchen. "Momma, we finished cleaning the table," she said.

"Good, I want you to take your sister to the house when Riza leaves," Dorothy politely said. "You did good today. Go get your sister."

Doris smiled and left the kitchen.

The others finished cleaning and trickled out to the house-slave house while Dorothy went upstairs to make sure the girls had put up their cleaning cloths. Afterward, she marched to Kenneth's room and knocked on the door.

Kenneth opened the door and stood blocking the doorway. "I didn't call for you, Dorothy," he said.

Dorothy calmly replied, "I know, but may I come in?"

Kenneth stepped back and signaled with his hand for her to come inside. He closed the door and stepped up to Dorothy, saying, "I saw that look you gave me, and that was improper. You need to be nicer to her. I like this girl."

"I apologize, but she was testing me. I know she was. She's smarter than you think. I know she dropped that spoon on purpose."

"I don't care. You have to ignore such things. Are Riza's habits becoming your own? I saw it in you...so don't you lie to me. You wanted to hit Reece."

Dorothy's slight frown disappeared when her eyes narrowed and she scowled. "I would black her eye if I had the chance. She picked on me. It wasn't right!"

Kenneth grabbed Dorothy and shook her. "You remember your place here! Stop it. I do like this girl, and she treats me good. It's what's best, and it'll allow me to keep my word to you better. With my momma happy and my old man proud of me, I can do more right by you. But you stay in your place, woman. Don't make me remind you again."

Dorothy placed her hand on Kenneth's face as she stared into his brown eyes and passionately kissed him. She kissed him again, and he released his grip and embraced her. The young couple fell into their desire, and afterward Dorothy took her time strolling to the slave house.

The one thing Reece can't give him is my love, she thought. *I've never pushed him before.* Dorothy leered. *I do have power... he can't keep his hands off me.*

On a late-March morning, Annabelle and Grace were braiding the twins' long wavy hair.

"Next time, I can do it myself, Auntie Grace," Rain said in Cherokee with her arms crossed.

Grace replied, "Watch that tone, little girl. The last time we let you do your own hair, you were in the mirror for more than two hours. So until you can focus and take care of your hair properly, you won't be allowed to do it like a big girl."

Rain pouted and rolled her eyes.

Annabelle stopped working on Jannie's hair and cocked her head, locking a look of reprimand on Rain. "Watch it, little girl," she said with each word deepening. "I swear sometimes you act like someone else in the family gave birth to you."

The women finished with the twins' hair, and the girls were sent off to help Lisa feed the horses.

Annabelle said with a smile, "I'm so glad I've gotten used to dealing with their hair. Only took us an hour."

"And soon they'll both be good enough to do it on their own, instead of taking more than two hours."

Annabelle sighed. "Did you see the eye roll?"

"Oh, yes, all of that was Lightning blood...undeniable."

"Jannie is the same when her anger rises...but Rain is so impatient. It's getting worse and worse." Annabelle frowned. "The last thing we need is another Lizzie. I feel her spirit get heavy anytime I mention Joseph's name. At first it's sadness, but then there's so much anger. And we don't have Elder Joyce anymore, and I just..." Annabelle shook her head as her brow furrowed and she exhaled. "I'm sorry. I...I shouldn't be this sad anymore, but—"

"I know. I'm still feeling her absence. Even though she's not truly gone, it hurts. I will give the girls more attention to help deal with their anger. We have to be honest with ourselves as to who they are. Rain is more like Lizzie, and she's not going to hold back, but Jannie is a quiet storm. But a quiet storm can be as dangerous as the one you see coming. Speaking of gone, have you seen Tsula at all?"

"I was so focused on the girls, I didn't even notice she left with Katelyn."

Grace's fingers drummed on her pregnant belly. "I don't want to get out of this chair, but let's go check on her," she said.

"Are you sure? I can go check on her," Annabelle stated.

"No, I need to keep moving around. If I go into birthing pains, it's Tsula's fault. Girl is making me worried while I still have to keep an eye on Lizzie. Lord Jesus, why are there so many difficult people in this family?"

The women went to Tsula's home and stood before the one-story house, knocking on the wooden door.

Tsula looked out of the window and then let them in. "Quiet, Katelyn is asleep," she said.

The two women followed Tsula inside, and Annabelle recognized the smell of burning sage. The sunlight shined through the living room windows, illuminating the house. The women sat down together at the small wooden table next to the crackling fireplace. On the table was a bowl with slowly burning sage.

"You were praying," Grace said.

Tsula brushed back a hair bang, saying, "I was. Katelyn fell asleep, so there was no better time to pray."

"How are you healing?"

Tsula shrugged. "I think just about the same as everyone else. I mean, Lisa is doing her thing with the horses, the boys got the fields ready for the crops, you look like your baby is going to shoot out of you, and Lizzie hasn't killed any White men recently, so I think we're doing okay."

Grace sighed. "Tsula."

Tsula grunted. "What? What do you want me to say? That I miss her? Yes, I miss her. Does that make you happy?"

"Tsula, it's not about what makes us happy," Annabelle said. "Everyone has been healing, and it wasn't like you to leave the house while we were doing the girls' hair. You always stay and have something funny to say."

Tsula bit her lip and shifted her gaze to her hands, then back to Annabelle. "I have nothing to give. My daughter won't get the chance to thank Elder Joyce for helping to bring her into this world. I always thought Katelyn would at least get old enough to say thank you, and—" Tsula's voiced cracked, and she exhaled. "Ugh, I swear the two of you are trying to make me cry."

Grace's brow lowered and she replied, "You know that's not why we're here. We're making sure you're not doing this alone. None of us need to be healing through this alone."

"Yeah, well, where's Lizzie?" Tsula asked as she scoffed and side-eyed Grace.

Grace leaned forward. "Don't try that. You know with her it's going to be day by day. It's the only way she opens up her heart."

Tsula drummed her fingers on the table. "Okay, fair enough." She smacked her lips. "I'm scared. There I said it...I'm scared. Like I said before, what are we going to do? She was the strongest of us spiritually, and we literally have no one else like her. Not Pastor Bluebird, not any of the other elders in the tribe. None of them have the gift of seeing, so now we're blind."

Grace adjusted herself in her seat and placed her hands on her pregnant belly. "She always told us to move by faith and not by sight. We can't fall into the trap of trying to understand it all."

"I believe her that Joseph is alive and that we will see him again, but how long will that be? How long will it be before those White people have forever changed him?" Tsula wiped away an escaped tear and grunted. "I swear the two of you came here to try to make me cry. I'm not Lizzie. I'm not... She's able to make it seem like she doesn't care. If there's anything I'm jealous of about that short, stubborn woman it's that she puts on a strong face."

Grace cocked her head. "That's not always a good thing. We both know closing out the people who love you isn't good. Elder Joyce worked hard to get Lizzie to release her pain."

Tsula's gaze fixed on Annabelle. "How are you doing in all of this, Annabelle?"

Annabelle fiddled with her fingers. "The nightmares have stopped, but I miss him every day. The girls are getting angrier and angrier. Between them and David, I'm not sure which child is going to release their anger in the wrong way next. The best I can do is keep filling them with love. I can't lose another child, Tsula. My spirit can't handle the loss of another child. It doesn't matter if the Father were to bless me with another baby. You can't replace one spirit with another."

Tsula calmly reached for Annabelle's hand and held it. "From one mother to another, I'm standing with you, sister," she said. "Every time I see you or the twins smile, I see him and it makes his absence feel worse, but I am with you."

"How about we smudge together?" Grace suggested.

Tsula nodded. "Yeah, I would love that. Besides…smudging by myself makes me feel like the ugly child nobody plays with because they smell and dig in their nose all day."

"Ew, Tsula, you come up with some of the nastiest ideas," Annabelle chuckled.

Grace chuckled. "Okay, let's pray before the baby wakes up."

Each of the women smudged themselves with the smoke of the burning sage. Afterward, they held hands and prayed for Joseph's safe return and for healing.

CHAPTER 14
The Missing Puzzle Piece

DAYS PASSED AND THE REPLANTING of the cotton began on March 30th. The slaves used double plows pulled by two donkeys to prepare the fields, the men moving the tools as the women and children planted the cotton and Masters Kit and Rice watched. Cecil began to sing hymns, and the boys joined in on the hymns.

Joseph's hands began to throb and hurt. "I hate this," he murmured. "I wish we could light the fields on fire."

"Don't say that. If Master Rice was to hear that, you would get whipped," Tom whispered. "They're looking for any reason to give us the whip."

Joseph grumbled, "I wish Jesus would come down and hit them with lightning."

Tom's brow lowered. "You sound like Riza. Are you okay?"

"My hands hurt really bad, but I know if I ask to rest, I'll get beat."

"We're almost done. Don't move as fast."

Joseph sighed. "All right, I'll do that."

Joseph and Tom continued planting cotton behind the plows, their attention soon drawn by a familiar brown carriage arriving at the mansion. "I think that's Mrs. Judy Mays and Mrs. Daphne," Joseph said.

Tom replied, "I guess Mrs. Wilma wants company. Susie told

me Mrs. Daphne always picks on Riza. She always tells Mrs. Wilma Riza should be hung."

"She sounds like a normal White woman to me. I think Mrs. Daphne is scared of Riza."

Tom joked, "Riza scares me too sometimes." The two boys chuckled and went about their work beneath the warm sunlight.

———◆———

Judy Mays and Wilma sat in the living room on a crème-colored couch as Riza poured tea for the women and the brown grandfather clock ticked nearby.

"I'm so happy you came by, Judy Mays," Wilma said. "I was concerned that you and Daphne's visits would happen less often with our secession and Abraham Lincoln now taking office. We're better off on our own, governing how we do things down here in the South."

"I'm curious about Mr. Lincoln's policies, but I do disagree with any abrupt removal of slavery," Judy Mays said. "I would've visited earlier in February when the snow had melted, but I had family matters to attend to."

Wilma put down her tea. "What dealings are happening in your family?"

Judy Mays casually replied, "Nothing major. My sweet Megan was ill and needed my attention."

"The poor dear. You should've had one of your slaves take care of the beautiful girl so you could've had some time to regain some strength. You look like you haven't slept at all."

Judy Mays chuckled. "Oh, no, I wouldn't have left her with my slaves. I enjoy caring for her needs, and I see no reason to give the responsibility to my slaves."

"My goodness, Judy Mays. Why have slaves if you won't use them?" Wilma sat up. "I did also take care of my children when they were ill. Though I did leave the rest of the care to the house slaves so I could socialize as needed. When Kenneth would become ill as a child, and even as a teenager, Dorothy took good care of him. Now that I think of it, I see why Kenneth has such sympathies for her."

Judy Mays folded her hands. "I think sympathy is a powerful show of character."

Wilma cocked her head. "I agree, but not toward a slave, dear. You do that with slaves and soon they forget we are not equals in any form. I think my household is enough of an example for you to know why sympathy in some cases can be wrongfully interpreted."

"I think the South has forgotten its place and the creation of our new government back in February is greatly disrespectful. Mr. Lincoln has not even been in office for a month."

"Riza, get us some crackers," Wilma said, then she watched as Riza hurried to the kitchen. "I want us to be careful with this subject matter around Riza. I believe she has learned her lesson, but it is unwise to tempt a tame lion with a rack of lamb. If she learns any more of this, I have no doubt she'll speak of it to the other slaves. The possibility of freedom would no doubt test the order around here."

Judy Mays's eyebrows lowered. "Do you believe Riza would be able to get all the slaves to turn on you?"

"I wouldn't say *all*, but enough for us to have to pull out the rifles. I enjoy Riza, though I wish that child was a little dumber for my own peace of mind."

"She certainly reminds me of Annabelle a little. I've always felt Annabelle ran away for different reasons than why Riza attempted her escape."

Wilma eyes widened. "Why do you say such a thing?"

"Riza started her life as a free child and has reason to return. Annabelle was born on my papa's plantation, we grew up together, and, though it's seen as distasteful, was heavily favored by me and my sisters. Unlike the other slaves, Annabelle had no reason to run away…that I could think of. She was actually safe on that plantation."

"It is hard to not develop some form of attachment with them, isn't it? Kenneth certainly shows that with Dorothy. What is this world coming to? Disobedient slaves and rumors of war will do nothing but continuously divide us until we fall."

Riza returned to the living room with a silver platter holding crackers in a glass bowl. "I agree, division is the last thing we need in our country," Judy Mays said. She exhaled and brushed off some lint from her green-and-white flowered Victorian dress. "I'm interested though, in seeing the new Indian boy you have. I've never seen him."

"Surely seeing Riza and Susie are enough. Besides, the boys are meant to work out in the fields."

"I'm interested in seeing what this one looks like. I wonder if he's different from the ones I've seen elsewhere."

Wilma dismissively nodded. "I have no issue with it. Riza, go tell Susie to have Joseph come here. Actually, bring Tom too so she can compare, and make sure they don't have any mud on their shoes."

"As you wish, Mrs. Wilma," Riza politely said. Then she walked away with a glance at Judy Mays.

Susie went out to the cotton fields and told Joseph and Tom to follow her to the mansion. As the boys walked up the porch stairs, she made them take off their shoes so they wouldn't track mud inside. Then she brought the boys before Judy Mays and Wilma.

"Well done, Susie. Now go finish the rest of your chores in the study," Wilma said.

"Yes, Mrs. Wilma," Susie said as she walked away.

"So he's the new half-breed I've heard so much about," Judy Mays said with a welcoming tone. "Good afternoon, Tom."

Tom nervously replied, "Good afternoon, Mrs. Judy Mays."

"Both of you can step forward a little more. I'm not snobbish like Mrs. Daphne."

Joseph and Tom slowly took two steps forward as they looked at Judy Mays.

"What do you think?" Wilma asked.

"It's obvious Tom is a half-breed…he's taller too, and the other one, yes, I can see he has those eyes. Very interesting. So you're Joseph? You can speak."

Joseph nervously replied, "Yes, ma'am."

Judy Mays examined Joseph with her blue eyes as Riza watched with great interest. "I expected you to be older. Running away with Riza and rebelling are not things we see often in children."

Joseph gulped. "It was a mistake, Mrs. Judy Mays. I'll never do it again."

Judy Mays grinned. "I'm sure you won't, little boy. I see Tom is still a handsome little thing for a mixed-blood, Wilma."

Wilma pleasantly replied, "I said the same thing to Calvin. We have great plans for Tom."

Judy Mays's eyes remained anchored on the boys. "I'd have great plans for him as well." She raised her voice, "Susie, please come here." The other children's eyes widened a little at hearing Judy Mays say please.

Susie quickly returned from the study and stood next to the boys. "Yes, Mrs. Judy Mays?" she asked.

"Which one of these boys has an Indian mother?" Judy Mays asked.

"Tom's mother is Natchez."

"Interesting...the Natchez. I remember seeing those people when I was a child. Well, I apologize for not giving much notice to you before, Tom. I'm sure you're a talented boy. Susie, take Tom back to the fields quickly. That's all I needed to know for now."

"Yes, ma'am." Tom followed Susie to the front door, and the two children returned to the cotton fields.

Joseph breathed heavier while Judy Mays stared him down with her focused gaze. "I've learned something interesting about you, Joseph."

"What would that be?" Wilma asked.

"It seems he told Riza a great deal about his past, and I find it fascinating," Judy Mays said.

"Why would you find the past of a Negro interesting?"

Riza bit her lip as she stood at attention and watched. "Even a child like this can have an interesting past. So your mother is a Negro woman, correct?"

Joseph nervously replied, "Yes, Mrs. Judy Mays."

"Riza tells me your mother's name is Annabelle. Is that true?"

Joseph looked at Riza with a slight frown.

"Don't be so concerned, boy. Riza hasn't betrayed you. I want to know, is your momma's name Annabelle?"

Joseph's gaze went downward. "Yes, ma'am, it is."

Wilma let out a weak gasp as she slightly missed putting her cup down on the tea table, causing the tea to spill. "Impossible! You couldn't possibly believe that this half-breed child is hers? Not *your* Annabelle?"

Judy Mays tapped her finger on her knee. "It's a rare name for a slave." She scoffed. "But that's not good enough information to be sure."

Wilma sighed. "Riza, come clean this tea up."

Riza went over to the table and started cleaning up the tea as Judy Mays rested her chin on her hand and asked, "Where was your momma born?"

Joseph stuttered, "I d-don't really know, but s-she was from Missouri, not Mississippi. I know—"

"Calm down, Joseph. Breathe and continue."

"She's from Missouri because she always writes letters to it and my papa takes them there."

Judy Mays stood up. "Is your momma about as tall as me? Don't lie, boy."

Joseph gulped. "She's almost as tall."

A smile arose on Judy Mays's face as she sat back down. She ate a cracker, then said, "I imagine you wouldn't know too much about your momma's past. A smart momma doesn't tell her child too much. Do you have brothers or sisters?"

"I—"

Abruptly Riza started to cough loudly as she cleaned up the spilled tea on the burgundy carpet.

Joseph looked at her and rubbed his sweaty hands.

"Riza, what was that coughing?" Wilma demanded.

"It's quite all right," Judy Mays said.

"No, I won't tolerate such an obvious interruption. Riza, you apologize this very instant."

Riza stood up. "I'm sorry, Mrs. Judy Mays, for my cough," she said.

"Apology accepted," Judy Mays said, smiling. "I understand

your thinking, and I find it adorable, defending him. Joseph, I want you to be honest with me, and I'll be honest with you. Have you ever seen any scars on your momma's back…scars that look more like stripes than normal scars."

"I have no memory of seeing my momma's back. I think I was too young to know anything when my momma would undress in front of me."

Judy Mays continued to smile while she listened to Joseph. "I suppose your momma was smart enough not to let you know. What an interesting boy you are."

"Can we really believe this?" Wilma asked. "Just by what we know?"

Judy Mays sat back. "Well, Wilma, what are the chances? Besides I needed my entertainment. Isn't that right, Riza? If you allow yourself to get bored enough, anything can start to happen. We'll start having crazy events like men pulling wagons with a donkey sitting in the driver's seat. Could you imagine the ludicrous nature of it? A donkey going hee-haw and whipping men!" She started to giggle, causing the children to also giggle.

Wilma chuckled. "My word, Judy Mays, your imagination," she said.

Judy Mays's eyes locked onto Joseph's smile, her own smile dropping from her face as her eyes widened. "You have your momma's smile."

Joseph stopped smiling and let out a weak gasp.

A small furrow formed between Judy Mays's brows. "Smile again, boy."

Joseph gulped and half-smiled.

Judy Mays's voice deepened again. "Smile for real, Joseph."

Joseph's eyes shifted to Riza, and she nodded yes.

Judy Mays caught Riza's signal and narrowed her eyes. Looking back at Joseph as he smiled, her jaw dropped. "Your momma's smile," she murmured. Judy Mays let out a weak scoff. "You're going to remain respectful here, aren't you, Joseph?"

Joseph gulped and nervously replied, "Yes, Mrs. Judy Mays."

Judy Mays nodded. "Riza can take him back to the fields, if that's all right with you, Wilma."

"Umm…well, yes. I don't see a problem with that. Riza, take Joseph back to the fields, and you be quick about it. Immediately come back here!"

Riza hurried to the front door, and Joseph followed her.

"Wait a moment," Judy Mays abruptly said. "Joseph, tell me this and know that you won't face any punishment for the truth."

Wilma looked at Judy Mays with a skewed frown and her brow drawing together.

"Can you read?"

Joseph bit his lip as he looked at Judy Mays. "Yes, Mrs. Judy Mays. I can read," he said uneasily.

"Who taught you how to read?"

"My momma, my aunties, and my papa taught me."

Judy Mays leaned forward. "So can your momma read well, and does she speak like me…like a White woman?"

Joseph froze and his eyes widened.

"Joseph?"

"Yes, ma'am."

Judy Mays's brows drew together. "You can go now."

Joseph walked to Riza, and the two left the mansion.

"So what do you think?" Wilma asked.

Judy Mays answered, "I don't believe this is real… I'm not entirely confident, but I do have a strong sense that he is her son. I'm not surprised that he knew so little. That's why I didn't ask for a last name. I'm sure she would have changed it again."

"I'm appalled that he knows how to read. He has no right to have such knowledge. Curse those fools in Missouri. I'm sure that's where his mother illegally learned."

Judy Mays sighed and took a sip of tea. "It was me…I was the one who taught Annabelle how to read and write. We were children and used to read the Bible together and any other book I could get my hands on. It was the secret I kept from anyone else in my household."

Wilma lightly hit her knee. "Judy Mays! How could you do something so reckless?"

"I was young. I was stupid. I found myself caring deeply for her. She was my best friend. Weird, isn't it? I broke many rules in my father's household and remained rebellious until my adult years."

"Don't be so harsh on yourself. You wouldn't be the first to take pity on a Negro. Though it's surprising someone of your stature would do so."

"Yes, well, I've learned that feelings are capable of breaking barriers. Riza is a strong example of that. She cares for Joseph, and she knew why I asked if that boy had siblings. She's a clever Mohawk girl. I enjoy her." Judy Mays put down her teacup. "Annabelle was last seen in Missouri, in a town called Mercy. I know that because of the Williams family that lives only two miles from my father's plantation. Ruthanne Williams. Her brother Ruben recognized Annabelle and almost captured her, but Ruthanne outsmarted him."

"Why would Ruthanne do such a thing? I remember that redheaded girl and that nice little temper of hers."

Judy Mays pressed her lips. "I believe Ruthanne had a change of heart. For whatever reason, Ruthanne helped Annabelle and has been at odds with the rest of her family because of what she did. I'm almost certain this child is Annabelle's son."

Wilma humbly replied, "If that's the case, by law he belongs to you. I have no issue with the exchange, and I can easily explain this shocking discovery to Calvin."

Judy Mays took a sip of tea. "What a year this has already turned out to be. I can't help but feel God has had mercy on me. I've been given the missing piece to a puzzle. However, I do feel I need to think about this."

"Well, we have no interest in selling any of the Indian children at all, but if it turns out your Annabelle is his mother, it would be only right for us to give him to you or your father."

"There is no rush, no rush at all." Judy Mays took another sip and then stared into the teacup in her hand as the tea slowly moved around. A small crease formed between her brows, and her nose crinkled. "He has his momma's smile."

As Riza and Joseph strolled to the cotton fields, she told him, "Joseph, you can't tell her you have brothers or sisters. It's too dangerous."

"Why can't she know that? If she knows my momma, wouldn't she help me go home?"

"Weren't you listening? She thinks your momma was a runaway slave of hers, and by law, any children of hers are her slaves. From what I know, your momma wasn't freed. That makes you belong to Mrs. Judy Mays by the law."

"I thought she was just interested in having me as a slave. You mean if she knew I had brothers and sisters, they would go after them too?"

"The White men would. So don't speak about them. It's the best thing you can do."

Joseph frowned. "She seemed kind of nice, unlike Mrs. Wilma."

"She is different from Mrs. Wilma, but she's still a White woman. Don't get your hopes up with her freeing you." Riza sighed. "She's the only White person I've liked down here. She would play guessing games with me. I'm sorry I mentioned your momma's name. I felt comfortable with her." She and Joseph arrived at the cotton fields as the other slaves worked tirelessly to nurture the new cotton. "Hold onto hope, Joseph. I think the next time we will get away." Riza hugged Joseph.

"Okay, I'll keep hoping, and it's okay. I know you didn't tell Mrs. Judy Mays to hurt me."

"Goodbye, Joseph."

"Goodbye, Riza." Riza jogged to the mansion.

As Joseph worked in the fields, he prayed, "Father, please protect my family. I'm afraid for them."

That night, Joseph lay awake in deep concern over what might happen to him and the danger he might have put his family in. He'd told Bo and Stella about the possibility that his mother was originally Judy Mays's slave earlier in the day, and both of them agreed it was wise for him to remain silent about his siblings. Both of them had been separated from their siblings over the years and didn't want Joseph to experience any more pain. He prayed for the protection of his family. Prayer was the only weapon he had, and he believed his prayers would be answered.

CHAPTER 15
The Key

THUNDER BEGAN TO SHAKE THE skies and rain broke free of the clouds. Blue eyes stared into the burning flames of two candles sitting on a brown coffee table in front of a lit fireplace. The silence of the room was punctuated by the crackling of the fireplace. Judy Mays sat back on the burgundy couch and folded her hands, her lips slowly forming a small frown.

"What bothers you, my love?" Edgar asked.

Judy Mays shook her head, her gaze moving to take in the fire, and she replied, "I'm not even sure, Edgar. I have so many mixed emotions right now."

Edgar leaned forward. "Why would that be?"

Judy Mays scoffed and slowly ground her teeth. "One of the mixed-blood children on the Plecker plantation may be Annabelle's son."

Edgar's eyes widened as he slow-stepped over to the burgundy couch. "Are you serious?"

"I wish I wasn't."

"How do you know this?"

"A boy at the Plecker plantation was taken from Indian Territory. Speaks perfect English…just like his momma."

"Judy Mays, Annabelle wasn't the only well-spoken Negro. Surely it must be—"

Judy Mays's brow furrowed, and her nose crinkled. "The

boy's mother is from Missouri...Mercy, Missouri. I kept telling myself it's just a coincidence."

Edgar sighed and crossed his arms. "What changed your mind?"

Judy Mays shook her head, and her eyes began to well up as she looked at Edgar. "His smile. He has her smile."

"Then surely this can be used to find her and bring her back. I know you may not want to tell your father about this discovery."

"I haven't felt this much confusion in a long time. I mean, she just ran away. I know there's no joy in being a slave, but... Right now, my anger is rising faster than my sadness."

"I will go to Mr. Plecker and speak with him."

"I don't want you to do that."

Edgar's brow drew together. "My love, why?"

"I honestly think the boy might be safer there right now. Papa can't know about the boy...not yet. Joseph has already gotten into trouble once on that plantation. If he figures out that I fully believe who he is, then he might try to make another escape."

"Why would he run away?"

"I'm sure Riza has told that boy the truth by now. If he has siblings, they also belong to my family. That intelligent girl unknowingly exposed Joseph. Ugh, I'm sure the Mohawk will do whatever she can to correct it."

"Then I agree we should wait."

"That little boy is my family's property. That's the truth, but either way, I can't let the laws of the South ruin my chances of finding Annabelle. Part of me wants to choke her, and the other part just..." Judy Mays inhaled deeply, and a tear fell from her eye that she quickly wiped away. "She belongs here, with me. I hate all of this, Edgar."

"My love, I know this upsets you."

Judy Mays replied, her voice dripping with sarcasm, "It's funny how God will answer your prayers, but when an answer angers you, it feels like a curse."

"I believe the best thing we can do is make sure we keep track of the boy. It's the best way to find Annabelle."

Judy Mays slammed her fist on her thigh, saying, "I want the boy!"

Edgar's mouth fell unhinged. "Judy Mays, I—"

Tears fell from Judy Mays's eyes and a growl rumbled from her voice. "She had the nerve to do what she did! She ran, knowing the consequences. Instead of coming to me with her problems, she ran and then..." She roared, "Ruthanne helped her run again!" She knocked a glass bowl off the coffee table, onto the floor. Tears streamed down her cheeks as she looked at Edgar. "I'm sorry. I'm...I'm sorry I can't get that day out of my head. Then he shows off that beautiful smile...the smile she gave her son. I feel so divided, and I shouldn't."

"It's okay to feel anger in this, my love. But you know better than anyone, she wouldn't have run away if everything was okay. She had you and your sisters but still chose to run away. There must be more to the story."

Judy Mays huffed and let her gaze drift back to the fire. "I know there's more, but—"

Edgar calmly put his hand on her shoulder. "Then let her tell you on the day you see her again. As you said, you don't want Joseph to run again."

"Joseph is my missing puzzle piece, but Riza is the key."

"Why do you say that?"

"You've met the girl, dear. She's a natural leader...an Indian rebel. It's only a matter of time before she makes a better plan to escape. She's no true slave."

"I think you need to get her full trust again if we're to win this game."

"I agree. I already gave her motivation to try again by telling her the truth."

"Then for now it's settled."

Judy Mays crossed her legs. "I'll play the game as needed... and keep myself in Riza's good will." She withheld her smile. "I can't help but to like the clever girl as I've watched her grow."

"Well, then, you won't need to pretend and can focus more on getting more from Joseph. Then Annabelle can be sought after."

"I agree, and I need to be prepared."

"For what, my love?"

Judy Mays began to caress her chin with her fingers. "She's a mother now. With that comes the wrath of a mother. I'm sure if she can, she'll return like a summer storm to get her baby boy." A leer slowly materialized on her face as she said, "After all, he has his momma's smile."

<hr>

Albert Brooks held onto one of Annabelle's letters that had been encased in plastic. "The old stories are meant to remind us of how our ancestors persevered," he said. "No matter what it is, the truth should be told."

"I don't know what I would've done if I were Annabelle, Daddy," Liz said.

Albert pursed his lips and frowned. "There are few things in my mind that're darker than hearing the fear in your child's voice. It's almost as troubling as seeing your child killed in front of you." He gave the picture to Liz.

Liz's brow lowered as she looked at the old picture of a woman.

"At first I thought I was doing all of you a favor by not telling you this, but now...I'm glad I spoke up," Albert said.

"For Joseph to be found by Judy Mays...she must have wanted revenge. Is that why you didn't tell us this?"

"A broken heart can be a dangerous thing, depending on the person."

Liz's eyes welled up. "She changed, didn't she? Did she keep Joseph away from Annabelle? Her face scowled as she added, "What an evil w—"

"Now, calm down, sweetie. Even people with good hearts have evil within them. Situations can bring out the worst in us, but even so, we have a choice on how we respond to the trials of life. It's the only thing we truly have control over. Which wolf we feed."

"But did Judy Mays make the right choice?"

"Good intention doesn't make a right decision."

Liz's eyes locked onto her daughters, Christina and Elisa,

and then back to her father. Her siblings and mother's focus also remained fixed on Albert. "Annabelle went after Joseph, didn't she?"

"The Father has the final say, and this is why we need to trust that the whole story is bigger than what we can see. The strength given to a mother should never be underestimated. Now, with that said, we will continue our story."

TO BE CONTINUED

I hope this adventure was an enjoyable experience for you and that you will visit your favorite retailer to leave a review because your feedback is priceless!

ABOUT THE AUTHOR

Hi, everyone! I'm Marcus, from the south side suburbs of Chicago. I'm a descendant of two Native American tribes. I have two degrees in zoology, love the Olympic Games, and I am into Native American history, especially regarding issues that have divided families. Some of the stories I enjoy creating focus on parts of history rarely talked about and revolve around genealogy and interracial relationships, particularly between African American and Native American communities, that cause us to reflect on the choices we make, especially in our teenage and young adult years. This focus is to help young adults see the bigger picture earlier in their lives. God's greatest commandment is to love each other. I hope to fascinate your minds, to educate, to make you think about your family, and make you reflect on your own choices in life.